MAGGIE SHAYNE

"Shayne crafts a convincing world, tweaking vampire legends
just enough to draw fresh blood."
—*Publishers Weekly* on *Demon's Kiss*

"Maggie Shayne demonstrates an absolutely superb touch,
blending fantasy and romance into
an outstanding reading experience."
—*RT Book Reviews* on *Embrace the Twilight*

"Maggie Shayne is better than chocolate.
She satisfies every wicked craving."
—*New York Times* bestselling author Suzanne Forster

"Maggie Shayne delivers sheer delight,
and fans new and old of her vampire series can rejoice."
—*RT Book Reviews* on *Twilight Hunger*

"Maggie Shayne delivers romance
with sweeping intensity and bewitching passion."
—*New York Times* bestselling author Jayne Ann Krentz

MAGGIE SHAYNE

Twilight Fulfilled

Recycling programs for this product may not exist in your area.

ISBN-13: 978-0-7783-1267-3

TWILIGHT FULFILLED

Copyright © 2011 by Margaret Benson

For questions and comments about the quality of this book please contact us at Customer_eCare@Harlequin.ca.

www.Harlequin.com

Printed in U.S.A.

To my editor, Leslie Wainger,
who has been with this series from its birth. With this book,
Wings in the Night is eighteen years old, and twenty novels,
novellas and an online read long, but it never would have
survived toddlerhood, nor grown into the body of work that
it has become, without the steadfast support, wise guidance,
and true love of its co-mommy.

Thank you will never suffice, but I'll say it anyway.
Thank you, Leslie, with all my heart.
—Maggie

Well, I suppose I am forced to admit, the above gooeyness goes
for me, too, though my version will be far more dignified and
less...drippy. Still, it is undeniably true that Leslie Wainger's
guidance had been invaluable. Except, of course, for those rare
occasions when she cut or shortened my scenes. Still, no one is
perfect. And she really is a wise and wonderful woman.
For a mortal. So, thank you from me, as well, dear Leslie.
You are one of those rare humans that I can honestly call "friend."
—Rhiannon

1

Coastal Maine

It was the blackest, rainiest night the forgotten and overgrown cemetery had seen in centuries. Ancient tombstones leaned drunkenly beneath the bones of dead-looking trees, while gnarled limbs shivered in the cold. Arthritic twig-fingers scratched the tallest of the old stone monuments like old, yellow fingernails on slate. And the surviving vampires huddled together around an open, muddy grave.

Brigit Poe, part vampire, part human, and one of the only two of her kind, was dressed for battle, not for a funeral. It was only coincidence that she wore entirely black. That breathable second-skin fabric favored by runners covered her body from ankles to waist like a surgical glove. Over the leggings, she wore tall black boots, with buckles all the way up to her knees. The chunky four-inch heels provided extra height, an advantage in battle. And the weight of them would add more potency to a kick. Her black slicker looked as if she'd lifted it straight from the back of a cowboy actor in an old spaghetti western. It was long and heavy, with a caped back, but it did more than keep the rain away. Its dense fabric would help deflect a blade.

She could have wished for a hood. She could have wished for a lot of things, topmost among them: for the task she faced to fall to anyone other than her. But that wasn't going to happen.

As she stood there, watching each vampire move forward to pour ashes into the muddy hole, her twin brother walked up to her and plunked a black cowboy hat onto her dripping-wet blond curls. She had, she'd been told, hair like Goldilocks, the face of an angel, the heart of a demon—and the power of Satan himself.

Black hat, she thought. It figured. In that spaghetti Western she'd been envisioning, she definitely would have worn a black hat. Her brother would have worn a white one. He was the good guy. The hero.

Not her.

"It's not going to be easy," he told her. "Hunting him down. Killing him."

"No shit. He's five thousand years old and more powerful than any of us."

"Not exactly what I meant, sis." James—known

to her as J.W. despite his constant protests—looked her dead in the eyes. She pretended not to know what he was looking for, even though she did. Decency. Morality. Some sign that she was struggling with the ethics of the decision that had been made— that she must find and execute the ancient one who had started the vampire race.

Only days earlier, her brother had located and resurrected the first immortal, the ancient Sumerian king known as "the Flood Survivor." He was the original Noah, from a tale far older than the Biblical version. His name was Ziasudra in Sumerian, Utanapishtim in Babylonian.

A prophecy, the same prophecy that had foretold the war now raging between vampires and the humans who had finally learned of their existence, had also said that the Ancient One, the first immortal, the man from whom the entire vampire race had descended, was their only hope of survival.

Or at least, that was what they had thought it said. Turned out, their ancestor was actually the means of their destruction. Still believing the Ancient One was their salvation, J.W. had used his healing power to raise Utana from the ashes. And the man had returned to life with his mind corrupted by thousands of years spent trapped, conscious, his soul bound to his ashes.

Believing he'd been cursed by the gods for sharing his gift of immortality and inadvertently creating the vampire race, he'd set out to destroy them all. One look beaming from his eyes, and they were annihilated. He'd killed many vampires already.

Human vigilantes had killed even more.

The end of their kind, it seemed, was at hand.

Unless *she* could stop Utana from his self-appointed mission.

"What I meant," her brother went on, "was that killing someone who can't truly die, knowing that all you're really doing is sentencing him to spend eternity, virtually buried alive—"

"Are you trying to tweak my conscience, J.W.?" she asked, irritated. "It won't work. I don't have one. Never have. That bastard's killed hundreds of my kind. Our kind. I've got no problem taking him out before he can eliminate the rest of us. No problem whatsoever."

Someone cleared his throat, and she looked toward the open grave again. Thirteen survivors of the recent annihilation had scooped up the dust of their beloved dead and brought the remains here, to this abandoned and long-forgotten cemetery in the wilds of Maine.

Those gathered included ten vampires: Eric and Tamara, Rhiannon and Roland, Jameson and Angelica, Edge and Amber Lily, Sarafina and the newly turned Lucy. In addition, there was Sarafina's mortal mate, Willem Stone, and the mongrel twins,

Brigit herself and her brother, J.W. The supposed only hope for the dark half of their family.

Rhiannon, their unofficial aunt, her long, slit-to-the-thigh gown dragging in the mud at her uncharacteristically bare feet, poured the final jar of ashes into the hole, threw the jar in after them, then tipped her head back and opened her arms to the skies. The rain poured down on the pale skin of her breasts, almost completely exposed by the plunging neckline of her bloodred gown. Her long black hair hung in wet straggles, and her eyeliner was running down her cheeks, mixed with rainwater and tears. She was not herself.

"I know you can hear me, my friends. My family." Her voice broke, but Roland moved up behind her and placed his strong hands on her bare shoulders. Then slowly, he slid them outward, following the length of her arms upward, his black cloak opening with the motion, sheltering her from the rain. He clasped her hands in his, his arms open to the skies just as hers were.

It was a beautiful image. And heartbreaking at the same time.

"I know you can hear me," Rhiannon said again. "And I trust you've found that we, too, enter paradise when we leave this life. We, too, are worthy of heaven. We have souls—souls that feel, that love, that live, a thousand times more powerfully than those of the mortals who call us soulless monsters."

She closed her eyes, drew a breath. "Be well, there in the light, my beloved ones. Be well, and fear not. For those you've left behind will survive." She opened her eyes, and they were cold and dark, more frightening than ever, ringed as they were in black. "And I swear by Isis Herself, you will be avenged."

She lowered her arms slowly, but Roland still held them, and he wrapped them around her waist, enfolding her in his cloak and in his arms as if they were one.

"It is done, my love. Come, we need to brief our little warrior before we send her off into battle."

Rhiannon turned, meeting Brigit's eyes, holding them. There was so much there, Brigit thought, staring at her mentor, the woman she most admired, most wanted to be like and whose approval she most craved. And truly, had never been without. There was love in those dark-ringed eyes. Love and grief and fear. A lot of fear.

Fear in Rhiannon's eyes was something so unusual that it shook Brigit right to the core.

J.W. tightened his hand on her shoulder. "It's going to be all right, little sister."

"Easy for you to say. Your job was to raise our living dead forebear. I'm the one who has to deal with him now that he's up and rampaging."

"Come," Eric said. "Let's return to the mansion. It's unsafe to be out in the open for long, even here."

One by one, and two by two, they filed out of the cemetery together, taking a soggy path that wound from the old graveyard along a narrow and twisting course to the towering structure that sat alone on the rocky, seaside cliff. The ocean was as restless tonight as the skies, as the vampires and their kin made their way higher. Winds buffeted them, howling and crying as if they, too, mourned the loss of so many.

Brigit walked alone. Normally she and J.W. would have been a pair, side by side, the only two of their kind and yet opposites in every way. But now he had his mate, the beautiful, brilliant Lucy, a vampire now. And Brigit was…she was alone, and facing the biggest challenge of her entire existence. A challenge she didn't want and wasn't sure she could handle.

And yet, she was all but on her way. Her bag was packed and waiting at the mansion. She'd been waiting only for the funeral rites to conclude.

Up ahead, Rhiannon, in the lead—where else?—reached the mansion's door and stood, holding it open while the others entered the crumbling ruin.

Brigit was last in line, and as she passed, Rhiannon put a hand on her forearm. "We'll have a talk before you leave," she said softly. "Wait in the library."

Great, Brigit thought. One more delay, and it was as inevitable as it would be unpleasant. The elders must want to brief her before she left on what was undoubtedly a suicide mission. Just what she needed. A lecture before dying.

Downtown Bangor, Maine

The oldest being on the planet, the first immortal, the original Noah, stood trembling on a village sidewalk in the pouring rain. He wore a dripping wet bed sheet, wrapped in the old style around his body, covering one shoulder. He'd arrogantly refused to don the clothing that had been offered him when he'd first been resurrected. The type of clothing that he now realized was necessary if he hoped to become invisible among mankind in this strange new age. People looked askance at him, ordinary humans, mortals, dashing past him from their speeding mechanical conveyances to the small and poorly designed buildings that lined the streets. In and out they ran, as if the rain would melt them. Up and down the streets they rolled in those machines. *Automobiles. Cars,* he'd heard them called.

He wanted to know how they worked. But later. First he wanted to become invisible. He would prefer dead, but death wasn't an option for him right now.

Right now he had very few options, in fact. But he did have needs, and the immediate ones were urgent enough to distract him from the problem of attracting too much attention. That would come after his initial needs were met. He needed warmth, shelter from the ice-cold, unforgiving rain. So much rain.

It would have been a blessing in his time—unless it went on too long. He wondered briefly whether this rain was normal in today's civilization, or whether the gods, the Anunaki, had yet again decreed that mankind must be brought to its knees.

Utana shook off the shiver of apprehension that thought induced and tried once again to keep his focus on his immediate requirements. He needed food, lots of it. His belly was rumbling, twisting and gnawing at him, demanding sustenance. And water—he needed sweet water to drink. Those things were first. The rest could wait. The garments to help him blend in with the mundane commoners as thick on this land as fleas upon a desert dog, the knowledge he so craved and must acquire in order to make his way in this world, the mission he must accomplish in order to extract forgiveness from the gods—all of those things could come later.

Food. Water. Shelter.

Those first.

And so he looked at the buildings he passed—red brick or wood, no beauty nor art to them, with wide openings in the walls that appeared to be empty but, he had learned, were not. In the rain it was easier to see the droplets on the hard, transparent walls. When dry, the things—windows, they called them, made of a substance known as glass—were nearly invisible.

And yet, not quite.

He moved closer to one of the windows, drawn by the smell of food, only to pause as he stared at the image he saw there. The image of a man, wearing exactly what he wore and moving exactly as he moved. Clearly a reflection, he thought, lifting his hand, watching as the image did the same. Much like what one would see when looking into still water.

He tipped his head slightly and studied his image in the glass. It was no wonder, he thought, that the mortals were disturbed by him. He looked menacing. Wild. Standing in the rain, letting it pour down upon him, while they all raced for cover. He allowed it to soak his hair, his garment, his skin. And he was bigger than most of them, too. Taller, broader. He sported several days' growth of beard upon his face. Dark it was, and dense, and he noticed that most of the people he encountered kept their faces shaved to the skin. A few had allowed their beards to grow, but they were trimmed carefully, tame and neat.

He pushed a hand through his long, onyx-black hair, shoving the dripping locks backward. And then he returned his attention to the window, and to the people he could see beyond it. They sat at tables, enjoying bountiful food that was brought to them by smiling servants who seemed content with their lot.

Finally something that made sense to him.

He watched for a while before going to the door through which others came and went. As he started to push the door open, a man appeared and stood blocking it. Skinny, but tall enough, and smiling even though his eyes showed fear.

"I'm sorry, sir, but we're full tonight. Do you have a reservation?"

Utana looked from the man's head to his shoes, and up again. "I know not...reservation," he said. "I wish food."

"Well, um, right. But as I said, we're full tonight." He lifted a hand, a helpless gesture. "No room."

"Bring food here, then. I wait." Utana crossed his arms over his chest.

"Um, right. From out of town, are you?"

Utana only grunted at the man, no longer interested in conversing with him. Silence would best convey that the discussion was over.

"Yes, I see. Well, the thing is, it doesn't quite work that way here. I do have a suggestion for you, however."

"I know not suggestion. Bring food. I wait."

"Why don't you try the soup kitchen? Methodist church at the end of the road. See? You can see the steeple from here."

He was pointing while he babbled, and Utana only managed to understand a word here and there. He was learning the language rapidly, but interpreting the words spoken in the rapid-fire way of the people here was still difficult. He followed the man's pointed finger and saw the spire stabbing upward into the sky. "Ah, yes, church. I know church. House of your lonely god."

"Yes. Yes, that's it. Go to the church. They'll have food for you there, and a place to sleep, as well, if you need one."

Utana nodded, but he was more enticed by the smells coming from within, and impatient with the man, who was clearly trying to send him away without a meal. It was all very good to know there would be a bed for him at the house of the mortal's singular god. But there was food here now, and he wasn't leaving without partaking of some of it.

So he simply pushed the skinny man aside and continued opening the door. As he was about to enter, another man ran up and pushed against the door from within. But Utana pushed harder and shoved the man back hard, sending him flying into the wall, where he caught himself with one hand, rubbing the back of his head with the other.

Utana walked into the food place.

There was noise at first, people talking, and the clinking, chinking sounds of their ridiculous eating utensils and dishes. But as their eyes fell upon him, the eating and conversation ceased, and dead silence ensued.

Utana eyed the tables, the food, the stares of the stunned diners, no doubt surprised by the appearance of a large, dripping wet man, dressed in what James of the Vahmpeers had told him was meant to be used as bedding, but he cared not. He was focused only on food, on sustenance. His nostrils flared as he caught the scent of beef, and his gaze shot to its source.

A man in an odd white hat came through a swinging door in the back of the room, bearing in his arms a tray laden with so much bounty he could barely carry it. Each dish was covered by a lid of shining silver, and yet the aromas escaped, and Utana's stomach churned in its need.

He did not hesitate. He strode toward the small, food-bearing man, who froze at the sight of him. His frightened eyes darted left and right as he debated whether to stay where he was or to retreat. In three strides, Utana was there, taking the tray. Then he turned and walked back through the room. People rose from their tables, backing away from the path he cut. Two people stepped forward instead, and tried to block his way, but he moved them aside with a simple sweep of his powerful arm, sending them tumbling into a nearby table.

The table broke, its contents toppling into the laps of the diners who sat there, even as they scrambled to escape. A woman screamed.

Utana moved past the ruckus to the door. Servants shouted after him, asking what he thought he was doing. But he ignored them all, carrying his bounty into the street and through the pouring rain, in search of a sheltered spot in which to eat.

In a moment he spotted one of the humans' wheeled machines, a large one, with a back like a gigantic box and a pair of doors at the rear that stood wide open. Utana marched straight to it and easily stepped up into the box. He set his bounty on its floor and pulled the doors closed behind him. Making himself comfortable, or as comfortable as he could be while still wet and freezing cold, he lifted the shining lids one by one, bending closer to smell. He had no idea what most of the dishes contained, except for the one that hid the large joint of beef he'd been smelling. It was still warm, brown on the outside and oozing with juices. He picked it up and bit in, and the flavor exploded in his mouth. Tender and luscious, pink in the middle, the meat was the finest meal he'd had since reawakening to life. He leaned back against the metal wall of the box, chewed and swallowed, and sighed in relief.

One need, at least, had been met this day.

Washington, D.C.

"Congratulations, Senator MacBride," the Senate Majority Leader said.

He'd just sailed into the room where she'd been waiting for over an hour, hand extended as he crossed toward her.

Rising, she accepted the handshake. He wore a huge smile—one of those toothy crocodile smiles she'd learned how to identify her first week in office. So she prepared herself for the storm of bullshit that was sure to follow.

"Thank you, Senator Polenski. And might I ask what is it I'm being congratulated for?"

The veteran senator just waved a hand in the air. "Your new appointment. But please, sit down. Relax. I'll ring us up some refreshments and tell you all about it." Walking to his desk, he reached for the phone. "What would you like? Coffee? Perhaps something a bit stronger, to celebrate?"

"I'd really prefer to know what I'm celebrating first, Senator."

He set the phone back down and perched on the edge of his desk. She was still standing right between the two cushy chairs in front of the desk, on a carpet that was so deep, her sensible two-inch pumps nearly became flats.

He met her eyes. "You've been named head of the Committee on U.S.-Vampire Relations."

She lowered her head, laughing softly. "Fine. Fine, I'll have coffee. You can tell me all about it as we sip."

He was stone silent until she had stopped laughing. She weighed the tension in the room and realized that he hadn't been making a joke. Lifting her head slowly, she met his eyes, tiny blue marbles beneath a head of thick white hair that always looked windblown. "Come on, Senator Polenski, you can't be serious."

"I'm completely serious. Word is out that they exist, thanks to that idiot former CIA operative and his tell-all book. Most of them—and a good number of ordinary human beings, as well—have been wiped out by vigilante groups at this point, but our intelligence agencies believe there are a handful remaining. Surely you've been following all of this in the news."

"I…I didn't think it was…real." She sank into one of the chairs, the wind knocked out of her. "I thought the official stance on the late Lester Folsom was that he was demented and suffering from delusions."

"It was. Unfortunately, no one bought it. So now we need to own up. They exist. It's real. John Q. Public is terrified, and scared citizens are dangerous citizens, MacBride. We need someone to get a handle on this. To calm the public. To see to it that these…creatures are contained, monitored and dealt with."

She must have given away her gut-level reaction to his words, because he averted his eyes, and added, "As fairly and humanely as is practical, of course."

"Of course," she said.

He nodded. "You will act as the conduit between the CIA and the Senate. You'll gather all the information available and ride herd on the man in charge of this mess, Nash Gravenham-Bail. Freaking mouthful. Rest assured, he isn't going to accept your involvement easily. You're going to have to ride him hard, do your own digging, know when he's holding back and how much and push for more."

"Get him to tell me everything. I understand."

Rafe Polenski shook his head. "Gravenham-Bail will never tell you everything. But get as much as you can. Bring the rest of us up to speed, put together your committee members and with them, come up with a plan of action for us to consider."

She blinked three times, shook her head and looked away.

"Well? What do you have to say?"

She drew a breath, opened her mouth, closed it again and drew another, searching her mind for words as her brain clogged itself up with questions. Clearly no one in their right mind would want to take this on. This was the modern-day equivalent, she thought, of the Bureau of Indian Affairs, and

God knew that hadn't gone too well. For the Indians, at least.

Vampires. Good God. Vampires.

They were pushing this assignment onto a junior senator from the Midwest. Someone they thought was too naive to know better. Someone easily manipulated, easily controlled. She was none of those things. But she hadn't been in office long enough for them to realize it. She knew exactly what was happening here. This wasn't going to succeed, and someone was going to have to take the fall when the shit hit the fan. She had just been appointed to be the one.

She knew all of that.

And she also knew that she couldn't turn the post down. One did not turn down Senator Rafe Polenski. The man was a legend.

"Well?" he asked, waiting, already knowing her inevitable answer.

She met his calculating eyes, and knew she was well and truly trapped. But maybe knowing what was going on would give her an advantage. Maybe she could outwit the snowy fox himself and live to tell the tale. Maybe she was a little smarter than this old-school, old-boy network member knew.

"Your decision, Senator MacBride?" he asked pointedly.

"Scratch the coffee," she said. "I'll have vodka."

Mount Bliss, Virginia

Jane Hubbard exited a taxi, and stood looking at the front of a massive and beautiful building. Winged angels made of stone flanked the tall, wrought-iron gate, which had opened to let the taxi enter. It had proceeded along a circular drive with a giant fountain in the center, where a statue of the beautiful St. Dymphna stood, holding a lighted oil lamp—with a real flame, no less—in one hand, like something straight out of Aladdin, and a sword in the other. The sword pointed downward, its tip piercing a writhing dragon at her feet, and water spurted upward from the slain serpent, arching gently back down again into the pool below.

The building had once been known as the St. Dymphna Asylum, as attested by those very words engraved into the white stonework above the entry doors, but was now known as the St. Dymphna Psychiatric Hospital. A more modern sign just beyond the gates said so.

But the place didn't look modern. It looked a century old. Maybe two. And as comforting as the angels and the saint were, Jane felt a shiver of apprehension when she studied the chain-link fence that enclosed the manicured lawns.

Melinda, at her side, squeezed her hand. "It'll be like a vacation, right, Mommy?"

"That's right, honey. That's right."

Jane had no reason to mistrust her government. The official who had shown up at her door had been female and kind. She'd known about Melinda's condition—the rare Belladonna Antigen in her blood. Jane had known, too. She'd known that the condition made her baby bleed like a hemophiliac. She'd known that it made donors extremely hard to find. And she'd known that it meant her daughter, now seven, probably wouldn't live to see forty.

What she hadn't known—had never even suspected—was that it made her a favorite target of creatures that were not supposed to exist. Vampires, the federal agent had told Jane, were real. All the hype in the news of late had been true. And while most of the monsters had been killed by the vigilante movement sweeping the nation, there were still some at large. Any human being who possessed the Belladonna Antigen was at very great risk of being victimized by them.

Especially now that humans and vampires were virtually at war.

And so the government had set up a haven for these rare humans, a place where they could go and be protected, cared for and absolutely safe, until this vampire problem was under control.

Jane would do anything to protect her little girl. It was the just the two of them. Had always been. Melinda was special. She was more special than even the government or her own doctors knew. Jane had always protected her.

And that was what she was doing now. Protecting Melinda.

Holding her little girl's tiny hand, she stepped through the arching, churchlike, wooden double doors of St. Dymphna's, and wished she could shake the feeling that she was making a terrible mistake.

2

Coastal Maine

Brigit sat in the library of the beautifully restored
Maine mansion that had been the home of a pair
of vampires who were now among the missing:
Morgan and Dante. She thought, however, that
the simple fact their home was still standing was a
very good sign. If it hadn't been burned, then their
neighbors probably hadn't yet branded them vampires and decided to murder them in their sleep. No
roaming band of vigilantes had yet targeted them.

Morgan's mortal sister, Max, and her husband,
Lou, had lived there, as well. Having an identical
twin who was mortal was probably an extremely
good cover, Brigit thought. But they had headed
for safer ground, not wanting to be accidentally executed, as a great many innocent mortals had been.

Their brethren must consider it collateral damage

when they killed their own. If a body remained after the fire, then the victim must have been innocent. If no body was found, the victims had clearly been vampires and burned to ash. That thinking made as much sense as witch dunking. If you drowned, you were innocent. Oops.

The de Silva mansion was empty but intact. The power was still on. The house had heat and indoor plumbing, phone and internet. It was all good. Brigit wished she could stay.

But she had an assignment, and it wasn't going to be a pleasant one.

As the elders filed in, all of them having changed into dry clothes, and pink with the flush of a recent meal, Brigit waited, wondering what they would have to say to her.

Rhiannon entered first, wearing one of her signature gowns, floor-length, thigh-high slit, plunging neckline. This one was teal-green, a color Brigit hadn't seen on her before. It went well with her raven hair. She was far more than an elder vampiress. She was Rianikki, a priestess of Isis, daughter of a pharaoh. She knew about magic and could do things no other vampire could.

Behind her came her beloved Roland de Courtemanche in his old-school tux and black satin cloak. Probably unwise of him to keep wearing something that might as well have been a flashing Vampire Here sign, but that was his call. He'd been a medieval warrior knight, was wise beyond questioning and had a fierce side that he kept very well contained.

Eric Marquand, Roland's best friend, came next. A nobleman, a physician and a scientist, Eric had nearly been beheaded during the French Revolution. Roland had visited him in his cell on the night before he was slated to meet the guillotine, saving his life and making him over.

Sarafina, the beautiful, fiery Gypsy, came last, skirts and scarves trailing, bangles and earrings jingling as she moved. She was the missing Dante's aunt, but more like a sister to him. And worry marred her brow.

The four sat at a table, embodying more than four thousand years of living, of wisdom, of knowledge. And yet there were some troubling absences among the elders of their kind. Damien, the first vampire, once known as Gilgamesh. The Prince, who had become known as Dracula down through the ages. They'd struck out separately with their respective mates to try to locate survivors and bring them to safety. But it wasn't safe out there. Not even for them.

Although these ancient mighty beings who surrounded her now had practically raised her, Brigit saw them through fresh eyes on this night. She felt awe at their presence, their power, and found herself bowing her head slightly before taking her own chair at the long table.

It was Rhiannon who began, with a story that Brigit already knew by heart.

"Utanapishtim, Ziasudra, onetime Priest King of the land of Sumer, was beloved of the gods, and so when they sent the great flood to wipe out mankind, he alone was spared. In return for his loyalty, the gods bestowed upon him the gift of immortality. There was only one caveat—he must never attempt to share the gift with any other human."

Rhiannon fell silent, her gaze sliding, adoringly but solemnly, to Roland, who nodded once and picked up the tale. "The great king Gilgamesh— the man we know today as Damien—was in deep mourning for his best friend, Enkidu, who was more than a brother to him. Enkidu was like the king's shadow self—like a twin who is opposite and yet the same," he said, with a meaningful look straight into her eyes.

Brigit understood.

"King Gilgamesh blamed himself for Enkidu's death. He wanted only to find a way to restore life to his friend. And so he wandered into the desert in search of the only immortal—the flood survivor. And he found him. The king commanded that Utana share the gift of immortality with him, so that he could share it, in turn, with Enkidu."

Roland stopped there, turning to Sarafina, who

took up the thread. "Utana could not refuse his king, and so he gave him the gift. But despite becoming immortal himself, King Gilgamesh could not recover his friend from the Abode of the Dead. And because Utana had disobeyed the gods, he was cursed. His eternal life was taken from him—but his immortality was not. And later, when he was murdered by an evil one, Utana died but did not die. We know now that his spirit remained, trapped with his ashes, lo these five thousand years."

Eric took over from Sarafina at her gentle nod. "There came to light a prophecy, a stone tablet from Utana's time, that told of the destruction of the vampire race and suggested that only by raising Utanapishtim from the dead could it be averted. This prophecy spoke of the twins who were neither vampire nor human but both combined, the two who are like no other and yet opposites, who would save our kind. But parts of the tablet were missing. Broken. Hidden away, so its true meaning was unclear."

Eric then looked at Brigit, holding her eyes until she knew she was supposed to fill in the rest. She cleared her throat, nodding. "And so the good twin, the one who was born with the gift of healing, found Utana's ashes and restored life to him. But Utana's mind was warped from thousands of years of imprisonment, and he turned on his own people, decimating the vampire race he had never intended to create. And those who remain believe it is only the evil twin, who was born with the power of destruction, who can return him to the grave—his prison— and save what few remain of vampire-kind."

Everyone in the room nodded.

Rhiannon spoke again. "Utana believes that he can only be free of his curse by undoing the wrong he committed so long ago. He thinks he has to wipe us out, so that when he dies again, he will move on to the afterlife, rather than returning to the horror of the living death where he spent more than five thousand years."

"I know."

"We know very little about his strengths, his powers," Rhiannon said. "Except that he can blast a beam of light from his eyes that is much like the explosive beam you yourself can project."

"And that he can take the powers from others," Brigit added, with a look toward the closed door, beyond which her brother lingered, somewhere, with their parents, Edge and Amber Lily, and the others. "We know that, because he took J.W.'s healing gift away from him."

Everyone nodded sadly.

"We don't know how to kill him in a way that will free his spirit," Roland said softly. "We only know that the first time he died, he was beheaded and his body cremated, at least according to the tablets. And while it grieves all of us to think we might be condemning him—our own forebear—to return to that nightmarish state, he has left us with no other choice."

Brigit nodded. "I know."

"We also know," Eric said, "that he can sense us, feel us, just as we can detect the presence of one another, and of the Chosen. There's a bond, a connection. We believe that he is using that bond to follow us, even now."

Brigit frowned; this was the first she'd heard of that. "What makes you think so?"

Eric rose, crossing the room to take a remote control from a nearby shelf and aiming it toward an elaborately carved, antique-looking cherrywood armoire. The armoire's doors swung open, revealing a large, state-of-the-art flat-screen TV. Eric thumbed another button to turn it on, and another to activate the DVR and choose a local news broadcast from a few hours earlier.

Captioned "Bangor, Maine," with today's date beside it, footage panning the interior of a demolished restaurant played out on the screen. Then the scene switched to show a S.W.A.T. team surrounding a delivery truck on a street that had been closed down, as a grim-voiced reporter explained, "An apparently mentally disturbed man trashed Succulence, a four-star restaurant in Bangor, this evening. The assailant took only food, but injured several people and caused enormous damage to the business. Police believe they now have this obviously dangerous man cornered in the back of a delivery truck a few blocks away from the restaurant. This is live coverage of the S.W.A.T. unit, as they slowly close in on the truck and—"

"No," Brigit said, getting to her feet, talking to the TV as if it would help. "No, no, get them out of there!"

A hand fell on her shoulder, and Roland said, "This is a recording, child. It's already happened."

The cops took cover and took aim, as someone lifted a bullhorn to order the man to come out with his hands up.

Brigit watched as the truck doors opened and Utana appeared. She'd seen the man before, but never looking like he did then. His makeshift garment—a toga made from a bed sheet—was torn, wet and filthy, his long black hair hanging in dripping straggles, his face shadowed by a wild-looking beard, his eyes dangerous.

He looked like she imagined Moses had, after his encounter on Mount Sinai.

And then she could see nothing but the beam that emanated from his eyes just before the picture went to snow. The screen flicked back to the somber, too-tanned face of an anchor at the news desk. "Our camera crew survived, and though they got additional footage, we can't show you more, out of respect for the families of the seventeen officers who were wiped out by whatever unknown weapon this madman was wielding. Frankly, it's just too gruesome for television. The man is still at large, and the National Guard has been called in to help with the hunt."

Brigit stared at the screen long after Eric had shut off the television.

"You have to stop him, Brigit."

She nodded. "And what are all of you going to do? You can't stay here. He's too close. He won't stop until he finds you."

"We're moving," Roland said. "The plantation in Virginia is isolated enough in the Blue Ridge Mountains that it should be safe…at least for a little while. We don't want to go too far until we've eliminated this threat and gathered as many of our own together as we can find. After that, we'll likely be forced to leave the country for a location more remote and isolated than anything the U.S. has to offer in this day and age. We're exploring several options now. But that's not for you to worry about."

"You have only one task to focus on," Rhiannon said. "Find the first immortal. Find him…and kill him."

Downtown Bangor, Maine

Utana had sensed the soldiers surrounding his temporary haven. All he had wanted was a meal, and a dry place in which to eat it. And he'd found both, though he had been surprised by the resistance of the food vendors when it came to sharing their bounty. Taking it by force had seemed ridiculous. Did they not realize he was a king? He had left the establishment in a mess, but it would be easily restored. He'd broken a table, perhaps some of the strange pottery food-vessels, as well. He'd had to use force on some of the humans. The mortals. That was what James of the Vahmpeers had called the ordinary ones. Mortals. Utana had intended them no harm, had used no more force than was necessary.

Well, perhaps a bit more than was necessary. He'd been agitated. And half-starved.

But then he'd found a shelter and filled his belly with the food, and he had never eaten its equal. Never. It was luscious, fit for the gods. He'd found a comfortable spot in the corner of the box that contained him, and he'd curled up, intent on napping, despite the fact that his clothes were still wet and he was shivering with cold.

And then, just as he'd been about to nod off into the world of dream journeys, he'd felt them all around him. He'd felt their fear of him, their hatred and their intentions. His punishment for taking a meal without compensation was to be death, it seemed. They carried weapons, he sensed it. And he knew by the vibrations in the very ether between them and himself that those weapons would be used on him without hesitation.

Yes. There was no question. He felt it. Violence. Barely contained, crouching like a tiger about to spring.

And so he had no choice. He wanted nothing from these humans. He meant them no harm whatsoever. It was his own race he must wipe from existence, not theirs. All he intended was to eat, to sleep and to be on his way. This devastation he was about to unleash was entirely their own doing.

Sighing in resolution, and with no small regret, he had opened the doors of his haven and meted out justice. He'd focused the beam from his eyes on the men who leveled their weapons at him. The light shot forth, a blue-white stream that widened, opening like the wings of a great, deadly bird, so that all of them were caught in it. The soldiers went still as the beam hit them. Their eyes widened as their bodies began to vibrate, frozen within the grasp of his power and unable to break free. And then, one by one, they exploded.

When it was over, an eerie calm fell over everything around him. The silent stillness of death. It was like no other emanation. When the souls fled the bodies of the living, especially in such massive numbers all at once, they left a vacuum behind. A space devoid of sense, of sound, almost of air.

Utana stepped down from the box-on-wheels,

and he walked amid the remains. True carnage, this. Pieces of the humans littered the stone like ground, and hung from the motorized vehicles and the tall, light-emitting poles, and from the lines that seemed to be strung everywhere in this world. It was a terrible waste of life, and all for nothing.

As he looked at the death and mutilation around him, he thought of the healing power he had taken from James of the Vahmpeers. He had not yet attempted to use it, but he had no illusions that it would be effective on bits and pieces of men. He would first have to sort them, leaving none out, nor mixing any together. Such a task would be impossible, and would take days—weeks, perhaps—even to attempt. No, it was of no use. Were they not meant to die this day, they would not have placed themselves in his path. The higher being knew far more than did the earthly one. Their fate had been sealed; there was no undoing it.

He picked his way among the limbs and gore, amid the tiny fires dancing from their motor-driven conveyances, and the smoke spiraling all around him. He saw more humans, watching from a safe distance, and he felt only fear and terror coming from them—no attack. Pausing, Utana bent low to scoop up a dead man's weapon. And as he held it, he closed his eyes briefly and absorbed its vibration through his palms. It took only seconds for him to understand how the weapon worked, how to use it, what it did. And so he gathered up a few more before moving on.

More soldiers would come after him. No army would let so many deaths go unavenged. He had not wanted war with the humans, but it seemed inevitable now.

His bare feet were cold as they slapped down on the wet stonelike substance with which modern man had apparently paved the world. The rain was lighter now. He would find clothing and shelter, a base of operations from which to work. The vahmpeers had moved to somewhere not far from this place. But they would know of his nearness now. Word of his deeds this night would surely spread. And then they would flee. If he hoped to catch up to them, to wipe them from existence, he had to find them before they did.

Washington, D.C.

"You can go in now, Senator," the curly haired receptionist said.

Marlene MacBride rose from the vinyl chair she'd been warming for the past twenty minutes, smoothed her pencil-slim skirt over her thighs and strode to the door. She was staring at the plaque that adorned it. Special Agent Nash Gravenham-Bail. As she lifted a hand to tap before entering, the door swung open, and she glimpsed a broad torso and a large file box coming toward her.

The box bumped her chest before she had a chance to move out of the way. She automatically gripped it, and the man behind it spoke.

"Senator MacBride. Sorry about the wait, but I think you'll find everything you need in here. Enough to get you started, at least."

Marlene lifted her stunned eyes from the box to the face of the man shoving it at her. It was the scar that caught her attention, as she would guess it did most people's upon meeting this man for the first time. It was a thin pink line, raised a bit, that began at the outside corner of his left eye and angled across his cheek to the center of his chin.

"Line of duty," he said. "Besides, it's intimidating. That's a bonus in my line of work."

She shifted her focus from his scar to his eyes. Wet cement, they were. "Mr. Gravenham-Bail?"

"It's a mouthful, I know," he said. "I still cuss my parents out on a daily basis for the hyphenated name thing. I mean, really, just pick one already. Make a decision."

She nodded.

"Easier if you just call me Nash."

"Mmm." He still hadn't let her into his office. She was standing in the doorway, holding a box that was getting heavier by the minute, and getting absolutely nowhere with him. "Look, Nash, I was expecting a meeting with you. So you could brief me on all this."

"Oh, really? I thought you'd want documents. Files."

"Well, those, too, but—"

"Look if you want a meeting, we'll set one up. Week after next?"

"I'm afraid that—"

"Barbara," he called, and started moving forward. Marlene had to either back up or let him walk right into her. He backed her into the reception area, pulling his office door closed behind him. "Barbara, schedule me a sit-down with the senator, here, for the next free afternoon I have. A full hour. And, uh, get someone to help her down with this file box, will you?"

"Of course, sir."

"Nice meeting you, Senator MacBride. I'll see you in two weeks."

He extended a hand to shake, looked sheepishly at the box that was occupying both of hers, then turned and was back in his office, door closed, before she could say boo. Hell, this wasn't going well at all.

Nash closed his office door, counted to sixty and picked up the phone. "Babs, she gone yet?"

"The elevator doors just closed on her, sir."

"Great. Get me a flight to Maine. Bangor, or as close to there as possible."

"Right away, sir."

Nash needed to get his hands on this resurrected monster, get him under control. He would not rest until every last vampire was obliterated. If even one remained, they would make others. Like damn lice. They were parasites. You had to pick 'em clean to end the infestation. And you had better get their eggs, too, unless you wanted to start the process all over again. In this case, that meant the so-called Chosen. Humans with the rare antigen in their blood that made them susceptible to the disease the Undead had dubbed the Dark Gift. It wasn't a gift. It was a freaking mutation. The only humans who could become vampires were the carriers of the Belladonna Antigen, so they would have to be eliminated, too. As soon as they'd served their purpose.

The Dymphna Project would take care of that. And by the time pesky Senator MacBride waded through the paperwork mountain he'd handed her, it would all be over.

But in order for his plan to work, he needed to find this Utanapishtim, this madman from another age, another world. He had to win the man's trust, so he could wield him like the weapon Nash intended him to be.

And then, when the war was over and humans were victorious, he would destroy the so-called immortal last of all, and end the age of the vampires for all time.

He was going to save mankind from the scourge of the Undead. And no junior senator from Nebraska was going to get into his way. No matter how good she looked in a skirt.

St. Dymphna Psychiatric Hospital
Mount Bliss, Virginia

Roxanne was the nurse on check-in duty on the day the odd little girl and her mother arrived at St. Dymphna.

And as it turned out, that was a damned good thing. Then again, she'd never believed in coincidence.

Roxy had been a friend to the vampires all her life. And her life was a long one. Longer than most of the folks who carried the Belladonna Antigen in their blood. They were known as the Chosen, and word was, they didn't live to see forty.

She'd seen a hell of a lot more than forty, but she wouldn't admit how much more. Not under torture. Besides, age was just a number.

Roxy had no desire to become a vampire. But she damn well wasn't going to stand by and watch them get wiped out of existence, either. Her vamp friends had been good to her. Saved her wrinkle-free hide more than once.

So when she got notification from Uncle Sam that she was to report to some out-of-commission loony bin with all the other Chosen, to be protected from vampire attack, she knew it was time to take action.

Vampires didn't prey on the Chosen. They were like spooky-ass guardian angels to them. Couldn't help themselves. One of her kind got into trouble, one of their kind showed up to bail them out. Usually did a little oogly-boogly mind shit on the way out, just to erase the memory and keep their cover intact.

Vamps weren't the only ones who could play oogly-boogly mind games.

Roxy had made herself disappear. As far as the government knew, she was on the run, avoiding compliance with their summons, while in truth she was right under their noses, with a false ID and a freshly minted nursing license, working as an R.N. at St. Dymphna's. Forged paperwork, a little witch-craft—yeah, she was a card-carrying spell-caster—and bam, she was hired.

And she was damned glad to be in the place, too, that day when she greeted the newest guests, Jane and Melinda Hubbard, at the front door.

The mom and daughter looked like two photos of the same person taken twenty years apart. And they looked scared, too.

"Hey, now. There's no call to look like that," Roxy said. "Know why?"

Melinda stared at her, huge blue eyes seeing

right through her, she thought. "Why?" the little girl asked.

Hell, the kid's gaze was so intense it sent a little shiver up Roxy's spine. But she shook it off and smiled. "Because *I'm* here. And I'm going to give you my personal promise that nothing bad will happen to you while you're here. You're gonna be my special friends. And no one messes with Roxy's friends. Okay?"

Jane smiled a little, hugging her daughter closer.

"She's like me, Mommy," Melinda said softly.

Roxy felt her smile die as Jane shot her a look. Quickly Roxy glanced around to make sure no one else had heard, and then she knelt down to put herself at eye level with the little girl. "I *am* like you," she whispered. "But that has to be our little secret, okay? No one else can know."

"Why?"

Roxy swallowed hard. She had not intended to tell these people—nor any of the other captives—who or what she was. It was too dangerous. Now she had a seven-year-old apparent psychic to contend with.

Roxy bent closer. "I might get into trouble if you tell. Okay, honey? You know how to keep a secret, don't you?"

"Uh-huh." Melinda eyed Roxy up and down. "Okay," she said. "I won't tell." Then looking up at her mother, she said, "She's good."

Roxy's brows went up. There was definitely more to this little girl than the antigen they shared. Speaking at a more normal volume, she said, "I'm gonna find you guys the nicest room in this place. Come on with me now. We're all up on the fourth floor."

As they headed for the elevators, Jane leaned in close. "What's going on around here, Roxy?"

Roxy glanced up and to the right, where the wall met the ceiling, meaning in her eyes. And she knew when Jane followed her gaze and spotted the camera mounted there. "Eyes and ears, hon," she whispered, a big, fake smile on her face. "Everywhere."

Jane nodded and lowered her head, face averted from the camera. "I'm just trying to find out if it's safe here for my daughter."

"Should have done that before you brought her here," Roxy said.

"Then we're leaving." Jane started to turn away toward the big entry door.

Roxy clasped her arm, and squeezed hard enough to get her attention and stop her in her tracks. "They won't let you leave. You didn't notice the armed guards walking the perimeter? The electric fence around this entire place? You're here now. And you'll have to stay here."

"But—"

"No buts. No choice." The elevator doors slid

open as Roxy released the woman's arm but continued to hold her eyes. Her false smile had vanished, and she realized it and pasted it back on again. "I'll do everything I can to protect you both. And when the time is right, I'll get you out of here."

"That's why you're keeping your...condition... secret?"

Roxy nodded as she hustled them into the elevator. "You want the zoo cages left unlocked, best have a monkey posing as a zookeeper, don't you think? Now come on. You blow my cover, we're all done for. And for heaven's sake, smile. You've gotta look like you're glad to be here. All right?"

"All right."

They stepped inside, all three of them, and the elevator doors slid closed. As they rode upward, Roxy added, in a very soft whisper, "Don't let them know she's different. That would be...bad."

The mother shifted her blue eyes to the little girl, who stood between the two adults, her knapsack on her back, a teddy bear peeking from the top. Tears shimmered in Jane's eyes, but she blinked them away and tightened her grip on her daughter's tiny hand.

3

Bangor, Maine

Brigit smelled death in the air. Death, grief, violence. And something more. She was standing above a demolished street in downtown Bangor, Maine. There was a taste to the night, a scent and a feeling. It smelled this way after lightning struck. After an electrical transformer had blown up, or after a breaker box had short-circuited.

And after she had used her power to blow something to bits.

She would have known what had happened here simply by that smell, even if she hadn't seen the news reports with her own eyes.

The streets were blocked off. Cops wearing black armbands in honor of their dead stood sentry at every possible access point. But they hadn't covered the rooftops. Local law enforcement agencies had a lot to learn about the Undead—and their mongrel kin.

Brigit stood on the roof of a hardware store, looking down at the mayhem. Burned-out vehicles, scattered debris. There were still body parts here and there, missed by the EMTs and the crews from the coroner's office, no matter how thorough they thought they had been. She could smell them. Charred meat had a distinctive aroma, and charred human meat had one all its own. It wasn't pleasant.

Her nose wrinkled, and she averted her face, closing her eyes against the onslaught of remembered images. But she couldn't stop the nightmarish scene from playing out in her mind just as it had so recently played out for real on the streets below her. She was too close, her mind too open. She saw the entire encounter play out in her mind's eye. Utana big and so powerful, but more utterly alone than any man had ever been, cold, wet and shivering in the delivery truck, devouring the stolen food with relish. She felt his awareness of being surrounded, his confusion as to why the humans would want to harm him when his goal was the same as theirs. To exterminate the vampires.

She felt his anger, and she felt, too, his reluctance to do what he had to do—followed slowly by his bitter acceptance of it. He believed the humans had left him no other choice. He believed it completely.

She pressed a hand to her forehead, willing the

images away, but they played out all the same. The beam blasting forth from Utana's eyes. The men—innocent men—being blown literally to pieces. And despite the horror of it, Brigit found herself compelled to examine the images more closely. How had he widened out the beam that way? She couldn't do that. She had to blow up one thing at a time. How had he managed to broaden its scope to include a wide range of targets all at once? She'd never been able to achieve such a thing.

Hell, if he was more powerful than she was...

No, she wouldn't think that way. He might be stronger, but she was smarter, faster, more at home in the here and now. Not to mention that she was sane. Oh, she supposed there were some who would debate that, given her hair-trigger temper. But she was at least saner than he was, this man who'd been buried alive for more than fifty centuries.

It wasn't his fault he was out of his freaking mind, she thought. But that thought, too, she shoved aside.

She started to turn, intending to track him down by following the essence he left in his wake, but then she paused, brought to halt by the vision still unfolding in her head.

Utana himself, his wet bedsheet toga dragging the ground, his long black hair clinging to his powerful shoulders and rain-damp chest, climbing down from the truck and walking slowly among the dead. She felt the waves of regret washing over him with so much force that they left him weak. She felt the tears burning in his eyes. And there were, inexplicably, answering tears welling up in her own.

And then, from directly behind her, he said, "Do you see? The humans—they gave me no choice."

Her head came up fast, chills racing up her spine at his presence. How? How had he snuck up on her like that? Why hadn't she felt his approach as she would feel the approach of anyone—mortal or vampire? Had he learned to block his vibrations from others? And at such close range? Impossible.

She turned to face him, trying to erase any hint of fear from her expression. Her eyes were level with his massive chest, and she had to tip her head back to focus on his face.

He met her eyes, and his flashed with recognition. "Brigit. The sister of James."

"Yes."

He lowered his head, perhaps unable to hold her gaze, and she sensed he might be ashamed of what he had done. "You are sent for to kill me?"

"Yes."

"Tell me of your brother and his Lucy. Are they...?"

"They're fine."

Unmistakable and unspeakable regret flashed in the depths of his gleaming jet-black eyes. "I wish not to harm you, sister of James."

"Don't worry, Utana. You won't."

He blinked twice, a frown appearing between his brows. But as he lifted his head and met her eyes again, she saw something more there. A hint of a spark. Perhaps he was rising to the challenge.

"I wish there were another way," she said. "I hate having to do this to you."

He almost smiled as he repeated her own words back to her. "Don't worry, Brigit. You won't." And then his teeth bared in a full-on grin. He was very pleased with himself, no doubt at his flawless repetition, right down to the inflection and tone.

She lifted a hand, palm up, fingers loosely resting against her thumb, as he spun and raced across the rooftop, putting some distance between them. She focused on him, flicked her fingers open and released the powerful, deadly beam from her eyes.

As if he felt it coming, Utana tucked and rolled, dodging the flash of laser like light. The chimney behind him exploded. Bricks flew like enormous pieces of shrapnel, but he blocked them with one arm, even as he turned and fired a beam from his own eyes in her general direction.

Brigit dove out of the way, and Utana's blast of energy blew past her and kept going until it hit a window across the street, shattering it.

Below, the workers cleaning up after the massacre scrambled for cover. People shouted from their crouched positions, looking up and pointing.

From behind a vent fan, Brigit launched another bolt of destructive energy, then raced to the rear of the building. Even as he shot a beam back at her, she jumped, plummeting downward and landing hard in a low crouch that did little to absorb the teeth-jarring impact.

Springing upright again, she ran. Her feet pounded the pavement as she poured on every ounce of human speed she possessed, eager to lead Utana away from anyone who might be harmed in the cross fire. Not that there was any love lost between her and humankind. But her vampire family would frown on unnecessary bloodshed.

Except for Aunt Rhiannon, of course. She would love it.

Brigit dashed down an alley, trying hard to tune out the stench coming from the trash bins as she did. Behind her, she heard Utana land barefoot on the pavement, and an instant later he was hurling power after her like Zeus hurling lightning bolts after an unrepentant sinner, as she zigged and zagged to avoid being blown to bits.

Ducking behind a building, she pressed her back to the brick, panting hard to catch her breath. But not for long. She popped her head out just long enough to return fire, then jerked it back behind the wall again. Once, twice, three times. Each blast of power sucked more vital energy from her. More life force. More strength. She wondered if it was the same for him.

Peering out from behind the building once more, she didn't see him, so she made a dash for the edge of town.

He followed, no longer firing, just running.

Yes, she thought. Using his power of destruction must drain him, too. And he'd annihilated many already tonight. She had the advantage. Except that she was pretty sure he'd been stronger to begin with.

Running onward, she knew she needed more speed, more force. Though it would rob her of precious energy, she paused to call her vampiric self up to the surface. Her jaw began to pulse and throb as her incisors elongated themselves, and her entire body prickled with newly heightened sensation. And then, fully vamped out, she ran full bore. The preternatural burst of speed would, she knew, make her appear as no more than a blur in the eyes of a human.

And, she hoped, in the eyes of the first immortal, as well.

Miles melted away, but Brigit didn't stop until she stood in a wooded glen. There was a pond. There were trees. A nearly full moon hung low in the sky. It would be dawn soon. Leaning against a tree, she hung her head, caught her breath, let her body return to her more natural state. Her fangs retracted. Her skin felt almost numb in comparison to the heightened sensitivity of vampire flesh and nerve.

"I will wait until…you make ready."

She straightened, spun. And there he stood, tall and straight and barely winded. "God," she muttered.

"Utana," he corrected. "You are…powerful warrior. Strong. Smart. I expected not such challenge from one so beautiful."

"Don't try to distract me with empty flattery, Utana. It won't work."

He frowned, tipping his head to one side as if trying to understand the meaning of her words. "I ask again—do not make me kill you, woman."

She met his eyes, then had to look away. They were black as night, deep and full of misery. "You murdered dozens of my people."

"All my years—as priest, as king, as soldier, as flood survivor, as immortal—all my years, I tell you, never did I kill when I was able to find another way. But—this time, no choice was I given. The will of the Anunaki must be obeyed."

She felt his heart twisting with his words, as if he were holding back an emotional storm. There was pain in this man, and she hated that she could feel it. She didn't know why, and wished it would go away, so she tried to close her mind to his. "There has to be another way," she whispered.

"Another way, yes. A living death for me. I want only release, Brigit of the Vahmpeers. Release for the vahmpeers, as well. To release from the curse of living as demons, hated by the gods, forced to exist on the power of mortal blood. It is damnation for them. You cannot see with the wisdom of one as old as I, woman. But I remove your peoples' curse as I remove my own. I wish only to join them in the Land of the Dead, where we will make our peace. I cannot know that blessed release until I obey the will of the gods and destroy the last of the vahmpeers."

"Over my dead body."

"Yes, I fear it is so." He sent a blast, but she felt it coming.

And even as she lunged out of the line of fire, she realized with stunning clarity that she had known he was going to blast her before he had made a move.

That apparent psychic bond she'd been cursing only seconds earlier had enabled her to read him.

She hid behind a fragrant pine, hands braced on its sticky trunk, and she tried not to think before acting. She decided she would attack on impulse, without a plan, while reading his intentions as they formed.

Popping out from behind the tree, she fired and scored a direct hit. The beam slammed the big man in his abdomen, the force of it bending him in two and launching him backward through the air. He hit a boulder and sank to the ground, only to roll to the side as she sent a second shot.

She ducked as he shot back. Her pine tree cover, five feet behind her by then, blew apart and went crashing to the forest floor, forming a huge barrier between her and Utana. Dashing to another cluster of trees, Brigit shot again, blindly this time, and then she ran on.

It must have looked, from above, as if an invisible giant were stomping across the forest, each step snapping trees as if they were toothpicks.

And yet no further hits were scored. He pursued her, his pain washing over her in waves that were almost as debilitating to her as they must have been to him. God, why did she feel him so powerfully?

He was getting closer. Brigit turned, lifted a hand to fire and felt an enormous force, like gravity times ten, pulling her straight to her knees. She shot all the same, but he sidestepped the blast and walked slowly toward her.

Lifting her head, she watched him approach. She raised her hand, palm up, but for the life of her she could not generate enough energy for more than a slight flash from her eyes. It made a popping sound as it crested in the air between them.

Utana reached her and then sank to his knees, as well, facing her. They knelt there, as close as they could be without touching. Their eyes met, locked. "I can…fight…no more," he whispered.

"Neither can I."

Three panting breaths, and then his hand cupped the back of her head and he brought her face to his, smashing his mouth to hers, kissing her with all he had. Several days' beard brushed soft against her chin, and they tumbled to the ground, limbs entwined, as fire burned in Brigit's veins and she wondered just what the hell had come over her— over him.

Exhaustion won out over passion in the end. Their kiss, though heated, began to cool, as, wrapped up in each other, they sank into an exhausted slumber on the floor of the decimated forest.

When Brigit stirred some hours later, the sun was beating down. The birds were singing a riotous chorus.

And Utana was gone.

She got to her feet and stood in silence, absently brushing the leaves and twigs from her clothes, and turning in a slow circle. But he was nowhere near. She didn't feel him anymore.

She relived the battle, her mind replaying every blast she'd sent and every one he'd returned. She walked back through the forest, noting where she'd been standing, running, diving, with the benefit of clear-minded hindsight.

Swallowing hard, she shook her head. He could have had her. At least three different times, she realized, she'd been exposed. An easy target, her back to him. And he'd sent bolts of power, not at her, but at nearby trees, toppling them.

He could have killed her. But he hadn't.

And then she relived that kiss. That earth-shattering, mind-blowing kiss.

"Damn, what am I doing?" She pushed a hand through her hair, and closed her eyes.

Utana had managed to force his eyes open before the sun rose. Pain still throbbed in his body from the single blow she had landed in their battle of the night before. And yet, as he'd studied the beautiful woman in his arms, he was overcome with feelings that were counter to his purpose. He told himself that it was little more than the natural urge to possess her. That any man would feel the same. It was only nature. He was male, she was female. And he wanted to take her, there on the floor of the wooded glen.

And yet, from within, came the knowledge that he denied and refused to hear. The same knowledge that had held him back from destroying her, and had made him hurl his bolts far from her soft and pleasing form.

Passion he could understand. Tenderness? For his enemy? No, that would not do. And while he wanted her, and thought she might not object too strongly should he take her, he held back. He told himself that it was because to mount her here and now would mean to stir her to wakefulness. And then the battle between them would no doubt begin again. And he was still in more pain than he cared to be—for a fight.

She was no ordinary woman. Perhaps she would not be owned. Indeed, according to James, women in this strange world were equal to men and able to choose. He'd thought it a joke. But truly, he had never known a woman like this one. She might very well be the equal of any man he'd ever known. At least in battle.

Perhaps in passion, as well. The kiss they had shared had been as eagerly returned as received. And fiery, too.

But no, he had a mission—a mission of the utmost urgency, assigned him by the Anunaki. He'd suffered too much at their hands to give up on the task they had given him. And truly, there must be just cause. The gods would not order the destruction of an entire race unless it were truly necessary.

He could not doubt them. He had to do as they decreed. He would not defy them again, for the suffering he had known for doing so once—just once—had been beyond human endurance. Should he cross them again, he could not even imagine what punishments might await him.

And so it was that he eased himself from the embrace of the sleeping female and rose carefully to his feet. For a moment he stood looking down at her as she slept, one hand pressed to his belly, where the skin was burned to black. Her hair was the color of sunlight. Pale yellow gold, and there were leaves of green and gold clinging to its curls. Her eyes, closed now, were the most unusual eyes he had ever seen. His people, all he had known, had eyes the color of onyx stone. Black eyes, to match their hair and their brows. But Brigit—she had eyes like the eyes of Enlil, the God of Air and Sky. Palest blue, with rims of black outlining the color. Her eyes seemed as if they could see through him.

Wise, she was.

Perhaps her words ought to be heeded.

No. She was woman, working on his resolve as only a woman could do. He tore himself away and began trekking through the forest. He needed to distance himself from the beautiful warrioress Brigit, because when near her, he could sense nothing else. Even his pain faded beneath the onslaught of that which was her. Her scent, her vitality. With distance, he would once again be able to home in on the essence of the surviving vahmpeers and resume his pursuit of them.

He hated the task that lay before him. He resented the gods for putting it upon him. And yet he dared not refuse.

Miles later, though, it was still Brigit he felt even as he emerged from the forest onto a road. She had filled his senses, leaving room for nothing else. He was in terrible condition. His clothing, the white robe James had called "toga" was filthy. Dry now, at least. But filthy. His body likewise.

He paused then, beside the road, and tipped his head up to the heavens. "I have no offering to proffer," he said in his own tongue. The new one still felt awkward to him, despite his ability to learn facts by touching objects. "Yet I beg of you, ancient and mighty ones—take this task from me. Allow my offspring to live. Free me of this curse. Surely I have suffered long enough."

He closed his eyes and waited for a sign. When none came, he sighed, resolved, and tried again. "If you will not relieve me of this mission, then at least provide me with the means to achieve it. I require shelter. Clothing. Food."

Again he closed his eyes, and waited.

He did not have to wait long. One of the humans' mechanized carts rolled to a stop beside him, and even as he stood there watching, a man got out. He was tall and very lean, and his eyes were the color of pale stone. He bore a battle scar upon his face that spoke of power. Utana recognized the man—had met him once before. The man emerged from the cart—car, Utana corrected himself mentally—and stood facing him.

As Utana stared at the man, preparing himself to blast him should he move aggressively, the newcomer dropped to one knee, genuflecting, lowered his head and said, "Oh, great and mighty King Ziasudra. It is indeed an honor to kneel before you."

Utana felt his brows lift. The rush of pleasure at hearing his old name, even spoken in such a terrible accent, and at being addressed as was befitting a king, was tinged by doubt and suspicion.

But he withheld judgment, watchful and wary. "Rise, mortal, and tell me what you want of me."

The scar-faced man lifted his head but did not rise. "Better to ask what you want of me. Do you remember me, my lord?"

"You were held captive by Brigit of the Vahmpeers. You were among those she called…vi-gi-lants."

"Vigilantes, yes. And it was you who set me free. You saved my life, my king. And now I can finally repay that debt. If you will allow it."

Utana shrugged. "What do you want of me?"

"You are the Ancient One, the flood survivor, Utanapishtim, are you not? The first immortal? Beloved of the gods?"

Utana narrowed his eyes on the human. "I am. But that does not tell me who you are, nor how you know these things that few mortals of your time know."

"My name is Nash Gravenham-Bail," the man

said. "I have been awaiting your coming, which was foretold to the leaders of my nation. I am a powerful man within my government, my king. But as of right now, I am your servant, sent to tend to you on behalf of my president."

Utana frowned. The leaders of this world knew of his resurrection? "I know not…pres-ee-dent."

"It's our word for king."

"Ah." Then the king of this land knew of him, as well?

"Will you come with me?" the man went on, still down on one knee. "I have a house for you. Food. Clothing. All you require and more."

"Why?" Utana asked. "Why wish you…to help me, human?"

The man lowered his eyes. "I don't blame you for being suspicious of me, my friend. The truth is, my president and I have no love for the vampires you've come to destroy. He wishes to honor you as is befitting a ruler, even one from another time."

"And you?" Utana asked.

The man bowed his head. "I, too, believe in the old gods, the Anunaki. Enki, Enlil, the great Anu, the fierce Inanna. I, too, wish to do their will, to solicit their blessings in this world where few even know their names. Helping you will give me a way to please them. I believe it is what they want of me." He licked his lips, perhaps nervously. "And as I've already said, you saved my life when you freed me from the vampires. And I am deeply grateful for that."

At last, Utana thought. Something he could understand, something he could relate to. And yet, he must be cautious. This world was not his own, and this human, though they had met before, was still a stranger to him.

He would go with this man, but he would exercise extreme wariness and care. But he was wise and powerful enough, he thought, to risk it. And the rewards of food, of shelter, of a base from which to work while he healed from the painful wound delivered by the lovely warrior woman Brigit, were far too tempting to resist.

"Be it so," he said to the man. "My vizier, you shall be. Rise, Nashmun," he went on, giving the man a name he preferred, "and serve me well." As the man stood upright again, Utana leaned close. He stared intently into the human's cold gray eyes. "Betray me not, Nashmun. My wrath knows no mercy."

4

At 7:00 a.m., in a truck stop not known for safety, Roxy, wearing a black pageboy wig and large round glasses, along with skintight leggings, a leather jacket and matching boots, sat at a table in the back and waited. She looked like Velma from *Scooby-Doo,* if Velma had joined a biker gang. The senator came in, looking nervous as hell, and as out of place as a goldfish in a barracuda tank. She clicked through the place in her sensible two-inch navy blue pumps that matched her blazer that matched her skirt, looking around in the most obvious manner possible.

"Shit," Roxy muttered. She quickly got up and made her way past the crowd of patrons, mostly large men and a few large women, talking loudly, chugging coffee and eating meals big enough to feed a small third-world village. She gripped the senator by the forearm and leaned in close. "Could you be more obvious?"

With a sharp look her way, the senator frowned. "Are you—"

"Endora," Roxy said. She'd had to pick a phony name when she'd emailed the senator, and her favorite TV witch had seemed like a good enough choice. "We need to make this fast."

"I'm all for that."

"Did you tell anyone you were coming here?"

"Yes."

Roxy stopped walking, sent her a look.

"My private security guy, the guy who screens my email. And no one else. I wasn't going to come here alone."

Roxy glanced toward the entry, a big glass door.

"He took the limo around back, but I can get him back here fast if needed."

"Gave you a panic button, did he?"

The senator averted her eyes. "Your message said this was about my new committee post. That you have information I need. What is it?"

She was a pretty thing, Roxy thought. And she had that idealistic fire in her eyes she'd glimpsed before in young politicians. Before they'd been around long enough to have it extinguished by the good ol' boys who wanted to keep the status quo.

"This way."

The two made their way to the table in the back, and Roxy slid into her chair and shoved a mug of coffee across the table. "I ordered for you."

"I prefer tea."

"You drink coffee today."

Roxy sipped her own, and the senator followed suit. Without further delay, Roxy said, "There's a former mental hospital called St. Dymphna's in Mount Bliss, Virginia, that's been commandeered by the DPI. You know about the DPI, right?"

The senator blinked rapidly, lowered her eyes. "I'm afraid that's—"

"Classified. I know that. Look, Ms. MacBride, I don't need you to tell me anything. I already know. I'm just trying to determine how much *you* know."

"I…know a lot."

"Not as much as you think, I'll bet, so I'll start at the beginning, and that's the DPI. Division of Paranormal Investigations. A black ops division of the CIA in charge of investigating vampires. It's been committing the kinds of crimes against other living beings over the past couple of centuries that make Saddam Hussein look like Mother Theresa. Only difference being their victims were vampires. Not humans."

The woman's eyes widened as she searched Roxy's.

"Yeah, I can see that's something you didn't know. Well, here's the thing. Right now they're rounding up all the human beings with the Belladonna Antigen and stashing them in St. Dymphna's."

The senator swallowed hard. "Humans with the antigen have been targeted by...vampires more than any other group of—"

"That's bullshit. Propaganda. Who told you that?"

"It's part of the research I was given by—"

"Research. Their research has been done by capturing perfectly innocent people who happen to be vampires and torturing them. Killing them. Experimenting on them."

"Look, I don't know who you are or why you think I'd believe—"

She'd started to get up, but Roxy gripped her wrist and jerked her back into her seat. "Humans with the Belladonna Antigen are the only ones capable of becoming vampires. Vampires sense them, and are compelled to watch over and protect them—even if it's to their own detriment. They can't help themselves. They're incapable of harming the Chosen, which is what they call those people."

Senator MacBride held Roxy's eyes. "Are you sure about this?"

"I'm the oldest living person with the antigen," Roxy told her. "I'm sure. Vampires have saved my life many times over the years, and I've seen them do the same for others. They're my friends. *Not* evil.

Not monsters. And no matter what the DPI tells you, those humans being rounded up and stuck in that asylum are *not* there for their own protection."

"Then why…?"

"I don't know. But whatever the reason, you can bet it isn't good. You need to look into this."

The senator nodded. "I will."

"Don't take too long." Roxy pushed away from the table, dragged a twenty from her pocket and slapped it down. Then she headed for the restroom at the end of a long narrow hallway in the back. Glancing behind her to make sure she was unobserved, she ducked into the men's room, rather than the women's, and moved quickly into the second stall. Unseen. Perfect. She pulled large jeans and a pillow for padding out of the bag she'd stashed there earlier, switched her jacket for a bigger one, ditched the wig and glasses, donned a moustache and beard, pulled on a billed cap with a bulldog logo on the front, and headed out again. She walked right by the senator on her way out, and the woman didn't even give her a second glance. She was on the phone, probably with her security guy.

Outside, Roxy saw what had to be the senator's car pulling to a stop. Off to one side a man in a long dark coat stood watching. Not the senator's bodyguard. Someone else.

Roxy had known this was dangerous. She was

glad she'd taken the precautions she had. Because either Senator Marlene MacBride was being watched...

...or *she* was.

Near Bangor, Maine

Brigit stood high on the hilltop, overlooking the winding road below, and watched as Utana spoke with a tall male mortal. The man's back was toward her, and she observed only that he was thin and wearing a brown "duck" type coat against the chill of the early morning. He drove a big SUV, dark green in color. It fit in here, just as his coat did. Perhaps he was a local. One of those bleeding heart, trusting types who took in strangers.

The idiot didn't know what kind of power he was playing with. Or what kind of danger. Utana was a time bomb. A killing machine with a warped mind.

There's so much more to him than that.

Now where had that thought come from?

Utana's face was visible in the early-morning sun. She'd deliberately stayed far enough away that she hoped he wouldn't sense her, but God knew she could still sense him. Not the killing machine part of him, but the man. The man who, she realized, had wept at the sight of all the carnage he'd caused. The man who'd kissed her as if she were the first shelter he'd seen on an endless trek across a burning desert. As if she were his first sip of water.

And she had to kill him.

God, what the hell was wrong with the world, anyway?

She sighed and dragged her attention back to the scene unfolding below. In spite of her mission, she found herself feeling ridiculously glad some Good Samaritan was taking pity on the once great king. Oh, she had no doubt the guy would regret it later, once he realized that Utana was completely off his rocker—a fact the stranger should have picked up on from the simple fact that Utana was wearing a filthy bedsheet like a toga.

Wait, something was happening. The local was opening the passenger side door of his SUV. Holding it as if he expected Utana to get in.

Hell, no, Brigit thought. There was no way he would trust a stranger, much less a mortal one.

Utana turned then, gazing in her direction as if he sensed her there. She sidestepped, ducking behind a bushy-boughed sentinel pine.

And then she heard him, speaking to her with his mind as clearly as if he were standing beside her, saying his words into her ear, his voice deep and resonant and sending chills up her spine.

I will not kill you yet, Brigit of the Vahmpeers. His thoughts were clear, their meaning overriding his broken English. *When I have done the rest, I will ask the Anunaki to spare you. Perhaps they will agree.*

A red haze of fury rose up in her, and she stepped out from behind the tree. *You'll let me live to see all those I love die before me? And you're expecting my gratitude for that?*

It is all I can do.

He lowered his head, bent low to get into the car. *Hey! Where the hell do you think you're going? Don't you know better than to trust strangers? Hey!*

But he got into the car anyway, and the man closed the passenger door, then went around to the driver's side and got in. The car moved away, and Brigit had no idea where it was taking her quarry.

She was cold, tired, hungry and pissed. She was frustrated as all hell and wishing for a way to shirk the duty that had fallen to her to carry out. And she had a long walk on her hands, back to Bangor where she'd left her car and her supplies.

But she needed to know where this idiot was taking Utana before she acted on any of those pressing matters. And so she set off on foot, calling on her superhuman—though not quite vampiric—levels of speed and endurance to pull it off.

She followed the SUV to a small no-tell motel on the outskirts of Bangor, grateful that they were at least heading in the same general direction as her car. The two men got out and opened a door a third of the way along the single-story motel. Room 6, she noted.

And then, as she stood there, an aroma turned her

head around. There was a diner across the street. Her stomach growled like a pit bull at the smell of used French fry grease. God, she needed food. She didn't know what was going on in that motel room, but she would have a clear view of it from the diner. She could watch just as easily from a table along the front wall, with a big fat plate of empty calories in front of her, right?

Right.

So she straightened away from the telephone pole she'd been leaning against and walked across the cracked blacktop to the greasy spoon.

She laughed, because that really was the name of the place. The Greasy Spoon.

The bell above the door jangled when she walked in, and a woman said, "Just sit wherever you want, hon. Coffee?"

"Yeah. A gallon or so," Brigit answered without looking.

Then she slid into a booth along the front, her eyes still on the motel across the street.

A filled coffee mug clunked down in front of her. "Are you the wife, or the P.I. working for the wife?" the waitress asked.

Brigit darted a glance the other woman's way and got stuck. She'd expected the clichéd red or blond beehive with pencils sticking out. Instead, she saw a careworn face, silver-gray curls and a smoker's wrinkled upper lip. "I'm sorry?"

"You're watching that *mo*-tel like it's gonna get up and run off if you turn your head. You got a husband having a fling behind your back?"

"Oh." She got it now. "No, no husband." She showed off a bare ring finger. "Just a friend I'm going to, uh…surprise."

"Uh-huh. You want food?"

"Something fast. What's ready?"

"French toast can be on your plate in ten minutes."

"Make it five and I'll double your tip."

"Deal."

Four minutes later Brigit was wolfing down a stack of syrup-drenched, piping hot, buttery French toast that was actually pretty damned good.

She slugged down the coffee, getting up and digging in her pockets for cash.

"The breakfast is five bucks honey," the woman called from behind the counter. "And here's a coffee to go, on me." She slid a capped, extra-large cup across the counter.

"Thanks. I'm grateful." Tossing two fives onto the counter, Brigit grabbed the cup and turned. She needed the caffeine boost. She was blocking her presence from Utana as thoroughly as she could, mentally maintaining an invisible and impenetrable shield around her aura. It was exhausting, and yet vital.

The men were still in the motel room. What the hell were they doing in there?

She left the diner, cup in hand, and glanced up and down the winding road. The motel was covered in white clapboard siding, with brick-red trim, shutters and doors. Each door bore a metallic, gold-toned number. A sidewalk ran along the front, and the semicircular strip of blacktopped parking had room for one vehicle per door.

A smaller, square detached structure bore a sign that said Office.

Behind it, there was a big empty rolling field full of brambles, briars and weeds. And that, she supposed, was where she was going to have to go. Sighing in resignation, she headed up the road until she rounded a bend and was out of sight. Then she jumped the ditch and jogged far enough into the giant weed patch to be invisible, and from there she began making her way back toward the motel.

She emerged from the weeds directly behind it and began counting the windows, trying to match them up with the doors in the front. When she got to the one she thought went with Room 6, she crept closer.

The window was a little too high for her, but she located a loose cinder block beneath the oblong fuel tank in the back, dragged it closer and stood on it. She took a quick peek inside, then ducked down, blinking in shock.

Her eyes had registered the following: Big. Male. Naked. Wet. And effin' ripped. The makeshift toga had been hiding a chest that made her heart beat faster and a backside that made her knees go weak. Damn.

Drawing a breath, she closed her eyes slowly, then opened them again and peered through the slightly fogged glass one more time.

Utana was standing beside a shower stall, staring at it as if in wonder. He was buck naked, and she couldn't take her eyes off him. She had a three-quarter view, and it was the shoulders that got her first. Rippling, bulging, beautiful. Every muscle was visible beneath his smooth, tanned, hairless skin. Then his chest, broad and thick, and then the abs... And as he turned a little more, the blackened section of skin where her blast had hit home. As she focused there, she felt the pain he was still in. He was trying to overcome it, trying to function in spite of it, and, for the most part, he was succeeding in keeping it buried.

He was one powerful man.

Her gaze slid downward—down to his pelvic bones and...

Oh, for the love of...well, it figured he would be hung like a stallion, didn't it?

She blinked and forced herself to look elsewhere. But it was not safe. His hard butt had just enough curve and dimpled inward at the sides. His thighs were like tree trunks. His calves like banded steel.

God, all right already. She had work to do here.

She had to kill him. She had to destroy that beautiful work of art just beyond the glass. She could probably do it right then. He was so busy staring at the shower, as if he were completely awestruck by the device he'd just made use of. His hair was still wet. He'd shaved at some point. That was probably what had been taking so long. She didn't imagine his newfound pal had had an easy time showing him how.

Utana dragged a towel from the rack and wiped himself down with it, taking great care on his injured belly.

And then he turned to the sink and twisted the faucets as if for the first time, like a child. As the water ran, he cupped his hands beneath it, and a smile split his face wide. He cranked the faucets off, then back on, then off again.

A moment later he was doing the same with the light switch. On, off, on, off.

Brigit lifted her hand, palm up, fingers loosely resting against her thumb.

His white teeth were perfect, the joy on his face exquisite, despite his pain. He flicked the light a few more times, then gazed at the toilet. Bending, he picked up the lid and stared inside. His smile faded. A frown drew his glorious black brows together as he studied it, tipping his head this way and that. He lifted the tank lid, peeking inside, and his frown grew deeper. Replacing the tank lid, he hit the handle, and with a whoosh the toilet flushed. He jumped back, eyes going wide, and then that smile reappeared. Closing his eyes, he placed both hands on the tank and closed his eyes as if listening, or feeling for something.

Of course, she reminded herself. He could understand how something worked by laying his hands on it, absorbing the information by touch. That was what he was doing now.

Eventually he took his hands away. "Ahh, that is what you do," he said, his voice loud enough for her to hear beyond the glass. "I guessed well."

Brigit drew a deep breath and began calling up power from the depths of her. She waited to feel it rising up through her feet, heating her legs, filtering into her spine like magma rising through a volcanic chamber. But it didn't.

Utana was done with the toilet now. He was picking up articles of clothing that had, apparently, been provided to him by the local Samaritan. He held up the trousers and looked at them doubtfully.

Turning, he yanked open the bathroom door and strode, naked, back into the room, apparently complaining about the pants.

Out of sight. Out of reach. She'd had the chance to save her people, and she had let it slip away. Again. What the hell was wrong with her?

Oh, but that smile…those eyes…told her more clearly than anything what was wrong with her.

She'd stopped seeing him as a killing machine. She'd seen him, just now, as a *man*. A man who could feel joy in the wonder of hot and cold running water, and electric lights. Like an innocent child, rather than a ruthless killer. A man whose death would mean his return to a state that was a lot like being buried alive.

Exactly like being buried alive.

No one deserved that, did they? Surely there had to be another way.

Slowly she withdrew from the window. She was going to have to follow them still farther, because she was certain now that this motel was not their final destination. If only she had her car.

"My king, you are about to experience something you've never even imagined."

Utana was feeling much better since his bathing, though still hurting immensely from Brigit's blast. He ignored the pain—something a warrior and king must become adept at doing. It was part, he thought, of being alive, being in a body again. And after being trapped without one for so long, he appreciated even the pain. He felt good, too, about his cleanly shaven face and the minty taste the "teeth-brushing" had left in his mouth, despite still being exhausted, in pain and uncomfortable in the modern clothing he'd reluctantly agreed to wear. The pants, in particular, felt confining and strange.

He looked across the car at his newfound vizier, doubt in his eyes. "You know not the wonder of my...imagines."

"True enough." Nashmun was driving, but he pointed up at the sky with one hand. "Have you ever imagined that?"

Scooting lower in the leather seat of the car, Utana tipped his head to stare skyward as the odd-looking bird passed overhead, and he nodded. "Yes, the large birds who soar, but whose wings do not move. I have seen and wondered on these."

"They're not birds, my friend. They are airplanes. Very much like the car in which you are riding now. They are machines, made by man, to take us from place to place. But instead of traveling on the ground, as we do in the car, the airplanes fly through the air."

Utana shot him a look, then craned his neck to see the bird again. "It is not possible."

"Of course it is. We're going to ride in one very soon, to take us to your new home."

"We are...to fly?"

"Yes. You'll love it."

Shaking his head as the airplane-bird moved out of sight, vanishing into the clouds, Utana said, "It is a strange world."

"I'm sure it is. Your English is coming along beautifully, however."

With a grunt and a nod at the device on the seat

beside him, Utana nodded. "The voice that speaks into my ears is…help."

"It's an iPod. And the word you want is *helpful*."

"Helpful. Yes." He studied the man, his stomach fluttering with excitement over what was to come, and yet his mind was occupied with matters far more important. And one beautiful woman whose kiss still lingered on his lips. "Where do we fly?"

"There's a house awaiting you—almost a palace, really. It's where certain foreign royals stay when they visit my nation's leader. And I've procured it for our use for…well, for as long as we're likely to need it."

A palace. It was certainly time, Utana thought. He had been treated with far less respect than his station demanded by the people of this land so far. And yet that, too, wasn't his highest priority. "In… the direction of north?"

"South, actually."

Utana shook his head firmly. "I must go north. My mission lies in the north."

Nashmun sent him a steady look. His eyes appeared honest. "I want to help you in your mission, my king. But you need a home base. A place from which to plan and launch your attack. You need to heal from that wound you have," he said, with a nod at Utana's midsection. "And to regain your strength, and learn more about the way this world works and how to make your way in it."

"They will escape me. I will know not how to find them again."

"You can feel them. Sense them. Can't you?" Nashmun shrugged, not awaiting a reply. "Besides, I doubt it will be necessary. They'll be sending someone after you before long, if they haven't already."

Utana lifted his brows. "Someone?"

"An assassin. To kill you, Utana. They know you have no choice but to wipe them out. And they will try to murder you before you get the chance." Nashmun tightened his grip on the wheel that let him steer the car. "That's what kind of scum we're dealing with here. They're not human. They don't have human emotions, or even common decency. They would do this, take the life of the man who created them—a man who should be as a god to them, a man they should fall on their knees and worship— they would take the life of their own king, their own father, in order to protect their own putrid existence."

Utana lowered his head. Indeed, the man was correct. His people had already sent an "assassin" to try to kill him. A fiery, powerful, sexy assassin he would rather ravage than battle.

And yet, he couldn't really blame the vahmpeers for doing so. He had, after all, destroyed a great many of their kind.

"It will be better to let them run awhile," Nashmun was saying. "Let them find a haven they think is secure. They'll start to think they've escaped you, start to relax their defenses a bit. Meanwhile, we will be gathering information. We'll know everything about where they are and how many of them remain. When we move in, we'll take them by surprise."

"Not *we,* Nashmun. *I. I* will be the one to send them to their deaths."

Nashmun shrugged. "As you wish, my king. But either way, it will be easy. Fast. One attack, and it will be done. And then you can live out your days in peace, knowing that when you die, the gods will allow you entry into the Land of the Dead, where you will find rest at long last."

"I will not live long past my children," he said. "I have no wish to do so."

Utana lowered his head, his heart bleeding in his chest at the thought of finishing the task he had already begun. Oddly, his first attack on the vahmpeers had not hurt him the way only thinking of the next one did. It had not hurt him at all. His mind had not been fully restored then, he thought. He had lashed out like a long-caged and oft-tormented lion, whose door has been left open. It had felt like release.

Now it felt like a crime. Even though he knew it was the will of the gods, it felt wrong in his soul.

And he wished with all he was that there was some other way. Even though he knew there was not.

"You're injured and weak, my king. In only a few hours you will be home. I promise, you'll be glad you let me help you."

Utana nodded, then let his head rest against the back of the seat. He was injured. Brigit's white-hot power had delivered a powerful blow. He'd used every bit of energy he could raise to keep her from killing him. And there was simply nothing left.

"That's it, my king. You relax. Try to get some sleep. It's all going to be better in no time. You'll have food, servants, a physician to examine your wounds. You'll be treated the way a man of your stature deserves. And you'll be far more equal to your task when you recover and regain your strength. I promise."

5

Brigit followed, still on foot. She was exhausted from her battle with Utana. Fighting the oldest immortal had drained her. Predictable, but she tended to see herself as ten feet tall and bulletproof.

Only in hindsight had it hit her between the eyes like a damned mallet that he most likely could have annihilated her if he'd wanted to. But he hadn't. She *had* landed a blast. He was probably hurting like hell. Unless he healed rapidly like she and her brother did. Or during the day, the way vampires did. Or if he'd used the healing power he'd taken from her brother, James, to heal himself. If he even knew how.

She wondered about that. About the extent of his powers. About the whys and wherefores of how his brand of immortality worked. She wondered if even he knew the answers to those questions. He was the only one of his kind, after all. Who the hell was he going to ask?

She knew that feeling a little too well. Yet another thing they had in common, she and the big guy. The beam of light from the eyes—the power to 'splode things, as she'd put it when she was a toddler, just figuring it out and getting yelled at for damn near every little explosion. The immortality, or at least, for her and J.W., apparent immortality. And the lack of anyone else in the world like them.

Of course, she had J.W. But he wasn't really like her, either. His power was a good one. He was the healer. Hers was the opposite. She was a destroyer.

Like Utana.

He must have missed her on purpose. There was no question. His aim wasn't that bad. He certainly hadn't missed any members of that S.W.A.T. team that had surrounded him in downtown Bangor.

She reminded herself sternly that he hadn't missed many of the vampires he'd attacked, either. Her friends. Her family. Tortured to the point of insanity by five thousand years of living death or not, that was unforgivable. Good to keep that in mind.

At any rate, she'd had a few hours sleep—yeah, in his arms, on the forest floor, like a pair of star-crossed lovers or some shit, but even so, she'd recovered some of her energy, even though she'd been expending it rapidly by following the big guy and his mysterious rescuer on foot ever since, all the while cloaking her presence. The food had helped, and the route the stranger was taking with his oversize green SUV helped even more. It took them right back through Bangor.

Sighing in abject relief, Brigit veered off from her pursuit. She jogged left, as they headed straight through the city, then right, into the drugstore parking lot where she'd left her baby-blue 20th anniversary edition Ford Thunderbird.

God, she loved her car. She had the key ring in her hand before she reached it, hit the remote starter button and unlocked the doors. By the time she slid behind the wheel, her baby was purring and ready. Relief washed over her like a warm bath. Another thing she was missing. For just a moment she leaned back against the headrest, closed her eyes and breathed.

Yes, she had inherited superhuman strength from the vampiric side of her ancestry. She could run very fast, and very far. But it wasn't as easy for her as it was for her Undead relatives. She had to breathe, her heart had to pump, it wasn't the same at all. It took a lot out of her.

But her pursuit was not yet ended. And her respite had to be brief.

Without wasting any more time, she got back on their trail, pulling out of the lot, then zooming along the side street parallel to Main, until she reached the edge of town and headed toward the highway. She could still see the tail end of the green SUV up ahead. Pressing down on the gas, Brigit thrilled to the roar of the engine and the feeling of power beneath her. She didn't even have to max out her horsepower, though, before she caught up enough to be sure she wouldn't lose them

She eased off the accelerator, keeping a safe distance and hoping Utana wouldn't notice her so near. If she let her focus waver, even a little, he might sense her. She certainly felt him. He was a keen, sizzling awareness that seemed to come to life in every cell of her body. Every nerve ending seemed acutely attuned to his energy. His life force. His... aura. The closer she got to him, the more her skin tingled and prickled and *felt*. Every part of her was uncomfortably aware. Like when her teeth became sensitive to heat and cold. That kind of overpowering feeling, of being too sensitive, too aware. Too... vulnerable. Yes, vulnerable. Damn, she didn't like that at all.

The SUV was turning off. Okay, okay, she needed to stop getting so distracted. She frowned as she approached the exit, noting the signs for Eastern Main Airport. She assumed they meant "airport" in the loosest sense of the word, because they were, at this point, in the middle of nowhere, and because this was not a place she'd ever heard of. It clearly wasn't a commercial airport.

Good God, they were going to fly? The Good Samaritan was going to get a surprise when he tried to put a five-thousand-year-old Sumerian on an airplane. Utana wasn't all that stable on the ground, for God's sake. He was probably going to freak.

Beyond all that, Brigit wondered again who the hell the guy in the SUV was. Her suspicion that he was more than just a helpful stranger grew bigger. Because why would a helpful stranger feed Utana, clothe him, bathe him, shave him and then drive him to an airport?

Something was going on. She should have sensed it from the start. But she'd been so busy trying to sort through all the wishy-washy emotional bullshit, not to mention the fire and brimstone sexual bullshit, in her mind that she'd missed it.

Brigit followed them, staying as far behind as she could, over a circuitous and unpaved road. They bypassed several hangars, heading instead up a side route marked plainly as private. Though she imagined this entire place was privately owned.

No one stopped her as she tagged along, keeping their dust cloud in sight. Not yet, at least.

Far ahead of her, the dirt gave way to a winding strip of pavement. The SUV came to a stop at a manned security booth. After what she assumed was a brief exchange, the zebra-striped bar blocking the way rose up to allow the SUV entry. Not much farther beyond, Brigit saw a small black jet sitting on the tarmac. She could tell from the wavering vapors it emitted that its powerful engines were running.

A private jet?

Well, that clinched it. This Good Samaritan dude was definitely not the kindhearted local yokel she'd taken him for, despite what his jeans and flannel shirt and forest-green SUV might suggest.

Were probably intended to suggest.

The two men got out. Utana was moving under his own steam, and she hated the feeling of relief that came with the sight of him. She was supposed to kill him, not wound him and then worry about whether he was feeling it.

His stance wasn't as erect or powerful as was his norm. He was still hurting. As she watched him from a distance, she felt his pain and wondered again why the hell he didn't use her brother's stolen power to heal himself.

Seeing the man that way detracted from her view of him as an all-powerful, timeless, ageless, almost Satanic being. She was seeing him as a man, a wounded man, out of his time and confused. Then again, she'd been seeing him that way ever since he'd kissed her. Ever since she'd seen his childlike delight at running water and electric lights.

The two men stood for a moment, and she tried to see the look on Utana's face as he studied the jet. God, it must be amazing to him. Beyond imagining. And yet his face and reactions were hidden from her view.

And then she was distracted. The man at the

tiny booth was exiting it, looking her way, raising a walkie-talkie from his belt.

Damn.

She executed a quick U-turn and headed back to the parking lot. No garage. This airport was too small for that. She left her precious car in the lot, locking it up tight, and then jogged toward that winding strip of pavement again. As soon as she thought she was out of sight of any prying eyes she poured on the speed…and yet she was too late.

The small jet was already in motion, speeding down the runway like a black vampire bat, about to take flight.

Blow it up!

She swallowed hard, watching the plane as it roared down the runway, picking up speed. Lifting her hand, fingers to thumb, she focused her eyes on the jet.

Do it! It's what you came here to do. Hell, it's what you were born *to do!* Her inner voice commanded. *Kill him. Kill them both.*

She called up the power, and her hand trembled with her torn emotions. Dammit, what was she going to do? There could be innocent people on that jet. The pilot, any other passengers she may not have seen. Hell, she didn't even know if the Good Samaritan was deserving of being blown to bits.

Since when have you given a damn about innocent mortals?

That mental voice sounded more like Rhiannon's than her own.

Shit.

The plane was lifting off and no longer within her range. Or at least not within a range she'd ever attempted before. She'd hesitated too long. The decision was made. She would simply have to follow them. Unfortunately, she couldn't fly.

Striding purposely onward, she marched straight up to the small coffin-size booth where the security guard sat on his tall stool pretending he liked his job.

"I need some information," she told him before he could even ask her who she was or tell her this area was restricted or some such crap.

He looked at her, his eyes narrow with suspicion. "You're not supposed to be out here."

"Well, I won't be—as soon as you tell me where I should be." She flashed him a big, sparkling smile and tipped her head slightly to one side, like every blonde pop star in every publicity photo.

It had the desired effect. He smiled back. "What are you looking for?"

"I need to know if you know where that private jet was going."

He blinked. "And why do you need to know that?"

Her smile faltered, and she felt frustration rising up in her chest. He was going to be difficult. And she was really out of patience. Tired, sore, hungry again—she had, as her brother had often noted, an appetite like a lioness.

Sighing, she called up her vampiric powers, though not all of them. She didn't need to fang-up to exert mind control. Nor could she, by daylight, without risking severe burns, if not death. When she met his eyes again, however, she saw the reflection of her own, their unnatural glow shining back at her from his startled mortal ones.

But only briefly.

"Tell me where that jet was going."

"Virginia. Near D.C."

"What airport?"

"Private airstrip. Covington."

"Address?"

"Twenty-one-fifty Airport Drive."

"How creative. Who were the men I just saw boarding the jet?"

"Um, I don't know about the big guy. Never saw him before. The other one is here a lot—long hyphenated name. Graverson-Bailey or something like that."

"And what else do you know about him?"

He paused, his eyes shifting left as if to search his memory. She quickly touched his chin, drawing his gaze back to her powerful one. It wouldn't do to let her control over his mind slip, not now.

"I don't know, exactly. Something for the government."

"And how do you know that?"

"His ID. It's all official."

"What does it say?"

He blinked. "I don't remember…"

"Yes, you do, Jerry," she said, sparing a glance for the name tag pinned to his chest. "It's in your brain, just like a photograph in an album. Open that album, look at that man's identification card and read it to me."

His eyes went distant and even a bit cloudy. And then he was speaking in a haunting monotone. "Nash Gravenham-Bail. DOB, eleven ten sixty-two. Height, five feet eleven inches. Weight, one hundred sixty-four pounds. Hair, brown. Eyes, gray. Central Intelligence Agency, United States of America. Security Clearance, Level 6, DPI."

She felt her eyes widen as she turned to search the skies for the departing jet. But all that remained was its vapor trail.

Utanapishtim, the most deadly being ever to walk the earth, was in the hands of the DPI.

Because she had hesitated to act—because she'd been shaken by a kiss, like a high school girl with her first crush—the two most powerful enemies her kind had ever faced had joined forces.

What the hell was she going to do now?

6

Utana sat in a small but comfortable seat near a round porthole, and watched the ground beneath him grow smaller and smaller as they rose, carried in the belly of the oversize man-made bird, until at last they ascended into the clouds and the ground became invisible.

"We are flying," he whispered, awed. And then, despite the rolling and tumbling of his stomach, he searched the skies.

"What are you looking for, my king?" Nashmun asked.

"*An.* The abode of the gods."

There had been mild amusement in the other man's tone, though Utana did not look to see if the expression on his face matched it. Did Nashmun dare to laugh at him?

"No one has ever seen it. Though we have flown as high as the moon itself."

"No!" Utana's eyes snapped toward the other man to see if he was making fun of him, taunting his apparent innocence by telling such a wild lie.

But Nashmun appeared serious. "Yes. We've sent spaceships to the moon and beyond, but we haven't yet found heaven—um, *An,* as you call it."

Utana mulled on that for a moment and then nodded. "The gods made it…un-visible."

"Invisible."

"Yes. They do not reveal it lest man ascend before he is worthy."

"That's probably it."

Utana bent his brows, certain this time of the sarcasm in the other man's tone and expression. "You do not believe."

"My king, I don't pretend to know one way or the other. Many people in this time no longer believe in the existence of gods and demons." Nashmun shrugged. "Then again, most of them didn't believe in the existence of vampires until recently. So who's to say what's real and what's not?"

"*I* say," Utana told him, angered and insulted— shocked in fact—that anyone would doubt something as real to him as day and night, or sun and moon. "If the gods are not real, who sent the Great Flood? Who allowed me to survive it? Who granted me life eternal, and then punished me so harshly when I shared that gift? Who, if not the gods themselves?"

The man bowed his head deeply. "You are right, of course, Utana, and I'm sorry if my words offended you."

"Best you remember, Nashmun. In my time, I was not king only. I was priest, also. And while the mantle of rulership is temporary, the initiation into the service of the gods is forever. A priest once is a priest always." Utana turned his eyes toward the sky once more. "I will pray to them now. Surely they will hear me well, this close to their abode."

Nashmun nodded rapidly, perhaps made nervous by the passion with which Utana had spoken. "I'll, um, I'll go up to the cockpit with the pilot for a bit, to give you some privacy. But be very careful moving around. If we hit turbulence—um, rough air, heavy wind—" he clarified, gesturing wildly to illustrate "—the plane will shake. You might fall down." He started to walk away, up the aisle, then paused to look back. "Also, it would be unwise—dangerous, even—to make any fires inside the airplane, all right?" He opened his fingers, palm in front of his eyes, when he said the word *fires*.

Utana nodded, smiling slightly at the way the man gestured with his hands, as if he were speaking to a dull-minded person, or perhaps to one who could not hear at all.

The "fire" gesture reminded Utana of the way Brigit had flicked her fingers open when trying to kill him. Beautiful, the way she moved. Everything about her was beautiful. He'd committed a grave sin against her, as he'd held her in his arms the night before. Just as he had against her brother. And he wondered if it mattered, given that he was going to kill them both in order to fulfill the dictates of the gods. And yet he felt in his soul that what he had done was wrong. And he wondered if Brigit had yet discovered his crime.

The notion made him uncomfortable with guilt. She had hated him already. She would hate him more once she knew—if there were more hatred in her. And even as he acknowledged that, he remembered the way it had felt to hold her while she slept. The weight of her head upon his chest, and the warm whisper of her breaths against his skin. The scent of her.

An odd yearning seemed to open like a gaping hole in his chest, longing to be filled once again with her presence. Her nearness.

He put a stop to his thoughts. The feeling was doing him little good, and moreover, it was distracting him from an opportunity to speak to the gods from a place nearer to them than he had ever been before.

Easing himself from his seat, Utana faced the small row of windows and dropped to his knees, shifting several times before finding any comfort at all in the strange garments he now wore. Mankind had made many advancements since his time. "Pants," however, were not among them.

Bowing his head, he closed his eyes and spoke in his own tongue, that the gods might understand him better. He hoped they would recognize him in this strange land, wearing this foreign garb.

"Ancient and Mighty Ones," he said in the ancient tongue of his ancestors. "The Seven Who Decree the Fates. Enlil of the Sky, Anu of the Heavens, Enki of the Great Abyss, Nanna of the Moon, Inanna his daughter and Queen of the Gods, Ninmah the Lady of Earth and Mountains, Utu of the Fiery Sun. Gods of old, I call upon you now. It is I, Utanapishtim, whom you first knew as Ziasudra, your loyal priest and servant, the Flood Survivor, the Immortal One. Yes, it is I."

He paused, waiting in silence, giving them time to recognize him, to remember. Until the past few days, it had been a very long time since he'd prayed.

When he thought enough time had passed, he dared to open his eyes and stared out the portholes before him, almost expecting to see them staring back at him. But he saw only clouds and blue sky.

Again he bowed his head, closed his eyes. "Mighty Ones, I beg your forgiveness for my sins. Long have I suffered your wrath, but now my suffering is compounded anew. I beg of you, set for me some other task of repentance. Remove from me the burden of this path I walk upon. Do not force me to murder the children of my soul. The golden one, in particular, the beautiful Brigit, who is like the sun to me. Surely she is blessed by Utu, to shine as she does, and by Inanna, to fight so fiercely and possess so much passion. Surely you cannot wish for me to destroy a being of such splendor, such fire. For to do so would be a sin against life itself. Please, send me a sign. Please, ask of me anything else. Anything but this."

The man, Nashmun, emerged from beyond a small door near the bill of the great bird. "I'm sorry to interrupt. We'll be landing soon. You should sit, my king, in order to be safe."

Utana did not lift his head, for to reveal the tears that stained his cheeks would be to show far more weakness than he would ever reveal to another male. Instead he only nodded and returned to his seat, relieved that they had not traveled so far as he had feared they might, for only a very short time had passed since they had left the earth behind.

Nashmun took his spot beside Utana, retrieving, before he sat, a small black box that he had left upon the seat. Yet another of this time's amazing electronic devices. This one had buttons and a small glowing red light. Nashmun pressed one of the buttons, and the light went out. Then he dropped the device into his coat pocket. "You should buckle your seat belt, Utana. Just as you did when we first took off."

Nodding, Utana did so. Although he had to wonder how much good anyone might presume the thin band of fabric would do, should the machine fail and send them crashing to the earth. Still, it seemed easier to comply than to question. And it was, after all, not the most illogical thing he'd observed among modern man.

A very short time later Utana emerged from yet another "car," although this one was a far different sort of car from the one Nashmun had driven, and in fact he did not drive it at all. Instead a servant sat behind the wheel. This car was long and gleaming black, and as plush inside as a miniature palace. There were cabinets with refreshments inside, tiny discs of ice to make the beverages cold, kept frozen by a tiny box that stayed cold inside. An amazing luxury. Oh, to have had such a device in the desert!

And yet, even the luxury the vehicle afforded paled in comparison to the place where it eventually delivered him.

This was an actual palace, one unlike any he'd seen before. Smaller than a ziggurat, yes, but elaborate, and so beautiful it took his breath away. Its surface was covered in gleaming tiles and trimmed in gold. There were onion-shaped domes that reflected the very light of the sun. Its entryway was an elaborate double arch, with a pointy peaked center that had been raised up over a tiled walkway. That elaborate path of brightly colored tiles wound amid fountains and flowering plants of all sorts and led to a pair of golden doors.

Indeed, this place rivaled the palaces of his own time.

He tried not to show how very impressed he was, lest Nashmun become swollen with pride. He'd always found an overabundance of praise the fastest way to a lazy servant.

His vizier stood at his side. "It's amazing, isn't it?"

"It is…quite beautiful," Utana agreed. "He who lives here must be very important in your land."

"No one lives here, Utana. This place is kept for visitors, rulers and royalty from distant lands. For the time being, you may consider it your home."

Blinking in surprise, Utana said, "Mine alone?"

"Well, of course it will be fully staffed. And I'll be there most of the time, as well. But yes, this is your home…for as long as you wish it, as a matter of fact."

"It is…" Utana looked again, almost afraid to believe it could be true. There was a tall gleaming golden barricade, with bars that looked like golden spears with their points aiming skyward, that surrounded the palace grounds. "It is beautiful. I am grateful."

"Just wait until you see the inside," Nashmun said, smiling broadly and clearly delighted with

Utana's reaction. "Come." They walked beneath the arches, between the flowers and fountains to the golden doors. A uniformed servant opened them, bowing low. "Your Highness."

Surprised that the man was addressing him, and even more so that he seemed aware of his rank, Utana nodded at the servant and then gazed beyond the doors as they swung open.

The room before him nearly left him speechless. A huge, round, domed ceiling, gleaming golden fixtures. The room gleamed with light, and the floor was covered with plush, brightly patterned carpets edged in golden tassels. Jewel-colored cushions and pillows lay everywhere he looked. Tables of gleaming wood and colorful tiles spilled over with fruits and pastries, all of them presented in dishes of gold. A pitcher, too, with a golden goblet beside it, awaited him.

"I'm afraid we haven't hired all the household servants just yet. We have three fabulous chefs—er, cooks, and plenty of housekeepers. However, your personal servants are still being interviewed."

"I will require dancers."

Nashmun lifted his brows, then masked his apparent surprise and nodded. "Of course. I'll see to it. I'm sure there are other requests—commands—that will occur to you as you rest and recover here, my king. But aside from all of that, will this palace do?"

Looking around, Utana spotted stairs that began

as one, then spread away to become two, leading upward to the second floor. "Yes," he said softly. "This palace will do. It will do very well." Turning, and finally allowing a feeling of absolute relief to enter his weary body and wary mind, he looked into Nashmun's eyes. "You have done very well, my vizier. And I thank you."

He could tell that his servant was pleased. He nearly beamed at the compliments of his king. And Utana decided that he could trust this man after all.

Three days.

Three freaking endless days, Brigit had been casing the place that could best be described as the Taj Mahal's "mini-me" and trying to figure out a way to get inside. And now she'd found one.

It hadn't been easy. She'd opted to drive to D.C. rather than flying commercial. It was supposed to be a fourteen-hour haul, but she'd made it in ten, doing ninety and better most of the way, and stopping only for gas, food and the restroom.

It was worth the extra time to have her car and all her supplies with her. On arriving, she'd headed to the Virginia airstrip the helpful security guard in Maine had mentioned by name—with a little help from her mental powers of persuasion. Of course, by then the sleek black jet had long since landed, and the men who'd been aboard it were nowhere in sight.

She'd had to exert her vampiric powers over five different mortals there before she'd finally found one who knew where they had gone—one who worked for the limo service that had picked them up.

And so she'd managed to extract an address to this...this Arabian palace, where her quarry was being treated like a king by a DPI agent who only wanted to use him as a weapon against the Undead. Apparently this government bastard didn't realize that wiping out her people was already Utana's goal.

Unless he'd changed his mind.

Maybe he was experiencing the same feelings of remorse she'd been having. If she could just win him over, convince him that he was mistaken, that killing her people was not what his gods wanted him to do... That creating the vampire race was not the reason he'd been trapped, his consciousness bound to his ashes for five thousand maddening years. Maybe her efforts to talk sense into him were sinking in. Maybe the DPI had anticipated as much and was taking precautions.

It was tough to see inside from this distance, and she dared not get close enough to Utana to alert him to her presence before she was ready to move in.

But one thing she had learned while lurking around outside the grounds, always out of sight, had shocked her to the core.

She'd had her first full-frontal look at the phony

Good Samaritan who'd abducted her quarry, and she'd gasped aloud when she'd seen his cold gray eyes and the scar that marred his face from the left eye to the dimpled center of his chin.

She'd dealt with him before, though she hadn't known his name. He had a real problem with the Undead, and she had no idea why. But he was powerful, and he was smart. And she had reason to believe he'd been the true instigator behind the vigilante movement that had cost the lives of so many innocents, vampire and human alike.

She'd captured him once.

Utana himself had let the man go.

Damn, this plot was getting more mixed up all the time. Could Utana and Scarface have been working together even then? No. It was impossible. Utana had been resurrected on a yacht, at sea, by her brother. At the same time, Brigit and her vampire resistance movement had been tracking and engaging the bands of mortal vigilantes who'd been burning vampires in their homes while they slept by day, helpless to escape. And in one such battle they'd taken that scar-faced bastard prisoner.

She'd had him tied up in the basement of an abandoned church when her brother and his beautiful Lucy had shown up with the newly awakened Utana in tow.

Scarface had been wearing plaid flannel and denim then, trying to look like a redneck. Lucy, though, had recognized him as one of the DPI, after being held by them for one miserable night.

Still, Utana couldn't have known him before that. Somehow Scarface had convinced the Ancient One to let him go.

Utana had been confused, fresh from five thousand years of living death and not knowing who to trust. Hell, he wasn't much better off now. And the bastard was still taking advantage of it.

The glimpses Brigit had managed to grab from a distance, and the bits she'd managed to overhear, thanks to her preternaturally enhanced senses, told her that Utana was being treated like a sultan.

He had everything but a harem.

Until today. Today she'd finally caught a break. And if Nash Gravenham-Bail of the DP-freaking-I thought he could win Utana's loyalty by giving him a palace and a pile of bowing, scraping servants, then just wait until he saw what *she* had in store.

The dancers the king had requested were due to arrive this evening. There was a feast planned.

Dancers.

When she'd first heard two of the housekeeping staff chattering excitedly about the plans as they left at the end of their shift, Brigit had been whisked back to her teen years in an instant, back to her days as the bad twin, before anyone expected her to ever do anything worthwhile, much less save her entire race. She'd returned mentally to another palace of sorts, one of her aunt Rhiannon's posh, luxurious mansions. One that had no doubt been destroyed by now, by the vigilantes trying to wipe out every vampire in existence.

In her memories, a fire snapped and crackled in a round central fireplace, and Middle Eastern music wafted from unseen speakers. She stood, sixteen and not yet comfortable with the breasts that seemed to have grown overnight, dressed in an outfit that could have been stolen from the wardrobe room of *I Dream of Jeannie.*

She felt stupid and awkward. Nothing like Rhiannon, who stood facing her, looking like the Egyptian princess she was, in a flowing skirt of satin that rode low on her hips. A jade-green hip scarf, lined with bangles, was knotted over it, and the top she wore showed off her tiny waist and bulging cleavage. Her long dark hair was swept to one side, and she moved like water.

"Do as I do, child," she told Brigit for the umpteenth time.

"I'll never be able to move like that," Brigit complained. "And besides, why would I want to?"

Rhiannon stopped the swirling motion of her hips, the undulations of her torso, and crooked a brow. "Because I say so." And then her stern expression softened. "The Egyptian belly dance is sacred, child. And in the hands of a priestess, it is an act of magic all its own."

Brigit had begun to turn away, but her head and her attention snapped back to her aunt at one fascinating word. "Magic?"

Rhiannon nodded, her eyes all-knowing. "Powerful magic. You can make any man putty in your hands by the magic of the dance. He will fall at your feet, grateful you've allowed him to be there. He will eagerly do your bidding, give you whatever you ask." She snapped her hips one way, then the other, and her bangles rang like hundreds of tiny bells with every movement she made. "Just." Snap. "Like." Snap. "That." Shimmy-shimmy-shimmy.

Lowering her head, Brigit sighed. "All right. All right, then, if it's magic…show me again."

"Good girl," Rhiannon purred.

Drawing a breath and shaking away the memories of her childhood, Brigit made a mental note to thank Rhiannon when she saw her again. *If* she saw her again, because once she gained access to that mansion and got close enough to Utana to blow him to bits, she might not have an easy time getting out again.

But her people, what was left of them, would be saved.

Nodding, her decision made, she turned from her vantage point and headed up the winding pavement through the beautiful Virginia countryside to the place where she'd left her beloved car.

She smiled grimly, hating what she had to do,

but knowing it was necessary all the same. If she could make him believe her, see things her way, there might be a chance he could survive this. And if she couldn't, then at least she would be close enough to blow his oversize ass to smithereens.

She got behind the wheel of her baby-blue T-Bird, then sat there, using her smartphone to surf the internet in search of belly dance costume suppliers in the area.

She found only two. But that was all right. She only needed one.

She was going to find an outfit. And it was going to be...

Killer.

7

St. Dymphna Psychiatric Hospital
Mount Bliss, Virginia

Marlene MacBride, U.S. senator and current chair of the Committee on U.S.-Vampire Relations, stood at the wrought-iron gates of what had been a mental hospital, speaking into an electronic box. "I told you, I'm a United States senator, and I'm here to inspect this place. I have the authority of the President, and if you don't let me in right now, I guarantee you won't have a job tomorrow."

"Yes, ma'am," the nurse repeated. "If you could just wait a few more minutes, until Mr. Gravenham-Bail arrives, it would be—"

"I've been standing here for twenty minutes already!"

"Yes, and we've phoned him and he's on his way."

"And you are proving to me that you have something to hide. So I'm leaving now, and you can tell Mr. Gravenham-Bail to expect all funding for this and any other operations he's running to be pulled by day's end. Goodbye." She released the button, spun on her heel and stomped, furious, back toward her waiting car. Her driver-slash-bodyguard was leaning against the hood and keeping his eagle eyes on her.

He hurried around to open the door for her, but before she got in, another car pulled into the small parking area outside the perimeter fence, to the right of the building. Gravenham-Bail himself got out of that car and came hurrying toward her, smiling as if glad to see her, though the scar made the expression into something grotesque and creepy.

"I'm so sorry, Senator. If you had only called ahead, I'd have been here waiting."

"Calling ahead kind of defeats the purpose of a surprise visit, Mr. Gravenham-Bail."

"Please, call me Nash."

"How about I call you unemployed? That is, unless that gate opens within the next thirty seconds."

He made a sheepish shrug, then lifted a hand toward the gate in invitation. She sighed, irritated, but walked up to it. Gravenham-Bail poked buttons on a panel, and she watched, memorizing the sequence, and smiled when he shot her an odd look.

The gate swung open, and the man ushered her inside.

"I'd have been here sooner, but I'm staying just outside D.C., and it's a half hour drive. They've got me playing host to a…visiting dignitary all week. Shall I show you the grounds first?"

"I'm more concerned about the inmates, Mr. Bail." She dispensed with the longer version of his name and didn't much care if he found that offensive or rude.

"They're refugees, not inmates. They're here for their own protection, Marlene."

She winced at his use of her first name but didn't let it derail her from her topic. "It has been suggested to me that the…the vampire race are protective of these particular human beings. And that your purpose in gathering them all here might be… something about which you've been less than forthcoming."

"What a fascinating little bit of fiction. Did it come from the vampires themselves, or have they hired a spin doctor?"

Two guards in army fatigues stood sentry at the front door. They saluted him as he moved through, holding her elbow until she pulled it away, disliking his touch.

"We don't use much of the first floor, other than my office, to the left. Pretty much everything else is housed on the fourth. That's where all our guests are located."

She followed him to the elevators, then rode along with him to the fourth floor. She was going to take a look at the other levels in this place before she left this place, she vowed.

As the doors opened, she stepped out of the elevator into what looked like an ordinary hospital. There was a nurses' desk with several uniformed women behind it. They looked up, apologetic but welcoming, as she neared them.

"Ladies, this is Senator MacBride. Senator, these are two of our nurses, Sarah Newfield and Roxanne Corona."

She nodded at the women, but her gaze froze on the redhead. Her eyes were extremely familiar.... Wait! She was the informant who'd led her here.

Quickly, she lowered her head, not wanting to give the woman away, but from the look of interest in Gravenham-Bail's face, she might have been too late. Dammit.

"Why nurses?" she asked, attempting to cover. "No one here is sick, are they?"

"No, but with a few hundred people in one area, you're liable to run into health issues. And of course, the Belladonna Antigen they all possess presents health challenges all its own. We wanted to take every precaution to ensure that the people here are safe and sound. About half our staff are

R.N.s. We also have cooks, housekeeping staff, social workers and a crack security team.

"Ladies," he went on, addressing the nurses. "I'd like you to give the senator a tour of our facilities here. She's to be allowed to visit with the patients, talk to them to her heart's content and even explore the vacant floors and the grounds if she wishes." He turned to Marlene and bowed his head. "I have some business to attend to in my office. You can find me there when you're ready to leave, and I'll walk you out." He started for the elevators.

She hurried after him. "But—Mr. Gravenham-Bail, I really need to talk to you about your true motives in holding these people here." She glanced back at the desk, ensuring they were out of earshot of the nurses. "I've done some research. I know about...your mother."

The words took him aback. He went dead silent for a moment.

She had learned that Gravenham-Bail's own mother had possessed the Belladonna Antigen. She'd vanished without a trace when he'd been eleven years old. No amount of digging had turned up any sign of her since then.

"Was she murdered by vampires, Nash?" she asked softly, using his first name at last, but only as a tactic. "Or did she become one?"

He twisted his head to the left and then quickly right, as if his tie were too tight. And then he said,

"My office. After you finish your tour. See you then." With a chipper salute, he vanished into an open elevator. Its doors closed almost instantly.

Nash Gravenham-Bail sank into his plush office chair, picked up a remote and hit a button. A panel within the wall slid open to reveal a bank of monitors, each one showing a different part of the hospital. Still using the remote, he turned up the volume and controlled the cameras in order to followed the progress of the pretty little pain-in-the-ass senator and the redheaded nurse—who had apparently offered her services as a guide—as they moved along the fourth floor.

As he observed and listened, his office door opened. "You called for me, sir?"

"Yes," he said to the young field agent. "I want a background check run on that redheaded nurse. Roxanne Corona."

"Sir, there were checks run on every employee bef—"

"Run another."

"Yes, sir."

"And I want more information about the good Senator MacBride, as well."

The man frowned.

"Personal information. I want to know where she lives when she's in D.C., who lives there with her and what kind of security she has at night."

"Sir?"

He glanced at the kid, amused by the worried look in his eyes. "She's stepping into very dangerous territory. Backing us for federal funding of this place, giving us a way to keep the so-called Chosen safe from those bloodthirsty animals. They're liable to target her. We need to make sure she's safe. She's our biggest ally right now."

"Oh."

"You have a problem with that?"

"Uh, no, sir. It's just that…"

"Spit it out, kid."

"Uh, well, sir, she didn't seem like much of an ally out at the gate."

Nash smiled. "Women, right? Keep 'em waiting, everything else goes out the window. Especially if their hormones are out of whack that day. You know how it is."

The kid sighed, lowered his head. "Yes, sir."

"I want you to do this personally. I want you to find every flaw in her security and report back to me, so I can fill in those gaps. We need her. Oh, and one more thing."

"Yes, sir?"

"I want the combination on the digital locks changed. Today."

"Yes, sir. I'll have it done within the hour, sir." The agent turned and left the office.

Gravenham-Bail leaned back in his chair and watched the monitors. He didn't need much more time. But he needed a little.

Utana was restless.

Yes, he was in the very belly of luxury here, in this place. Servants scurried to attend to his every need. Daily, sometimes twice daily, he immersed himself in steaming hot baths of scented, oiled water, in tubs that could have held three or four people. His skin and hair were cleansed with the most incredible soaps and shampoos he had ever used, and the robes they brought him to wear, the silks and other shimmering fabrics, were of higher quality than he had ever known.

He had not once been required to dress in the detestable "pants" again. He'd complained so much the first and only time he'd had to wear the things that Nashmun had not dared offer him another pair. Instead he wore robes he was told were quite common among certain foreign leaders.

He was fed meals of such succulence he could not have imagined it. He need only request a given dish and it was delivered within hours. His rooms, in the upper part of the palace, were filled with soft light, with fragrant incense, with music whenever he wanted it. His bed was the softest he'd ever known, laden with coverlets and pillows, and surrounded by curtains of emerald and jade and blue.

And tonight they were bringing him something they said was "a surprise."

He was not a stupid man. He knew full well that Nashmun had motives that went beyond love for the old gods and gratitude to Utana himself. His first loyalty was clearly to his country's king—pres-ee-dent, Utana corrected himself mentally. And that was good and right. Clearly part of Nashmun's mission was to make Utana comfortable, and to keep him relaxed and content until his government deemed the time was right to continue with the mission of eliminating the vahmpeers.

And that, Utana knew, was the true reason he was being treated so well. These people, these humans, wished to use him as the ultimate weapon in their war against the vahmpeers.

It did not seem so evil of them. It was, after all, his own ultimate goal, as well. And he did not mind being treated like a god incarnate while he awaited the time. But yet, after only three days, he knew he could not long abide here. Luxury and idleness bored him. And the gods must be getting restless, awaiting his obedience. Nor was it Nashmun's place to say when the time was right. This matter was between Utana and the gods he served. The ones who had cursed him.

A tap at his chamber door interrupted his musings.

"Enter," he said. If nothing more, this time of

idleness had afforded him the chance to become far more adept at the language they called modern English. He was nearly fluent, though aware he still possessed an unusual accent.

Nashmun opened the door. "I am back, my lord. My apologies for being away for so long today. I had matters of state to attend to."

"I am not displeased," Utana said.

"I'm relieved. And very glad I made it back in time. Dinner is ready. And your surprise awaits with it."

Utana nodded. "I am curious, I admit."

"Oh, you'll love this. This is exactly what you need, I promise."

Nodding, Utana followed his vizier into the hall. They walked along its deep red carpet to the curving staircase that wound downward, and then through the entry hall to where double doors stood open upon what Nashmun had called the "ballroom." He'd had no use for it as yet.

However, tonight, there was a banquet awaiting there. The smells wafted tantalizingly from a table so laden with food that Utana was amazed it could still stand upright. All around the room were mortals—dignitaries, he presumed—and on a slightly raised platform in the far corner, men with musical instruments played softly. There were tall drums, stringed lutelike instruments, flute-pipes and others he did not recognize.

"What celebration is this?" he asked, looking around. "Is it one of your people's high holy days?"

"The celebration is in honor of you, my king," Nashmun told him. "These are some people who have been eager to meet you. The leaders of all the nations of the world have come to pay their respects to you, and to thank you for what you are about to do for us all, in freeing us from the scourge of the Undead." He lifted a hand, snapped a finger in the air.

The music stopped. The chatting and clinking of glasses ceased. And every head turned his way. The women wore glittering gowns, their hair piled high and glittering jewels adorning their earlobes and necks. The men wore dark suits and ties, save a few, who wore robes as he did. They all looked his way.

"I give you our salvation," Nashmun announced. "The ancient and mighty Utanapishtim, Priest of the Anunaki, King of Sumer, returned to us by the gods to save us from an evil we cannot hope to survive without his help. All hail Utanapishtim!"

"Hail!" they all shouted. And then, before his eyes, every head of state in the world genuflected before him.

Utana was overwhelmed, and his throat tightened too much to speak. "I...I do not know what to say," he whispered to his vizier.

"Say nothing, my lord," Nashmun whispered.

"Only accept their devotion and respect as you pass among them to take your seat of honor."

Nashmun walked beside him, leading him by a circuitous route among the kings and presidents and prime ministers to a cushion on a raised platform, slightly above all the rest. As he passed, Utana nodded to them each in turn. Finally he was seated in a velvet nest of comfort. Only after he sat did the dignitaries resume their chitchat, their drinking.

A servant brought him a platter of food, and another clapped his hands to indicate that the others were now permitted to begin their meal. Utana began to eat, interrupted every so often by Nashmun, introducing him to the guests who humbly approached. Each president and king and prime minister thanked him for his service and pledged fealty.

He'd had no idea that the entire modern world knew who and what he was. He was quite simply stunned. And he was pleased by the gifts they laid at his feet as they came to him. Gold, silver, jewels, fabrics.

For a time he was swept up in the adoration. But then he felt something...different.

Her.

A warm, tingling sensation danced up his spine, along the nape of his neck, tickling him there like the breath from her lips.

Brigit. She was near.

He felt her. Smelled her. Looking up, Utana searched the room for her beautiful face. What was she doing here?

"And now, my king, for your surprise," Nashmun said.

Glancing his way, Utana lifted his brows. "I thought all of this was my…surprise."

"In part. But there's more." Nashmun clapped his hands twice, and as he did, the musicians ceased their playing and began again with a new song. The drums were louder, more insistent. A door in the back of the room opened, as the lights dimmed low. And the women came through it. Dancers, dancers like the ones from his own time, with scarves trailing, and faces hidden beneath veils designed not to cover, but to entice. Their bodies moved, snakelike, as they entered the room single file, bellies bared and twisting, hips and breasts adorned with jingling coins, feet bare, except for ankle bracelets.

Their movements and the beating of the drums were impossible to separate. They were one, as they danced a serpentine path onto the platform, where they performed for him.

But his eyes were on only one.

The one in the center, who moved like no other, her eyes glued to his over the top of the veil that concealed lips he had dreamed of tasting again. Her hips snapped with the power of command, and her belly undulated as if with a life of its own.

Her eyes did not release his as she danced.

And he did not release hers.

"You are pleased, my king?"

"I am…more than pleased. You've done well. I would ask only one more thing of you, my faithful vizier."

Nashmun must have smiled. Utana felt him smile, but he could not look away from the beautiful Brigit long enough to know for sure. "I think I've already guessed what that might be, my lord. Several of the dancers are prepared to see to any other…needs you might have. In your chambers tonight."

"I want only one," he said, his eyes on Brigit.

Nashmun followed Utana's eyes to the beauty who danced like no other. He frowned slightly at her. "Who is…?"

But he stopped there. Utana saw Brigit's beautiful pale blue eyes shift to meet Nashmun's. He saw the power they held, those eyes, and he focused his mind on hers to hear her thoughts.

Yes, she told the vizier. *I belong here. You hired me personally. You trust me implicitly. I am your favorite in the troupe, and you will grant me anything I desire.*

Her hips began to shimmy as the drumbeat grew more rapid.

Anything.

Anything.

Anything.

"Yes, anything," Nashmun whispered.

"What did you say?" Utana asked, privately amused by his golden goddess's power over mortal men.

"Um, nothing. But yes, I'll see to it, my lord."

"Good." Utana lifted his cup, draining it of the wine it held, than handed it to his vizier, with whom he was more pleased than ever before. "More wine."

Brigit's skirt was made of several layers of shiny satin in a deep jewel-tone like the sea itself, and over them flowed sheer layers of paler blue and purple that mimicked the many shades of the sky at twilight. Her hip scarf of teal and green rode low, coins jingling with every move she made. Her belly was bare from hips to breasts, which were cradled in a heart-shaped scrap of material that somehow managed to boost her cleavage to a formerly unknown degree. The top was fringed in green, and at the end of each strand hung yet another coin-shaped metal bangle. When she shimmied, they shimmied, and the effect on the crowd was gratifyingly mesmerizing.

Idiots.

Sheer, oversize scarves draped from her arms, and she whirled them skillfully and far beyond the abilities of the professionally trained dancers who surrounded her. But then again, no vampire blood ran in their veins, nor had they been personally coached by an Egyptian high priestess who'd probably been there when the dance was invented.

They didn't have the power to influence the minds of mere mortals as she did. They didn't have the physical strength to move the way she did. She put them all to shame.

And just as she had hoped, Utana couldn't take his eyes off her. They were glued to her—and not to her face, either. She twisted her body in slow, sensual undulations that mimicked the heaving waves of the ocean. Those waves moved over her, from her thighs to her hips, to her belly, to her chest. Her arms, long and strong, were like cobras dancing to the tune of a snake charmer. Her hips circled slowly, then snapped to one side, circled the other way, then snapped again, and the bangles sang their hypnotic song, matching the drumbeats that pounded like the hearts of every male in the room.

Oh, she had him. He was getting hard just looking at her. She knew it. There was no way he was going to let her leave this palace tonight. He would insist on taking her to his bedchambers, and he would also insist on complete privacy, despite knowing what she was here for. She was willing it. And he would comply, despite his awareness that he would be risking his own life, and foolishly so. He would comply because his ego was too big to admit that she was any threat to him. And because his penis was going to be doing all the talking anyway.

No man could resist the magic of the dance when it was wielded as it was originally intended; as a ritual, as a spell, as an enchantment. As the embodiment of pure feminine power. The power of the goddess herself.

She felt that power rising in her, just as Rhiannon had always told her it would. Utana would not give her identity away to his lying, scheming, scarfaced sidekick. If he did, they wouldn't let her stay. And he wanted her to stay. He wanted it more than he wanted to draw another breath.

She had him.

He smiled, almost as if reading her mind, and she felt her eyes widen in alarm, realizing she'd been so caught up in her own sex appeal that she'd forgotten to block her thoughts.

Lifting a hand, he crooked a finger at her, beckoning her closer.

It would look odd if she refused. Clearly everyone here had been instructed to treat him like the King of the World. Poor Utana was the only one not in on the joke. This entire evening was some kind of giant deception. The people around him, claiming to be the current leaders of the nations of the world, were nothing more than actors, playing roles. Deceiving him, lying to him. All in the employ of the DPI. She almost felt sorry for him. And yet she, too, was deceiving him.

Straight to the grave, perhaps.

She sidestepped down from the raised platform, one arm up high, one out straight, wrists circling, hips snapping with each step. Her entire body took part in the dance as she writhed her way closer and still closer to him, feeling him, his desire, his arousal, his manliness, with every step she took. He rose to his feet as she reached him.

She stopped inches from his body, arms overhead, snaking over each other as her hips swirled in an endless figure eight that brushed his groin lightly with every pass.

He took the final step, closing the space between them, so that every inch of her body undulated against his.

"You have no idea how glad I am to see you, Lady Moonlight," he said for her ears alone.

She lifted her brows and spoke just as softly. "Your English has improved dramatically."

"I learn rapidly."

"But what's up with this Lady Moonlight bit?"

"It is what you remind me of. Moonlight." He ran the back of one hand over her cheek to her chin, to her neck. "Pure. Mystical. Secretive. Potent."

Shivering with pleasure at his touch, Brigit reminded herself that she was supposed to be making him lose his mind with desire, not the other way around. And yet she couldn't move away, could she? Not if she were going to keep this illusion intact. The others must continue to believe she was a part of this ridiculous charade. If she did anything out of character, the glamour she had cast over them would falter. She was only a quarter vampire. Holding a roomful of liars in her thrall was an effort.

Particularly with Utana distracting her this way.

"Besides," Utana said, "I presume you do not wish for my vizier to know you for who you really are. You took a grave chance in coming here—even with the veil, you are a woman few men could forget easily."

"I had to see you again," she whispered.

"And so you shall." He leaned his head closer, so that his nose was barely touching her neck, and he inhaled her scent as he moved up to her ear.

Her knees turned to water.

"You will continue to dance for me until I say otherwise. Or I will tell them who you are and have you arrested."

Her eyes widened. "You wouldn't."

"Dare you put that to the test?" His gaze intensified, holding hers.

Softly, almost against her own will, Brigit heard herself whisper, "No…"

Quickly she looked away. God, he was powerful.

"Your eyes will remain on mine. You will look at no other."

She bit her lip to prevent vocalizing her absolute consent. But he felt it all the same; she saw it in his satisfied smile.

"Return to the stage, then," he said, trailing his hand down her back, pausing on her backside and squeezing it hard. "And make those coins jingle all the way." He smacked her as she turned and obeyed, shimmying as she moved across the room and back up onto the stage, wondering what on earth she'd just got herself into.

8

Brigit fixed her eyes on Utana, and for the life of her, she could not look away. She danced as she had never danced before, the power of it rising up from some unknown and yet bottomless well within her. And she danced for him alone. Despite her mission, despite her lies, she felt as if this performance were real. As if he truly was her beloved king; as if she truly was his to command. As if her deepest desire and only goal was to give him pleasure as he watched the movements of her body.

When the troupe finished their performance and left the stage, Utana rose and pointed at her. "This one remains," he announced. And then he turned to the drummers. "Keep playing."

They glanced nervously at each other, and then at Scarface.

"Your heard the king. Play!" the man said.

The drummers played. And Brigit kept on dancing, twisting, writhing, as if she were possessed, under a spell, moved about by an unseen puppeteer whose will could not be denied.

Utana stabbed her eyes with his, sent his command to her by means of thought, not words. *Here. By me. You dance for me alone.*

Her throat went dry as she wondered just what the hell had taken possession of her body, her mind. But she moved to dance in front of him, and she realized it wasn't entirely against her will. She loved the passion in his eyes. The desire she was making him feel for her. It was heady. She felt powerful.

He moved closer to her, taking a seat in the softness of a huge cushion on the floor. He seemed to be enjoying the food, the wine, but she knew it was a lie. He was focused only on her, on her swirling, gyrating hips, level with his face.

She didn't know how much longer she could keep going. Her body was coated in a thin sheen of perspiration. She'd been dancing nonstop for two hours and then some. Then, finally, he leaned toward his so-called vizier and said, "Have her taken to my chambers. And…bind her."

Brigit sucked in a gasp, opened her mouth to protest and then bit her lip. It wouldn't matter. She didn't need her hands to blast him with her power. She liked to use her hands to help her focus and direct the energy, but it wasn't necessary. He was going to come around to her way of thinking, or he was going to be spread across the room in bits and pieces, whether he had her bound or not.

Gravenham-Bail's eyebrows went up, but he nodded and rose to obey, taking Brigit by the arm. She stopped dancing at last and stumbled from the room at his side.

They exited the ballroom, crossed the palace-like atrium and moved up the curving stairway to the left, then along a hall to the double doors of the king's suite of rooms. Along the way her escort paused to whisper to another man, who nodded and hurried away.

The scar-faced man flung the doors open and shoved her inside. "You've been paid very well," he said to her.

Although she hadn't, she had apparently done a very good job of convincing him that she was one of his employees.

"Very well," she replied.

"And you were told this might be a possibility."

"I don't think I agreed to the bondage bit, though."

"Well, it's not like you have a choice, honey. Shit, you were practically asking for it, the way you were dancing out there."

Behind him, the man he'd spoken to on the way upstairs appeared, bearing two pairs of handcuffs and several lengths of rope.

Scarface took them without looking at him and said, "Go on. Close the doors on your way out."

Brigit's alarm bells were going off.

"Give me your arms."

"Look, I'm not sure this is such a—"

He grabbed her wrists, yanking them forward. She could have pulled free. Hell, she could have blown him to pieces or just simply broken his neck. But that would have given her away. He worked for the DPI, and besides that, he knew her. If she removed the veil or relaxed the glamour she was still casting over him, he would recognize her as the leader of the vampire resistance who had captured him, ever so briefly.

If she gave herself away, she would wind up in a government lab as its favorite rat. The DPI had been hunting for the "mongrel twins," the only two of their kind, for decades. But more importantly, she would lose her chance to save her people.

So she relaxed her arms and let him cuff her wrists together, and continued keeping her face averted, her veil in place.

"Move over there," he said, pointing to the bed.

She did, swearing at him inside her head but never speaking a word aloud.

From somewhere far away she heard Utana, speaking to her with his mind. *If he touches you, call out to me, and I will kill him.*

Well, that, at least, was reassuring.

The man with the scar snapped a manacle to her left ankle and affixed the other end to the huge heavy bed's clawed leg. He had to move the heavy layers of bed curtains aside to even find it.

"That should do."

She could pick that bed up and hurl it at him if she wanted to, she reminded herself.

He looked at her.

She averted her face and muttered, "Don't even think about it, pal."

His lips pulled into a smile. "Not before my king, anyway."

And then he was gone, and she sighed in relief. He hadn't recognized her. Probably couldn't have described her face to another soul if his life had depended on it. Because it wasn't her face that had held his attention.

And for that she was grateful.

Brigit was left to bide her time and wait for Utana to come to her. And to plan what she would do when he did. She wondered why she had to give that any thought at all. She ought to just kill him. She could do so bound as easily as not.

Not immediately, though. She should wait at least until he took the cuffs off, so she could make her getaway when their confrontation was over.

That was her heart talking, though, not her brain. She could burn through the cuffs with the power of pure fiery destruction. She could free herself and blast anyone who dared step into her path as she escaped this house of lies. She didn't need to wait.

She should kill him the minute he stepped through those—

The double doors opened, and Utana stepped through, looking around the room and sending his thoughts to her as clearly as if he were speaking them aloud.

Say nothing, Lady Moonlight. I believe I am observed even here, though I have yet to learn how. Though they worship me as a king, I am not entirely trusting of my new devotees.

Oh, please, tell me you're not buying all this bullshit. She thought the words at him, even while her mind was elsewhere.

Her throat went dry as she stared at him. God, he was beautiful. Dressed in robes, not makeshift ones made from bedsheets like before, but a fine white tunic, with masses of burgundy satin that looped over one shoulder. He looked like the king he once had been.

And even as she watched, her eyes widening, he lifted the sash over his head. And then the robe. Beneath it was nothing. Utterly nothing. And she couldn't stop her eyes from roaming down his body. His skin was the color of light brown sugar, smooth and probably just as sweet to the taste. His chest was so broad and cut, it was almost ridiculous. His neck was corded, his biceps bulging. He didn't look like an ordinary man—hell, he didn't look like an ordinary vampire. Because he wasn't one, she reminded herself. He was something else entirely. He looked like a bodybuilder. Every muscle rippling beneath that desert-sun-kissed flesh as he moved slowly closer, his eyes never relinquishing their tractor-beam hold on hers.

Kill him, her brain told her. *Just call up the power and kill him. Get this over with.*

He was near her now, close enough to touch, and he clasped her shoulders, running his hands down her outer arms.

"You are so beautiful." He whispered the words softly, so no microphone would capture them. "Like no other woman my eyes have seen, Brigit of the Vahmpeers."

She shivered at his touch, and wanted more in spite of herself.

"We are mortal enemies," he went on, leaning low, running his lips over her ear and down to her neck. "You have come to kill me, have you not? To finish what you began in those northern woods, where you slept in my arms instead?"

She swallowed hard, telling herself to pull back from his touch, but instead tipping her head back, giving him more access, relishing the feel of his lips on her skin. She shivered as he moved her veil aside and mouthed her neck, loving the sensations rushing through her, making her tremble with delicious pleasure.

"I…I have no choice, Utana."

He sighed, hot breath caressing her so that her blood felt like thick molten lava.

"Unless…unless you give up this insane quest to wipe out my people."

"Like you, beautiful one, I have no choice. Know that it is not my will. Know that I feel as if a blade is twisting deep inside my heart when I think of the blood on my hands. Your people—they are my people, too."

Her eyes burned. "I can't let you kill them."

"I can't let them live."

"Utana, please—"

"Shhhh." His fingers removed the veil from her face. "These are not the words I want between us just now, my lovely moonlight dancer. No. I want sounds of passion from you, sounds of pleasure. Not talk of death."

"I—" She bit her lip.

"Say it. Do not deny me the truth. Not if I'm destined to return to the living death from which your brother raised me."

Trembling, she nodded against his head, his face. "I want you, too. God help me, Utana, I've wanted you since I first laid eyes on you."

"Thank the gods." He kissed her then, and she fell against him, lifting her arms, despite her handcuffed wrists, to lower them around his neck as she opened to his kiss, fell into it and felt as if she were plummeting headlong into a bottomless well of utter yearning.

Reaching behind his head, he freed her from the cuffs with no more than a flick of his fingers, never breaking the hold of his lips, his mouth. His hips arched against her, and her stomach knotted tighter, feeling his arousal pressing into her belly.

Nuzzling her neck, he slid his hand downward, breaking the chain that held her ankle…an act that reminded her sharply why had she had not done so herself. "They might be watching us, Utana. You said yourself, you felt observed here," she said as he moved with her along the side of the bed, and then, his arms around her, lowered her onto it, and himself with her.

The hand that was caressing her shin moved slowly up the outside of her leg, lifting her swirling skirts as it did. With a wave of that strong hand, the heavy curtains surrounding the bed reacted. They moved as if a gust of wind had caught them, closing themselves around the mattress. Closing out the whole world. The war that was raging between vampire and human. The horrible acts he'd committed. The hateful one that she must soon commit. All of that was gone.

"This is an oasis in the harshest desert sands," he told her. "This time, this place, this moment between us. A paradise we must savor to its fullest, for it will never come again."

"Yes," she whispered. She smiled against the top of his head as he moved down the front of her, kissing the swell of her breasts above the tiny top.

"Never have I seen the dance so…enchanting. So powerful. And it…is from my time, not yours."

"So is the woman who taught me," she whispered. "Give or take a few thousand years."

"I shall thank her one day."

Those words sent a chill through her as a visual appeared in her mind. The image of Utana meeting her beloved aunt Rhiannon—and then blasting her with the beam of his eyes, as he had done to so many others.

Her passion cooled, and she was racked with guilt. "Will you thank her before or after you murder her?"

She pushed against his chest, turning her body to one side as he blinked down at her in confusion. She closed her eyes. "I can't do this. Get off me."

"Brigit—"

"Get off." She shoved hard, throwing some of her preternatural strength into it, and he landed on his back beside her. He was breathing hard. Hell, so was she.

She steeled herself, called up that image of Rhiannon being blown to bits in order to fuel her resolve, and got to her feet.

"Are you leaving me, then?" he asked, as she crossed the room toward the door.

"Yes. In a moment, but first…" She couldn't meet his eyes. "I'm sorry, Utana. But there's no other way." And she lifted her hand, palm up, fingers lightly resting against her thumb, and she called up the power.

"Your heart is harder than I ever imagined," he whispered.

"Not really," she told him, tears streaming down her face. "This is going to shatter it. But I have no choice." And in one act of pure will, she opened the channels, for the power to rise up and shoot from her eyes as she flicked her fingers open. Tears were streaming, but she kept her focus and flinched at the moment when he should have been raining down around her in tiny pieces.

Except nothing happened.

Frowning hard, she stared at her hand, at him sitting there, as realization dawned. He hadn't even moved to defend himself. He'd just sat there, waiting. And he looked furious with her now.

"What…? How…?" She stared at her open palm, feeling no hint of the tingling energy she'd felt her entire life. *You…you took my power?*

That night in the forest, he admitted, speaking mentally, just as she had. *As you keep saying, Brigit, there was no other way. You would have killed me, as you have just proven, or forced me to kill you, and I did not want to do that.*

She released a short, clipped breath that was part

exasperated sigh and part bitter laugh, her head lowering. "But you're going to do it anyway. Your imaginary freakin' gods have commanded it, right? And you're not man enough to stand up to them."

He was silent, and when she dared peer up at him again, she saw that he was seething. She'd gone too far.

"I have beseeched the Ancient and Mighty Ones to make you an exception to their decree. Perhaps, however, you are not as worthy of that as I once believed."

"I'm not. Of my entire race, I'm the least worthy. I'm the evil one, the destroyer, or at least I was. I'm the first one you ought to murder, Utana, because I swear to God, if you let me live I *will* kill you. I'll find a way."

"And what god do you swear to, Brigit? An imaginary one of your own?"

Her eyes narrowed, and Brigit vamped up. Her fangs elongated as she surged toward him, growling low, and about to pummel him senseless with vampiric strength and speed.

He caught her wrists and tugged her against his chest, clasping her head and hiding it there against his hot skin. "Enough!" And then, silently, *Do not give yourself away, Brigit of the Vahmpeers. Nashmun will have you killed if he learns what you are.*

She stood there, tense and trembling. *No, he wouldn't. He'd put me in a lab somewhere, to be ex-*

*perimented on by doctors and scientists. You know
damn well my brother and I are the only two of our
kind.*

She retracted her fangs all the same. Then she
pulled away, dashing tears from her cheeks and
turning toward the door.

With her peripheral vision she saw him flick a
hand and heard the lock turn. "I'm afraid I cannot
let you leave, my lady."

She went still, an icy finger of dread dragging
itself down her spine.

"You will be my personal servant here for the
duration. You will abide by my will and do as I
command, for as long as I decree it so."

Turning slowly to face him, she said, "Do you
really think your right-hand man is going to allow
that? I'm a citizen in his employ." *As far as he
knows, that is.* "He has a responsibility to protect
me."

"He is loyal to a fault and worships me as his
king. He will do whatever I command—as, little
one, will you."

*He's using you, lying to you. He's playing you,
Utana.*

*Do you think I'm not aware of that? He treats
me well, and his nation honors me, because they
need me to do what I must do anyway.*

No. Holding his gaze she shook her head. *No,
Utana. Listen to me. All of those dignitaries at the*

celebration earlier were frauds. Those were not our world's leaders. They were actors, in Nash's employ, and not very good ones at that. And I'm ninety-nine percent certain our government leaders have no idea what he's really doing.

He was silent for a very long moment. And then, at length, he nodded. *I was one of the greatest kings of my time, Brigit. A priest to the most powerful gods of creation. I am not an imbecile.*

She shook her head in disbelief. *If you know he's using you, then why the hell are you here?*

Frowning, he waved a hand at the luxury that surrounded him. *Need you ask?*

No. No, he was lying to her now. Trying to save face, she thought.

Yet Nashmun must make me go on believing his lies, mustn't he? He must play the role, and so he will do as I command in this matter. He will keep you here, in chains if necessary, to see to my needs, in order to preserve the illusion he's worked so hard to create here.

Brigit searched his face, looking for a way to reach him and finding none. *When he has what he wants from you, Utana, he will kill you. And he will send me away to be tortured in the name of science.*

No mortal is capable of taking my life, he assured her, and his confidence and power came through with the thought. *And yet, once I have done the task the gods command me to do, I will have no great desire to go on living. Far better I join my people in the Land of the Dead, where I must send them before me. I deserve no less. But this I promise you, no one, mortal or otherwise, will lift a finger to harm you while you are in my care.*

Right, she shot back, and she sent her fury with the word. *Not until you get around to doing it yourself.*

He said nothing, simply walked past her and opened the door. She was not surprised to see Nash Gravenham-Bail on the other side, acting as if he had just been about to knock. She quickly turned away, lifting her veil over her face once more, as Scarface entered the room.

"I will keep her here as my personal attendant," Utana told him. "I will require an abundance of pillows and coverlets that she may have a comfortable place to sleep without crowding me in my bed. And, Nashmun, make it known that she is not to be permitted to leave this place under any circumstances without my consent. And make it known, too, that should any living being do her harm or touch her flesh in passion, I will wipe him from existence. Is that clear?"

"As you wish it, my king," the man said, bowing low.

The lying scum.

He darted a look at her, and she returned it briefly, with one so acidic that it should have melted his skin from his face. Then he backed out of the room, closing the door behind him.

Brigit watched him go, then turned, refusing to look at Utana, and moved to the window seat to sink onto its red velvet cushions and stare through the glass at the freedom they were all so sure they were denying her.

They didn't know her very well. Oh, sure, she would hang out here for a while. She could lie well enough to make Scarface and the entire DPI look like amateurs. So she would pretend to be beaten. But she had no doubt in her mind that she could walk out of this place anytime she decided to go.

And she would. Right after she murdered the man with the biggest ego she'd ever seen. He was a fool to keep her here. He should have thrown her out as fast as humanly possible. But instead he'd given her the opportunity to study him, to watch and observe and find his weakness. He must have one. And when she learned what it was, she would use it to wipe him from this planet once and for all.

She would be his prisoner—his harem slave, if necessary. But only until she figured out how to kill him.

9

His beautiful Brigit slept on the floor, in a well-cushioned, jewel-colored nest. Her oversize pillows were made of silk and satin and velvet. Her blankets were the softest to be had. Chenille, the servant had called them when she'd brought them into the bedroom. He liked the fabric well.

What he did not like so well, Utana mused, was the lovely warrioress's moody silence and lack of eye contact. She had brooded near the window-glass for a while, and then spent nearly an hour in the adjoining bathroom. Long enough that he had begun to worry, but when he'd tapped on the door, she had been snappish, assuring him that escape from his suite of rooms was quite impossible, something she said he was probably too dense to have figured out for himself, and that he needn't worry.

He'd mulled over those words ever since. Why would his vizier take precautions to prevent his royal guest from escaping his own room? Was he not free to leave this place by means of the front door, should he so desire?

Wearing a short nightgown, she'd emerged at length, her hair wet, her skin damp and fragrant from the bath. He'd wanted her more than ever, but she had only wrapped herself in a chenille blanket and nestled into her cushions. Within minutes she had gone to sleep. And no wonder. He sensed her exhaustion.

Perhaps, if he were honest with himself, he might admit that it was wrong to keep her here, a prisoner. She was far too important a woman to be treated in such a way. The would-be savior of her people. She must be held in very high esteem. He could only imagine what purpose she must suppose he had in holding her captive this way. He hadn't told her the real one.

He needed her here with him. She had known instantly what had taken him the better part of three days to even begin to suspect—and had still been unsure of. That Nashmun was deceiving him, using him to achieve his own ends. Brigit had known immediately that all the honored guests posing as world leaders at tonight's celebration had been liars, as well. Actors, she'd called them. Pretending to be kings and pres-ee-dents and foreign dignitaries of all sorts.

He'd allowed himself to be fooled. And the force

that had fooled him had not been any great powers of deception on the part of his fork-tongued vizier. No, it had been his own ego. He had wanted to believe the world of modern man honored and respected him. And so he had.

Even though he'd told Brigit that he had known the truth from the start, he had not. Though he should have. He was ashamed, and angry.

She knew. What was more, Nashmun was aware that she knew, thought her to be a part of his charade, one of the actors in his employ. Having not yet seen her face unclothed and recognized her from their brief, unpleasant acquaintance in the past, Nashmun believed her to be on his side. If they could sustain that illusion, Brigit might well gain access to information Utana might not be able to gather on his own.

He had no wish to remain here longer than was necessary. He'd been growing bored with the luxury already, even before he'd been made a fool of. He wanted only to regain his strength and was already well on the way to doing so. And then he needed to find the fleeing vahmpeers and commit the hateful act he'd been commanded by the gods to perform. He had to immolate them.

But perhaps, if he were lucky, the Anunaki would grant his desperate pleas and allow him to let this one live.

And perhaps her brother, too. For she would never wish to live if her twin did not.

Yes, he decided. He would petition the gods to spare James, as well. And in the meantime, Brigit was going to stay here to help him. Whether she liked it or not. Because a very strong suspicion was maturing within his mind. When the time came that he wanted to leave this place, Nashmun was going to try very hard to keep him within his control. To hold him here. A prisoner.

And Utana did not like being a prisoner.

He watched Brigit for a while longer as she slept, the notion of going to her in her nest of soft pillows niggling at him. The chambermaid had brought the nightgown that she wore. A soft, thin white gown that left her long, lean, firm arms bare, with ruffles at her shoulders and more along the hem, which came only to the tops of her thighs.

He had been planning to ask that more clothing be brought for her, but now he thought better of it. He would choose her garb himself.

In the morning.

Stripping off his robes, he slid naked into his bed. Alone. And he lay there trying to sleep for two full hours before giving up in frustration.

He decided to walk outside, in the gardens behind the palace, and clear his head. He needed the night air.

Surging from his bed, he dragged a luxurious

robe of red satin from the back of a nearby chair and pulled it on, looping the sash and yanking it tight, even as he strode toward the door.

"Where are you going?" she asked.

He froze, her voice stroking over his skin like a physical touch. "I'm going outside to walk amid the gardens."

"Can I go, too?"

"No."

She sat up, the blanket falling around her as she did. "Why not?"

His hand stilled on the doorknob. "Brigit, I am not accustomed to explaining my decisions, only to having them obeyed without question."

"Well, you'd better *get* used to it, pal." She rose and strode right up to him, which was almost funny, her being so small, her bare feet tiny and not much good for stomping, and her only power against him no longer hers to wield. "I'm going with you," she said.

He stared down at her. "The reason for my walk, Brigit, is to ease my frustration. Since you are the cause of it, your company would defeat the purpose. Do you understand?"

She frowned at him. "You're the one making me stay. How am I the one who's frustrating you?"

He shot his hand out to clasp hers, then brought it to his groin to press her palm there, only briefly.

Just long enough so that she felt his hardness. He saw her eyes widen.

Then he let go, and she jerked her hand back as if she had been burned.

"I have come to understand that taking a woman by force is considered the height of bad behavior—a crime, in fact, in your odd and twisted time. Even, I am told, for a king."

She took a step back, and he could see that she was shaken by his words, even though she rolled her eyes and made a disgusted sound in her throat. "You're such a pig."

"I am not a pig. I am a man. And I want you very much. I dislike intensely your society's insistence that I not take you until you consent to the act. It is maddening, even though I know it is only a matter of time until you do."

"In your dreams."

He smiled slowly, reached out to trail a finger over her cheek. "Those would be pleasant dreams, indeed, lady."

She turned and flung herself back into her nest. "Fine, go walk it off, then. For future reference, in my time, cold showers are considered an acceptable alternative."

He nodded. "While I am out, I will command Nashmun to send someone out to purchase clothing for you. It will be here waiting by the time we've had our morning meal. Is there anything in particular you require?"

My suitcases are in my car. It's parked in a pull-off about two miles north. But if you tell them that, they'll know I didn't arrive in that van full of belly dancers.

I'll get your belongings myself. I will tell them I went shopping.

They'll never let you leave. Haven't you figured it out yet, Utana? You're as much a prisoner here as I am.

He kept his emotions hidden, though her words troubled him, confirming, as they did, what he had come to suspect. *Even if that were true, they could not keep me against my will. You underestimate me, harem slave.*

She sucked in a breath, shocked, he knew, by the way he had referred to her.

I'll return within the hour, lady. And I will bring your things to you and prove to you that my situation is not as dire, my vizier not quite as duplicitous, as you presume. Until then. He bowed to her with exaggerated formality.

She called him something, a word he had not heard before: asshole. He told himself to find its meaning in the library downstairs before he returned. And then he left, closing his bedroom door behind him and turning the lock.

"King Utana?" asked the attendant who stood outside his chamber door.

There was always one stationed there, never the same one twice, and always male. They had a similar energy about them, these doormen. They smelled of authority, like enforcers. And their appearances were similar, as well. They wore short, cropped haircuts. Each also bore a tiny earpiece with a curling wire that ran behind his ear and vanished into the collar of his stiff modern suit. They always wore the suit. It was always the same. A white shirt beneath a jacket of darkest blue that matched the detestable pants. They adorned themselves with a sash of sorts, around the neck, always either blue or red. What had Nashmun called them? Neckties, yes. Neckties. As far as Utana could see, the odd things served no purpose except adornment, and he could not fathom why, as there was nothing remotely attractive about them.

No matter.

"I am going for a walk in the gardens," he told the man he had come to think of as one of his personal guards. Now he wondered if the man were there to protect him, or to keep him from leaving. "Do not let anyone in or out of my chambers until I return," he ordered, eager to see what the man's reaction would be.

"King, I'm not sure that's such a good idea."

"I did not ask what you thought about the idea."

Utana nodded at the chamber door. "Keep her safe. I will return within the hour."

"Yes, sir."

With a sharp nod, Utana walked away down the long corridor to the head of the curving staircase that swooped downward. He felt the guard's eyes on him the entire way, but the man did not move to stop Utana from leaving. Feeling a bit of relief that Brigit had been wrong in her assumptions, he started down the stairs, then paused, as he heard the doorman speaking again.

Utana stood very still and listened, his hearing far more acute than his chamber guard must be aware. Though it was puzzling, too, as Utana sensed no other being nearby to whom he might be speaking.

"The First is on the move," the guard said.

The First. That obviously referred to himself, Utana thought. But to whom was the man speaking?

There was a crackle of static, and understanding dawned. He'd heard that crackle before, when the servants of this palace communicated with one another by means of the ingenious devices attached to the cuffs of their jackets.

"Says he's going for a walk in the gardens," the guard said a second later. "Back in an hour, he says." There was more crackling, and then, "Right, will do."

Utana frowned, listening, but there was no further discussion, and his guard did not come after him but remained at his post, as Utana had instructed.

Or as the person he'd been reporting to had instructed?

Utana moved down the stairs then, no longer quite as confident in his ability to come and go as he pleased. He was beginning to suspect that Brigit's words had been correct, and he was eager to put them to the test.

He crossed through the massive domed room at the base of the stairs, which served as both entry hall and the central hub of the palace, with other sections extending from it in all directions save one, where the entrance was. It was like the body of a giant spider, with legs extending all around.

Utana took the hallway that led to the rear, following it past its countless doors all the way to the end, and then exited, finding the doors unlocked.

He stepped out into the palace's rear gardens, pausing to look around. But he saw no one, sensed no other presence there. The only sounds were those of the fountain's gentle cascade, rippling and splashing and peaceful, and the cries of a pair of night birds, calling out one to the other. *Caroo, caroo, caroo.*

The nighttime air touched his face, and he inhaled the scents of late-blooming flowers and fresh breezes. It was good here. And he felt no presence.

No one had followed him. No one waited to try to stop him from leaving, should he so desire. It was a relief to know that. True, Nashmun had his reasons for wanting to befriend him. Surely his desire to rid the world of the vahmpeer race was motivating him. But that did not make him the evildoer Brigit believed him to be.

Utana wandered the garden's paved footpaths for half an hour, wishing to the gods that the path was one of well-trod earth or grass, or even sand. This hard false stone on which he walked, which they called "pavement," was unnatural and hardly soothing. He needed his feet on the earth.

No matter.

He spotted the tall arching gate at the far end of the garden. He would go through it, and then around the manicured lawns to the front of the palace and the street beyond it, to find Brigit's car and her clothing. But first...

He paused, finding for himself a spot near the center of the garden that seemed isolated. Stepping off the pavement, he sighed in relief as his bare feet felt the cool earth against them.

So much better. A few more steps off the path and he was amid an abundance of rosebushes, standing in a small circle of grass more or less in their center. White blossoms surrounded him, and the night air was thick with their fragrance.

Perfect.

Utana stood there in the natural circle formed by the boundary of the thorny foliage and opened his arms. Tipping his head back, he stared up at the night sky, which was as thick with stars tonight as the garden was thick with roses. Indeed, the white stars and the white roses were very much alike. Both sacred to the moon, both formed in honor of the Queen of Heaven, Inanna, and in her image. As the beautiful Brigit herself must be. Oh, her hair was pale. Not raven, like Inanna's. But her beauty, bravery, spirit, even her temper, rivaled those of the Morning Star herself.

"Ancient and Mighty Anunaki," Utana said softly, "hear my plea. I, Ziasudra, Utanapishtim, Flood Survivor, your faithful servant, priest of the Ancient and Mighty Gods, King of Old, I call upon you. Hear my words!"

He paused, feeling the air, sensing that his gods were near. They heard him. He felt the tingling energy of their attention.

"Enki, Lord Earth, Enlil, Lord Air! Hear me! Anu, of the Heavens, Utu, Sun God, Nanna of the Moon, Inanna, Queen of Heaven and of the Morning Star, Ninmah, Mountain Lady! Give heed to my cry!"

The wind lifted, and a tiny swirl of fallen rose petals rose with it, forming a spiral in the air before him, then raining to the ground again.

They were here. They were listening!

"I ask you again for your mercy upon my people, who have done you no harm. Indeed, the sin committed was mine alone. And for that I have suffered, surely more than any man has suffered before. I ask you yet again, Ancient and Mighty Ones, the Seven Who Decree the Fates, I beg of you, humbled as a servant at your feet." With those words, he fell to his knees. His heart seemed to swell within him, and tears to burn in his eyes. "Spare them," he begged. "Spare me this bloody task which you have set before me. Punish me further if you must. But spare the vahmpeers. Or at the least, the moonlight lady and her brother, James, who bear only a hint of the stain of the condemned, and that through no fault of their own."

He bent his head as the rush of his desire went forth from within him, leaving him weak and empty. "I will do anything required to make it so. Send me a sign, that I might know your will. As always, I shall humbly obey."

He opened his eyes, nodded once, confident his gods had heard him at last, and that they had been pleased with his prayer, the roses, the scents. Yes, they must have been pleased. Soon they would send a sign. Their answer.

Utana walked back onto the paved footpath and approached the arching garden gate. He reached for the latch.

As his hand touched the metal, a blast of energy

hit him with a shower of sparks. The impact sent him flying backward, his feet leaving the earth as his body arched, and then he landed, his back slamming into the paved walkway, driving the very breath from his lungs. He lay there, face up on the ground, gasping for the breath that had been stolen away from him and feeling as if his palms were on fire.

His body seemed alive with a tingling, zinging energy almost too strong to bear, and his head pounded and throbbed as bursts of white light exploded before his eyes.

Was this the answer his gods had sent to him, then?

It was not the reply he had hoped for.

10

Brigit waited for him to return. The bedroom was dark except for the soft yellow glow of a night-light, its candle-size bulb glowing from a miniature lamp beside the bed.

It had been the better part of an hour. And she was worried. He was far too trusting of Nash Gravenham-Bail and his DPI cohorts. He had no idea what those bastards were capable of.

She did. She'd seen it firsthand. Her own mother—

No, she wouldn't think about that now. Not now. And why was she spending her time worrying about the well-being of her enemy, anyway? The man she'd been sent here to kill.

And yet, when he still hadn't returned ten minutes later, she worried all the more. Getting up from the mound of downy soft pillows, a bed so luxurious she'd decided she was going to create one for herself one day soon, she paced to the window and, parting the curtains, looked out.

But this bedroom didn't overlook the gardens behind the mansion, and she saw nothing but the waning moon and star-dotted sky.

And then, quite suddenly, the amber glow of the night-light flickered, dimmed to almost nothing, and then surged brighter than before. Then it went out with a soft popping sound, leaving the room dark.

Frowning, no longer content to wait there, Brigit spun to the door and was about to yank it open, not even thinking about the fact that it was locked, when her superhuman hearing picked up the radio crackling on the guard's belt. She paused and listened.

"Zone Three here. The First is down *hard.*"

"Shit," the guard muttered. "Zone One. On my way. What happened?"

"About twenty thousand volts happened," came the reply. "He grabbed the garden gate." And then she heard him jogging at a good clip down the corridor.

Brigit didn't hesitate. She pulled the door open and followed, only a few steps behind. And the guard, who quickly realized she was there, seemed to decide in an instant not to waste precious time doing anything about it. Luckily he seemed not to even wonder about the lock.

Despite their hurry, they didn't even make it half-way down the stairs before they were stopped by the sight of four guys coming toward them, carrying Utana between them, one at each arm, one at each leg, grunting as they started up the stairs. For a moment she couldn't take her eyes off Utana, unconscious, perhaps dead. But then some kind of psychic warning kicked in, and she glanced up in time to see Scarface rushing behind them.

Quickly she turned around and ran back up the stairs to the bedroom.

Seconds, only seconds, and they were stomping into the bedroom and dumping the big man onto his mattress, which sank beneath his weight. She quickly located one of the scarves from her belly dance costume and considered wrapping it around her face and head, so that only her eyes showed above it. But that would be suspicious. The room was dark, lit only by the lopsided moon outside the windows. And Nash was focused on Utana, not her. She tried to produce a quick glamour, enough to keep him from recognizing her should he happen to look her way, but her focus was on Utana, as well.

"Is he…is he alive?" she asked, as the men backed away from the bedside, giving Scarface himself access.

He didn't even look at her. "The fake concern is great, but you're supposed to be a prisoner here, right? Shouldn't you be happy about this?"

Swallowing hard, she nodded, moving closer to the bedside, despite the danger of being recognized.

"Quiet, he's coming around." Gravenham-Bail leaned closer. "Utana? My king, can you hear me?"

Utana's eyes moved beneath his closed lids. His lips moved, too, and his false friend tipped his head, listening intently, his ear near Utana's face.

"You were electrocuted," his vizier said, staring down at Utana in utterly false concern. "I'm so very sorry, Your Highness. I blame myself for not warning you of the electrified fences."

Utana's eyes opened then, but only to mere slits. "Wh-why?" he asked.

"For your protection, my friend. You're an important man. In this age, world leaders are not safe in their own homes." He shot a look across the bed at Brigit, then at the men who'd carried Utana. "I want everyone to clear out of here. I have a private physician on the way. Bring her up here the minute she arrives."

"N-no." Utana clasped Brigit's hand even as she turned from the bed. "She stays."

Licking his lips, Nash frowned. "All right. Yes. That's fine."

"You…Nashmun…go."

Nash blinked in shock. Catching Brigit's eyes before she quickly averted her face, his own narrowing, he nodded once, then turned and headed toward the door, motioning for her to come with him. "I'll bring Lillian up when she arrives," he said.

"Lillian?" Brigit asked, trying to pour her energy into the glamour she'd cast.

"The doctor. Same one who did the physicals on your dance troupe. She'll be here any minute. Try to keep him calm until then."

Brigit nodded, knowing this was going to be yet another problem, and waited until the man left the room, then quickly pushed the door closed. Turning, she hurried back to the bed. "Utana—are you all right?"

He nodded. "The blast was…not unlike yours. This garden gate nearly did your job for you, Brigit." Then he lifted a hand to gently stroke her cheek. "He did not recognize you?"

"No, but I think he's getting suspicious." She took hold of his wrist, turning his hand palm up and looking at the blackened flesh across his palm. "My brother's healing gift. You took it from him. Use it to heal yourself."

"I…tried. I know not quite how to…wield it."

"Then give it to me."

He frowned at her. "You…would heal me?"

"I want you in good shape so I can kill you later," she said, before remembering they were probably under surveillance. Her voice had been low—low enough, she hoped. Still, she dropped it to the merest whisper. "Can you do it? Can you give powers as well as take them away?"

"I can."

"Then do it. And hurry up about it," she whispered, leaning closer. "Apparently this doctor they're bringing saw all the dancers. She'll know I wasn't one of them."

"Trick her mind, as you did his."

"I can try, but it doesn't always work. Not all humans are as weak-willed as he is." Which was, in itself, a matter of some concern for Brigit. Why would the DPI put a man whose mind was that easily manipulated in charge of a case involving the Undead, masters of mind control? It didn't make sense.

He nodded. "I will suffer this pain until the... doctor...goes. She will know something is wrong if I am well. Then...we shall see. Go now. Hide yourself. I was wrong to make you stay and risk them finding you out. I wish no harm to come to you, Brigit."

She nodded and then retrieved a robe from where it hung on the far side of the bed. Her fingers brushed over his skin as she picked it up, and his eyes flared briefly in reaction, despite the pain he must be in. Pulling on the oversize robe, Brigit headed for the hallway.

As she stepped out of the room, Utana bellowed, "And do not return until I send for you!"

She scrunched up her face. "Damn men and their damned egos," she muttered. Then she looked at the guard, back in his spot outside the door. "Well, you heard him. Is it all right if I just go…I don't know, find a vacant bedroom and get some rest? It's not like I can get out of here, unless I want to get myself fried like his kingness just did."

The guy lifted his wrist mic, passing along the question.

"Gee, I love a guy who makes his own decisions."

He was unflappable, didn't even act as if he'd heard her. Then he got his answer and gave her a nod. "The next three rooms are vacant. Pick whichever one you want. But don't try to go any farther or go downstairs."

Then he looked up at the sound of voices. "Here comes the doc."

By the time he looked her way again, Brigit was gone.

Utana lay in the bed and marveled at the intensity of the pain. His hand felt as if he were gripping a hot poker. And bolts, like powerful echoes of the initial blow, kept shooting through the rest of his body, pulsing up his spine and hammering the base of his skull. Lesser shocks, much the same but on a smaller scale, shot out into his limbs, into his fingers and toes. It felt as if he were touching that damnable gate again and again.

Before long Nashmun entered, accompanied by the doctor, a woman with long, white-streaked jet-black hair. She immediately leaned over him, pressing an instrument to his chest.

He closed his hand over the thing, startled and not trusting these people. But as he cupped the thing with his uninjured hand, its meaning and use came clear in his mind. It was a tool, used to listen to sounds inside the body. She could hear his heart beating, and the air rushing in and out of his chest, depending on where she placed it.

She met his eyes. "It's all right, it won't hurt you."

"I know," he said, and he removed his hand and allowed her to continue. After a few moments she lowered the ends of the device from her ears, letting it hang around her neck, and pressed her fingertips to his wrist. Again she listened, looking at the time-keeping device on her wrist. Wristwatch, he reminded himself.

Finally she turned his hand over, and examined his scorched palm. "This is nasty."

"It…pains me," Utana said, understanding now that she was this society's version of a healer, and wondering what prayers and chants and herbs she would use to ease his suffering.

Turning, she opened the small black bag she had brought into the room with her and took out several items. She removed the top from a container of water and extended his hand over a small bowl made of that odd material that had not existed in his time. Plastic, Nashmun had called it. Everything seemed made of it today. Squirting the water from the bottle, the healer woman cleansed his burned palm.

It burned like new fire! He hissed and jerked his hand away.

"If infection sets in, it will be worse," she told him, and her tone was harsh, until Nashmun elbowed her. She glanced sideways at him, then met Utana's eyes, schooling her own features into those of a loving and devoted servant. "What I'm doing hurts now, my king, but I'll be fast, and it will feel much better when I've finished."

Utana did not see that he had any other options but to allow her to continue tending his wounds. He found himself wishing Brigit were there to mind-speak to him whether or not these people were telling the truth. Truly, she knew them and their ways far more than he did.

But that was not the only reason he wished for her presence. He thought there was no situation, nor time, nor place, nor environment, that would not be improved by her presence. His longing for her to be by his side was becoming a constant pang within him. A need demanding fulfillment.

Slowly he relaxed his hand and extended it once

more for the doctor. If nothing else, her ministrations would at least distract him from thoughts of his would-be assassin.

The healer-woman finished her painful cleansing of the wound, and then she opened a tube and squeezed from it an odd-smelling unguent. Quickly she coated his seared flesh in a thick layer of the stuff. Utana's eyes widened, as the magical concoction eased his pain, cooled the burn, providing unexpected relief.

"See?" she said. "That's better, isn't it?"

"It is," he agreed.

"Now we have to keep it clean. So it can heal." She was capping the tube as she spoke; then she unrolled a length of thin white fabric, and wrapped his hand around and around with it.

"A glass of water, please, Nash?" she asked.

Nashmun nodded, rushing into the bathroom. As he brought the water, the doctor pulled a bottle from her bag and shook out two tiny white objects. "Take these. They'll help with the remaining pain." She held them near his mouth, so he presumed he was to eat them. He accepted the pills, chewing them as she turned to accept the water from Nash.

When she turned back to him with the glass in hand, Utana was making a terrible face and running his tongue over his teeth to try to dislodge the clinging bitter bits. "These taste terrible," he complained. "What are they?"

"Don't spit them out. Here, drink!" She held the glass to his lips, and he drank, then drank again, eventually rinsing all the pieces down his throat. Gods, the things were awful.

When he could speak again, he asked, "What poison did you feed me?"

"It's medicine. We call it aspirin," she told him, and then she sent an apologetic look toward Nashmun. "It's all I dare give him. We have no idea how his physiology will react to any medication, after all."

"Understood. Thank you, Lillian."

"You're welcome." She looked at Utana again. "You will need to rest. You'll be tired, and your muscles will ache, for a few days. If you have any more pain than that, you need to tell Nash, and he'll send for me. All right?"

"Yes."

Nodding, she began repacking her bag.

Nashmun focused his attention on Utana. "Where were you going, Utana?" he asked. "Were you trying to run away from us?"

Utana narrowed his eyes, wondering if, at last, he might glean the truth from his so-called vizier. "I thought to go in search of clothing for Br—for my harem slave." He realized that he had no idea what name Brigit had given Nashmun, but he was sure it would not have been her true one.

Lillian looked up from her task, sending an unspoken question to Nashmun.

"One of the dancers," the vizier explained. "He took a liking to her, decided to keep her as his personal…maid."

Lillian crooked a dark eyebrow. "That's extremely inappropriate, Nash."

"We'll discuss it outside."

"You cannot ask the girl to—"

"I said we'll discuss it outside."

Lillian bit her lip. It was clear to Utana that she knew more than he did about events here. About who the dancers truly were, and what their duties entailed. Sending a quick look around the room, she let her gaze linger on the bed of pillows where Brigit had slept, and then on the clothes she'd worn to dance for him, hanging over the back of a chair.

"I'm going to want to speak to this girl personally," she said.

Nashmun said nothing to her. He spoke to Utana. "I'll be back momentarily, my king." Then he went to the bedroom door and opened it, standing there, waiting.

Lillian huffed, snapped her bag closed and strode out of the room. Nashmun went out behind her and closed the door.

Quickly Utana flung back his blanket and got to his feet. Weakness hit him as if it were a wave in the great sea. He gripped the headboard to keep from falling, closed his eyes and willed it to pass.

When it did, he moved as quickly as he dared to the door. His gait was unsteady, weak. Why did this have to happen to him now, just when he'd been beginning to regain his strength? He cursed the power of the garden gate anew in his mind, then reminded himself that he had asked his gods for an answer. And apparently they had delivered it.

Near the door he stopped and, bending, pressed his ear close to the wood.

"—think you're forgetting who's in charge of this operation," Nashmun was saying.

"And I think *you're* forgetting," Lillian replied, "that I've been asked to report to the director personally. And I don't think he's going to like this. There was nothing in the plan about providing him with a consort, for God's sake."

"I am aware of what was in the plan. Hell, I *wrote* the fucking plan."

"Then you know better."

"I know it's working," Nashmun said. "Look, he trusts her, is even attached to her already. She could be our strongest weapon. We can use her to control him."

"Why would she be willing to let us use her that way?" she asked. "Have you asked yourself that?"

"She's bucking for a promotion. Why else?"

Utana sensed the change in Nash's tone. He was

lying to the doctor. He knew something more about Brigit than he was letting on.

"Why else?" The woman sounded surprised by the question. Then she sighed. "You're a straight male, so perhaps you haven't noticed, but this king of yours is a handsome man. A powerful, beautiful, sexy man. You're playing with fire here, Nash. This girl could turn from our strongest weapon into our biggest problem faster than you can even imagine."

Nash was silent, his mind closed to Utana.

The woman sighed, then spoke again. "On the other hand, if she's truly loyal and as ambitious as you say, you're right, she could prove extremely useful in controlling him."

"That's all I'm saying. And besides, we won't need him much longer. The Dymphna Project is almost ready to go. I just need to remove another obstacle or two before we can launch Phase Two. If there are any vampires left alive, this plan will flush them out, bring them right to us. And once we have them all together, in one place…" He said no more.

Utana shivered.

The woman outside the door sighed. "Just to be sure, I'd like to go over this dancer's records, her psychological profile, her history with the Division. If I don't find any red flags, then…I'll back you on this with the director."

"That's fair enough."

"Which girl is it?"

"Um…hell, I don't recall her name."

"Have you seen her…during the day?"

Nash released a soft chuckle. "Yes, I've seen her during the day. I'd know if she were a vampire, for God's sake. Do you think I'm a rookie?"

Lillian sniffed. "All right. Get her name and text it to me. I'll pull her records when I get into the office tomorrow."

Utana had heard enough. And his head was swimming yet again. He managed to shuffle-step himself back to the bed and fell onto it. But even as he righted himself and pulled the covers over himself once again, he knew that there was a problem. A very large problem.

Brigit's identity was about to be exposed.

Brigit didn't come out of hiding until she saw out the window that the doctor and her shiny maroon SUV, which looked like something a soccer mom would drive, were gone. But she'd heard every single word.

And it was a damned good thing she had.

She had to get out of this place—and she had to do it tonight. But before she did, she had to find out exactly what they'd been talking about with this… Dymphna Project. What could they be up to?

If she were smart, she would find a way to get what she needed and get clear of this place without once setting foot back in the bedroom of her sworn enemy. Already, in searching the bedroom for anything she could use, she'd located clothes to wear as she made her getaway: a pair of jeans only a little too big, a sweatshirt, even socks and a pair of slightly tight tennis shoes. She should just go, just find a way out and go.

And in fact, that was exactly what she intended to do. Until she heard him calling to her mentally.

Brigit. Come back to me, Lady Moonlight. I have information you must know.

She frowned, going still, part of her wanting to block him from her mind and the rest of her wanting to run to him as fast as humanly possible. And all of her was just plain curious. What information could he possibly have for her?

Had he overheard Nash and the doctor's conversation, too? Would he actually warn her? Help her to avoid capture? And if so, why, when he was sworn to kill her in the end?

She pulled her borrowed robe tighter and tucked her borrowed clothing inside. Tiptoeing, she left the safety of the vacant bedroom and walked quietly back toward Utana's room. The same guard was still outside the door. Over the railing, she saw Nash Gravenham-Bail walking through a door on the far side of the circular atrium-slash-great room into what looked like an office. She paused, watching him. In the quick glance she was afforded while he moved through the open door, she saw a desk, bookshelves, a computer screen and a row of tall filing cabinets.

She needed to get in there, she realized suddenly. And then she resumed moving toward Utana's room.

The guard saw her approaching, and she smiled nervously, wondering if he'd seen the direction of her attention just then. He tapped the door twice, opened it slightly and said, "Your lady is back, my king."

"Good."

Nodding, the guard opened the door wider, letting her pass without more than a cursory glance. She couldn't tell a thing from the expression on his face.

Utana stared up at her when she reached the bed. "Are you feeling better?" she asked.

"The doctor eased my suffering, yes. But I'm... weakened. And flustered. And..." *You need to get out of here, Brigit. The healer-woman is going to check your name and learn you are not one of them.* "And I've missed you," he said aloud.

Her response to his words was a softening. A believing. Her response to his warning was even warmer, but her questions were still wary. *Why are you warning me? You are my enemy.*

I do not wish to be your enemy any longer, Brigit of the Vahmpeers.

If you are an enemy to my people, you are my enemy. You can't have it both ways, Utana.

She waited then. For what, she wasn't sure. Did she really expect him to betray his gods just for the sake of a passing attraction that he'd probably felt a hundred times before for a hundred other women? His real harem slaves. His real dancers. His real wives?

"Sit here beside me," he said, patting the bedside. "Please."

She turned away to take off the robe, letting the clothes inside fall to the floor, then kicking them under the bed. Then she sat near him, even knowing it was a dangerous thing to do. "Of course, my king," she said. *Did you hear anything else I should know about?*

His eyes shifted away from hers. *I need you to heal me, Brigit. I do not trust them.*

If he meant to distract her, he was doing a damn good job of it. Finally he believed her. Then again, it was kind of hard to deny what she'd told him, now that his so-called friends had electrocuted him for trying to leave. *You'll give me back my powers, as well as my brother's?*

No. I will give you the power I took from your brother. The power to heal. Not to destroy, for if I do, I fear you will destroy me.

She looked at him quickly, about to lie through her teeth and promise that she wouldn't. But he only shook his head. *You've just told me I am the enemy of your people, and therefore your enemy. And your honesty is…of value to me.*

"I won't help you if you don't give it back to me," she whispered, tears welling in her eyes.

"Then I will suffer," he whispered back. "But at least I will not die only to be trapped in a rotting body, my consciousness held prisoner by the curse of the gods. I cannot return to that."

Her eyes shot to his, guilty eyes, because she knew that was exactly what would happen to him if she killed him. And it was almost more than she could bear to think about. God, how could she sentence a man to that?

And yet how could she let him live, only to know he would murder everyone she loved?

This was impossible.

His hand was on her upper arm, and then his fingers brushed over her cheek, compelling her to face him. And when she did, he was far closer to her than she had known, his face only an inch from her own.

His hand cupped the base of her head, and his mouth found hers.

And God, it was heaven and it was hell all at once. How could she want a man so badly when he was going to destroy her entire family?

How could she be so weak?

So full of desire?

For him?

She opened her mouth to him, and his arms wrapped around her, pulling her chest to his as he kissed her so deeply it felt as if he were trying to steal her very soul. Or maybe he already had. Maybe he'd somehow taken possession of it when he'd stolen her powers. Like the devil himself, maybe he had that power.

God, she wanted him.

Her hands buried themselves in his long hair, and she fed from his mouth, thinking nothing had ever tasted so good. Nothing had ever made her want more so desperately.

His arms around her felt completely possessive, encompassing and safe. So powerful and strong, so very strong. She was protected, though that was not something she had ever wanted, much less needed. She was strong, self-sufficient and proud of it.

Why, then, did it feel so good to be wrapped up in him, safe from all the world?

When he lifted his head away, her eyes were glowing, and she knew it. She saw him see that glow and react in surprise. Passion brought out the vampire in her. Her fangs had elongated, and her mouth was hungry for a taste of him. The need burned in her, demanding satiation, as her eyes fixed themselves on the powerful pulsing in his throat.

"Beautiful," he whispered. "Even this part of you. So very beautiful."

She forcibly averted her eyes. This was not the time. "All of my kind are equally beautiful. Why won't you let them live?"

"I begged the gods to allow it. I asked them for a sign. And then the gate nearly killed me. I have my answer."

"That wasn't an answer from the gods, Utana. That was a trap, set for you by the evil people in this place." She lowered her head, blinking tears from her eyes. "Give me the power and I'll heal you."

"It is already done," he said softly. "Will you help me now, my moonlight lady?"

She nodded. "I owe you a favor. For warning me. Thank you." She rubbed her palms together until they were warm and tingling, and then she opened them and stared into them. "I'm not exactly sure how this works, but…"

His hands closed on her wrists, turned them until her palms were facing his chest. Then he lay back and closed his eyes.

If there had been a blade nearby, a dagger, she could have plunged it straight through his heart quite easily, she thought. And then she saw the silver letter opener on the nearby nightstand, and her mind got stuck on it. Its blade was sharp and four inches in length. Big enough, she thought, if her aim were true. She stretched out a hand to pick it up, barely moving the rest of her body, her eyes affixed to his broad, beautiful chest, expanding as he inhaled, tempting her hands and lips to touch and taste.

Her hand closed on the letter opener, and the pain in her chest was as deep as if she'd plunged it into her own heart.

11

Senator Marlene MacBride sat on the sofa in her D.C. apartment, files open and spread out all around her. She was fully aware that Gravenham-Bail had only given her what he wanted her to see, and even with that, she was horrified at the accounts she was reading. Accounts of vampires held in captivity, dying in captivity, in DPI-owned facilities. They'd been treated like guinea pigs.

She learned all about their kind as she read. About the aversion to sunlight, the need to feed on human blood, the tendency to bleed out, the super-human strength and speed, the heightened senses and the additional ones—like telepathy. But nothing she read led her to believe they were a gang of murderous monsters.

She was more troubled than ever.

The wine helped. She was on her third glass, and feeling far more relaxed than she had up to now.

Her visit to the St. Dymphna Hospital had left her pretty wrought up. Oh, everyone there was being treated well. But there were kids there....

One, in particular, had struck a chord with her. A little girl, about seven, with blond ringlets and blue, blue eyes that had seemed to look right through her.

She pushed the shiver of the memory aside. Her decision was made. She was going to pull the plug, and the funding, on St. Dymphna's. She saw no evidence that the people being put up there were in any sort of danger, nor any evidence that vampires were dangerous at all.

Her initial report would also recommend that Nash Gravenham-Bail be pulled from any operation having anything to do with vampires. He was clearly biased and not to be trusted on the matter.

That report was typed up and ready to go. She would hand it to her aide in the morning, to have it copied and sent on to Senator Polenski. Then she was taking a two-week vacation—she had a cruise booked, and a husband waiting. While she was away, Polenski could decide if he still wanted her to gather a committee to investigate this further.

In the meantime, sun and sea awaited her.

She finished her wine, set the glass down and decided to leave the files where they were until morning. She shut off all the lights and padded into her bedroom. Suddenly something heavy hit her in the head. Light exploded behind her eyes, and she was gone.

* * *

Utana was still lying there, vulnerable, arms at his sides, eyes closed. Trusting her. Wanting her. And she wanted him just as badly.

Brigit withdrew her hand, leaving the blade where it was. There would be another time, she told herself, though she thought it might very well be a lie.

She closed her eyes and called up the power from deep inside. She drew it up from the earth below, from the sky above, felt it streaming into her, green and gold, meeting in her middle and swirling there until her solar plexus pulsed with power. Mentally she split that sphere in two and streamed it out into her shoulders, down her arms and into her palms.

The heat in her hands increased. It burned strongly enough that her eyes were startled open, and then she saw the warm white glow emanating from her hands and vanishing into his body.

"It's working." He whispered the words urgently. "I feel it wor—"

"Shhhh." She kept the power flowing, sensed it spreading out inside him, following the veins and the network of nerves to every part of his being, and a moment later he slid his bandaged hand beneath one of hers and pressed it palm to palm, interlacing fingers, holding it there.

The energy grew hotter, pulsed harder, but only momentarily. And then it was fading, paling, receding.

She drew a deep breath and lifted her head. "Wow," she whispered.

He smiled up at her. "Thank you."

"You're welcome."

And for one brief moment they were just two people. Not sworn enemies, not immortals, not opponents in an Armageddon-level standoff.

They were just a man and a woman.

And then he was sliding his hands up around her shoulders and pulling her close, kissing her again. Waving a hand, he made the bed curtains all gather together without touching them, just as he had done before.

It wasn't his fault, she thought, as he pulled her body on top of his, moving against her, kissing her deeply, passionately, endlessly. It wasn't his fault. He was becoming saner all the time, more logical all the time. He was listening to her, believing her about Nash Gravenham-Bail and the DPI and their lies. He was believing her. And when his mind had time to heal from all those thousands of years trapped, buried alive... When his mind had time to heal, he would believe her about the rest. He would understand that there might be an explanation for his condition other than a curse from the gods. He would believe her when she told him that his gods could not possibly want him to wipe out her family. He *would*. If she could keep him away from them long enough, just long enough, for his mind to heal.

For his mind…

To heal…

And then she realized that maybe she could speed up *that* process, too.

He distracted her from those thoughts, distracted her thoroughly, by pushing the nightie she wore up her body, peeling it over her head and tossing it aside. Brigit found herself sitting astride the big man as he stared up at her in the darkness. His hands cupped her breasts, kneaded and squeezed. Then they slid around to her back and pulled her forward, and his mouth took the place of those hands. He suckled; he nipped. Her breaths came faster as sensations overwhelmed her. Almost as if she would drown in them. And they did not let up.

As he gently, relentlessly tortured her breasts, his hands cupped her bottom, lifting and squeezing, spreading and pressing. And then he slid one hand in between their bodies, finding her center, opening it and probing. He didn't take his time. He didn't wait for consent. He spread, and he entered. And when she pulled back, startled by the suddenness of the invasion, he gripped her, held her, made her take it. One finger became two, thrusting forcefully, burrowing deep and still deeper. Hard, he drove his fingers into her. Over and over. And in moments she no longer pulled away but rode his hand, meeting that driving force that was him.

He was a different man, from a different time. And this was not the time for lessons in wooing. He wasn't wooing, he was taking. Possessing. And she found herself knowing there was no going back now, and glad of it.

He withdrew his fingers. His hands closed around her waist and lifted her, pulling her forward and then yanking her hips down again, so that she straddled not his hips or his bulging erection, but his face. No time to think or object, no way to pull back from his powerful grip. He was devouring her. His tongue stabbing into her, his lips closing around her. Even his teeth pressed together, sending bolts of delicious pain shooting through her body before his tongue licked it all away again. He repeated the torment, alternating pleasure and pain until the two were one, and she embraced and welcomed and surrendered to them as the waves of ecstasy began washing over her.

But no, no, not yet. He lifted her again, hands still at her waist. He moved her as he pleased, with no effort at all. And a heartbeat later he was lowering her again, this time entering her as he did.

He was big. Huge. Her eyes widened at the depth to which he filled her and the feeling of his thickness. Her body stretched tight around him. No time to adjust to the full sensation, no time at all. He was raising her up, pulling her down, as his hips arched to push into her over and over, until she was once again on the brink of ecstasy. And this time he pushed her over and came crashing down with her.

He held her hard and moaned. She bit his shoulder to keep from doing the same, and when she tasted blood, her fangs elongated and sank into his flesh. She drank, and the climax racking her body intensified tenfold, and went on and on and on.

It was only as she lay atop him, her entire body limp with relief, that she remembered her earlier thought. Gently she slid her hands to either side of his head and, holding him there, she called up the power. She felt it rise, and as she guided it into him, into her beautiful, powerful, twisted man, she wished with everything in her that it would have the desired effect.

A soft beam of white light glowed from her palms.

Anunaki, if you're real, heal this man and save his people. And in so doing, save his soul. For I believe it's a soul worth saving.

Nash used IV needles and tubing, which he'd stretched all the way from the senator's bathtub to her bedside. It wasn't all that difficult. Two quick punctures to her jugular, a little tape to keep the needles in place. He thrust the other ends of the twin tubes far enough into the bathtub drain to keep any of the blood from being visible.

While she lay there, unconscious from a blow to the head, bleeding out, he walked around her apartment, arranging things to make it look believable. It had to look like there had been a struggle. How else would she suffer a head injury before the vampire drained her dry, proving to the world that they were every bit as dangerous as he had always said they were?

He tipped over a few pieces of furniture. He kicked the file folders, so their contents flew everywhere.

Then he took her little report and replaced it with the one he'd taken the liberty of typing up himself. His version said that she supported his work fully but was afraid that in so doing, she was putting herself at risk. The vampires wanted to stop him, the new report claimed. That must not be allowed to happen.

It was going to look great in the press. As if she'd had a premonition she might be targeted. The sensationalism-loving media ate up this sort of thing with a spoon. And it had been too damn quiet for their taste since the vigilante movement had been shut down, thanks to Brigit and her little resistance gang.

But she was in his control now—the pretty little mongrel. She thought he didn't know who the hell she was. She thought he was an idiot.

"Surprise, little Brigit Poe," he said softly, as he returned to the senator's bedroom to watch the blood pulsing through the tubes until it slowed to a trickle. And then stopped altogether. "My mamma didn't raise any idiots, before she took off with one of your animalistic relatives." He lowered his head, stroking the scar on his cheek, hidden now beneath the black ski mask he wore. He'd tried to stop the vampire from taking his mother away—tried with a hatchet. And his mother had turned on him, new-born fangs baring as she'd hissed like a wildcat. Her clawed hands had flashed, glass-hard nails cutting deep.

And then she'd vanished into the night with her Undead bastard of a protector by her side. She'd left him bleeding, his father weeping.

The weakling. If he'd been half a man, he would have used the shotgun he'd been holding in his trembling hands. Nash would have. In a freakin' heartbeat, he would have.

Fifty-two stitches later, Nash had known that destroying her kind would be his life's work. And if a few innocent humans had to die in the process, well, that was too fucking bad.

He looked down at the pale lifeless corpse in the bed. Too bad. Then he took the tubing from her throat and carefully began rolling it up, following it to the bathroom. Without spilling a droplet, he bagged up the tubing and the original report.

On the way out, he opened the balcony doors that looked down twenty stories onto the D.C. streets below. Then he left through the basement, emerging into the alley between buildings, same way he'd gone in. No one saw him arrive. No one saw him leave. And in ten minutes he would be back at the palace with the clueless king and his overconfident mongrel lover, whom he didn't dare leave alone for very long.

Brigit was shattered.

There was no other way to describe what she felt. This man who now lay in the bed beside her, snoring softly, his big powerful arms holding her to him as if she were some rare treasure that might escape him, his fingers stroking over her skin every now and then, even in his sleep—this man was like no other.

He'd made her body melt beneath his touch. He'd made her feel things she had never ever felt before. He'd driven her so out of her mind—literally, she'd existed only in sensation in those moments—that she'd vamped up. She'd bitten him, tasted his blood.

Tasted it still on her tongue, salty and sharp. And the tiny fang marks on his neck and shoulder, which would vanish at the first touch of sunlight, stood now like beacons, announcing how far he'd driven her.

She had to have help. She had to talk to Rhiannon. Or her mother, or maybe her brother…yes. James. James would understand. He was all into feelings and emotions and goodness and sickening nonsense like that.

She wasn't in love. It would be ridiculous to think this was love. It was sex. Mind-blowing, earth-shattering, soul-bending sex.

And she wanted more of it—she craved it more than she craved life itself. And yet she had to kill the one who'd given it to her. God, the world was one fucked-up place.

Maybe…maybe her attempt at healing his wounded mind would take. God, she could only hope.

Gently she slid out from beneath his massive arm, her bare feet lowering to the floor and feeling every fiber of the thick carpet against her soles in a way she wouldn't have before. Her senses were heightened—no doubt due to the power of his blood now coursing through her veins.

As she bent low, pulling the stolen clothing from beneath the bed and putting it on, slipping on socks but ignoring shoes as too potentially noisy, her chief awareness should have been on the camera that was no doubt tracking her every move, catching glimpses of her nudity. But she barely gave it a second thought. Her focus was completely on him. Every step she took away from him felt harder—as if a thick rubber band connected them, stretching thin, pulling tighter, the farther she moved.

Pulling her straight back to him.

I have to go.

Yes. Before morning, before that Cruella de Vil lookalike lady doctor called Lillian ran her fake name through the CIA's employee records and found out she didn't exist.

But before she left this place, she had to get into that office downstairs, because it seemed to her that was the most likely place to find out about this Dymphna Project—which seemed, from what she'd overheard, to be a trap the DPI was setting for the vampires.

What were they doing that was supposed to lure any remaining vampire out of hiding?

She had to know. She had to warn her family.

Knowing the ever-present stone-faced guard would be stationed right outside the bedroom door, Brigit went to the window, opened it and leaned on the sill to stare outside. A cool predawn breeze touched her face, and she inhaled deeply, appreciating the smells of the garden out back and the slightest bit of a chill in the night air. Below her and far to the right, around the corner of the house, was the garden where Utana had been injured last night. Its gate, in all likelihood, remained closed. She wasn't worried about that right now.

She wanted to get to the ground floor of the

palace without being seen, and she thought perhaps those side doors that led out into the garden might be her best bet. Locked or not, she could open them.

She just didn't want to set off any alarms.

She was on the far side of the bed from the spot where she suspected a hidden camera was mounted. With the bed curtains drawn, she had visual cover.

Satisfied no one would see her and moving so silently that no one would hear, Brigit slid her backside up onto the windowsill, then swung her legs around and dangled them over the edge. She took a fortifying breath and took one last look back at the sleeping god in the bed. He was spread out like a woman's dream centerfold, the blanket just barely clinging to his hips, so she could admire that chest, and she fought the urge to go back over there to slide her hands over it one more time.

What the hell is the matter with me? He wants to wipe out everyone I love.

Out of confusion. Out of the messed-up tangles of a mind trapped for thousands of years, buried alive.

She wanted him. And she was tearing herself apart trying to wrap her head around her feelings and their situation.

No time now. Hell, years might not be enough time to make sense of her feelings for him. She had to put them aside and just get on with this.

She pushed off from the windowsill, and for an instant there was the rushing of wind past her ears, through her hair, and then the ground caught her. Her feet hit, knees bent to absorb the impact as she squatted low, then bounced upright again, looking quickly around her and seeing no one. Good. Easy as pie.

So far.

She crept along the edge of the house and rounded the corner to where the rose garden began. Following its winding path to a set of double glass doors that led back into the palace, she gnawed her lip and searched for an alarm, a wire, a panel, anything that might give it away. Seeing none, she pressed a palm to the door's ornate pewter handle and closed her eyes, feeling.

There was an alarm on this door, but it was not engaged. The lock was, but that wasn't a problem. Edge, her father, was known as the most skilled mental locksmith among the Undead. And he'd taught her well.

She exerted her will on the door locks, and they turned. Smooth as butter.

Opening the door slowly, she tiptoed inside, down the long, vaulted corridor toward the atrium, the hub of the wheel-shaped palace. When she neared the atrium, she pressed her back to the wall and slowed down, silent, and watchful.

The atrium itself appeared empty. Desolate. And the energy of sleep permeated the place. She didn't feel anyone awake or alert anywhere, though she knew well enough that there were guards outside the main doors. They didn't need a human guard outside the garden entrance—not with twenty thousand volts of electricity protecting the garden gate. There was one guard upstairs, standing outside Utana's room, she reminded herself. If he moved a few steps forward and looked out over the railing, he could see most of the atrium below. And if he heard a sound, he would do just that.

She would have to be careful, and utterly silent.

Emerging from the hall, she glanced up toward Utana's room, but the guard was not in sight. Quickly she scanned all the other portals leading out from the atrium. Hallways and doors lined the thing.

The one she sought was a door almost directly across from Utana's room. She figured out which one it was—situated between two hallways. Yes, that had to be the one.

Okay. This was it. Three, two, one… She tiptoed rapidly across the imposing atrium, knowing that any noise at all was going to echo as if made in the middle of an empty museum. Her socks, however, made no sound on the marble floor, and she kept far away from any furniture to avoid bumping into it.

It seemed to take minutes. It didn't. And then she was outside the office door, pressing her ear to the wood and listening with every fiber of her mind, body and spirit. Listening, feeling, sensing.

No one inside.

Palm to the doorknob. Mind open, listening to her senses.

Locked. She squinted at the door, squeezing her flat palm into a fist and twisting it counter-clockwise. She heard the lock obey her motions and her commands by clicking open. The noise startled her, and she snapped her eyes toward the upper rail-ing, even as she opened the door and ducked inside. She was pushing it closed when the guard appeared, staring down into the atrium.

And then she paused there on the other side, fore-head to the wood, wondering if he'd seen her, or glimpsed the door closing, even briefly.

Hell, she didn't know.

She'd better hurry the hell up, then. Turning, she scanned the darkened room, glad of her vampiric night vision. Books lined three walls, file cabinets completely covering the fourth. A computer stood on a large desk in a corner.

There wasn't time to go through everything, nor to start trying to guess passwords or scroll through files.

No. Instead she moved to the desk and put Nash Gravenham-Bail foremost in her mind. She saw his face, the scar that ran from the outer corner of one eye down to the center of his chin. The gray irises,

YOUR PARTICIPATION IS REQUESTED!

Dear Reader,

Since you are a lover of paranormal romance fiction – we would like to get to know you!

Inside you will find a short Reader's Survey. Sharing your answers with us will help our editorial staff understand who you are and what activities you enjoy.

To thank you for your participation, we would like to send you 2 books and 2 gifts – **ABSOLUTELY FREE!**

Enjoy your gifts with our appreciation,

Pam Powers

**SEE INSIDE
FOR READER'S
SURVEY**

YOUR READER'S SURVEY
"THANK YOU" FREE GIFTS INCLUDE:
► 2 Paranormal Romance books
► 2 lovely surprise gifts

PLEASE FILL IN THE CIRCLES COMPLETELY TO RESPOND

1) What type of fiction books do you enjoy reading? (Check all that apply)
○ Suspense/Thrillers ○ Action/Adventure ○ Modern-day Romances
○ Historical Romance ○ Humour ○ Paranormal Romance

2) What attracted you most to the last fiction book you purchased on impulse?
○ The Title ○ The Cover ○ The Author ○ The Story

3) What is usually the greatest influencer when you <u>plan</u> to buy a book?
○ Advertising ○ Referral ○ Book Review

4) How often do you access the internet?
○ Daily ○ Weekly ○ Monthly ○ Rarely or never.

5) How many NEW paperback fiction novels have you purchased in the past 3 months?
○ 0 - 2 ○ 3 - 6 ○ 7 or more

YES! I have completed the Reader's Survey. Please send me the 2 FREE books and 2 FREE gifts (gifts are worth about $10) for which I qualify. I understand that I am under no obligation to purchase any books, as explained on the back of this card.

237/337 HDL FH9E

FIRST NAME	LAST NAME

ADDRESS

APT.#	CITY

STATE/PROV.	ZIP/POSTAL CODE

SUR-PAR-11
© 2011 HARLEQUIN ENTERPRISES LIMITED
® and ™ are trademarks owned and used by the trademark owner and/or its licensee. Printed in the U.S.A.

The Reader Service — Here's How It Works:

If offer card is missing write to: The Reader Service, P.O. Box 1867, Buffalo, NY 14240-1867 or visit: www.ReaderService.com

BUSINESS REPLY MAIL
FIRST-CLASS MAIL   PERMIT NO. 717   BUFFALO, NY

POSTAGE WILL BE PAID BY ADDRESSEE

THE READER SERVICE
PO BOX 1341
BUFFALO NY 14240-8571

NO POSTAGE
NECESSARY
IF MAILED
IN THE
UNITED STATES

cold and emotionless. The stone-brown hair. The powerfully square jaw.

And then she sharpened and deepened her inner vision, until she could see his aura. Orange with ambition, red with violence and black with hatred. Blotchy, but all of it backed in a sickly yellow, not a bright, sunny color, but more like the yellow of phlegm or infected mucous.

And it was an infection that drove the man. She knew that for certain then. An infection of the soul. Of hatred.

Yes, it was the yellow she should follow. The most powerful part of him was his sickness. She was curious as to its source but short on time to explore. And so she opened her eyes but kept them unfocused, blurred, and shifted her head until she picked up the yellow in her peripheral vision.

Everywhere he'd been in this room, he'd left his essence behind. And she followed it now from the doorway to the desk chair, and from there to the filing cabinets—one file cabinet in particular. The drawer he'd opened held his snotty essence, and he'd touched a lot of the tabs on the file folders, flipping through them. But one had a bigger residue than the rest, and that was the one she pulled out.

At first the pages inside made no sense to her. It appeared to be a mailing list—but no, not just names and addresses, but descriptions, ages, names of employers.

Who were all these people?

Not vampires. She would have heard of at least some of them if they were.

Interestingly, some were typed in black ink, some in blue and some in purple. Most had one of several boldface symbols beside their names.

She fanned through the pages. There were at least a dozen of them, with roughly ten entries per page, in two columns. A hundred and twenty names, give or take. And it wasn't until she got to the end of the document that she found a small notation.

Key

Black = Subject is unaware he/she possesses
Belladonna Antigen

Blue = Subject is aware he/she possesses
Belladonna Antigen but unaware of
connection to Hostile Non-Humans

Red = Subject is aware he/she possesses
Belladonna Antigen and fully aware
of connection to Hostile Non-Humans

Purple = Unknown whether subject is aware
he/she possesses Belladonna Antigen

✓ = In Custody

☆ = Arrest Pending

O = Whereabouts Unknown

X = Deceased

This was a list of human beings with the rare Belladonna Antigen in their blood. A list of the Chosen. And most had check marks beside their names, a few had stars and only a bare handful had the circle that marked them as whereabouts unknown or the X for deceased.

They were rounding up humans with the antigen. Yes, there had been discussion among the Undead that something like that seemed to be happening, because humans with the antigen had been disappearing ever since the existence of the vampiric race had become public knowledge.

Now there was no doubt why. The government had been detaining them and taking them…where? Clearly this was part of whatever trap Scarface was laying for the Undead. He knew the connection, the bond, between vampires and the Chosen, the way the Undead would watch over and protect those human beings who possessed the antigen that made them potential vampires.

It wasn't a choice the vampires made. It was a reflex, a need. There was no free will involved.

She shoved the file back into the cabinet and scanned the room. Where could she learn the rest? Where were the innocent humans being held? The desk called to her, and she went to it, opening drawers even as she hit the power button on the computer. She rifled the desk as the PC powered up, and then she quickly scanned the keyboard for traces of his snotty essence, finding it on the G, B and N keys. His password was NGB—his own initials. Figured, given his arrogance. Finally she clicked the internet icon and checked the history.

Her eyes skimmed down the column of recently visited sites, pausing on a familiar one—a mapping page. She clicked on "begin private browsing" so the computer wouldn't keep track of her movements, then opened a new tab and rode it to a popular networking site. Leaving that up, she returned to the original tab and skimmed the most recently requested driving directions.

St. Dymphna Psychiatric Hospital. Mount Bliss, VA.

She cut and pasted it into the search bar, and clicked return.

Then she drummed her fingers, waiting. Results popped up about the same time the office door swung open.

Scarface stood there, two armed men behind him, both pointing guns at her.

12

"What'cha doin' there, Brigit?" Gravenham-Bail smiled softly.

She was caught, and she knew it. But even that knowledge didn't stop her from noticing the way he was dressed. Black pants, a black turtleneck, black leather gloves, black tennis shoes. Black socks, even. What the hell?

"You're spying for the vamps? Aren't you?" he went on.

"Spying? Hell no. I'm just your loyal, belly dancing secret agent. I just was looking for a computer to…check my FaceSpace messages."

Her eyes darted to the screen, fingers inching forward. She jabbed the mouse button, closing out the mapmaker and search tabs, leaving only the FaceSpace page up, then quickly lifting her hands palms up, and stepping back from the computer. "See for yourself."

She wasn't feeling the least bit confident as she met his eyes, but she tried to look as if she were telling the truth.

He shook his head. "What are you really doing here, Brigit?"

She took an involuntary step backward but stopped herself, knowing it was a sign of weakness he would not be likely to miss. "You know that's not my name, Nash. You hired me personally." She echoed her words with her thoughts, pumping them into his brain with all the force she could muster.

"Honey, that wasn't even working at the beginning. Did you really think they'd put me in charge of eliminating the Undead if I was that easy to manipulate? Besides, we've butted heads once before, you and I."

She nodded, giving up the lies. "Okay, okay. So you know I'm not who I say I am. I was working for the resistance. I'm a human being, as you well know, having seen me in daylight, who happens to believe vampires ought to have civil rights just like everyone else, and—"

"Enough with the lies." Nash nodded to his cohorts. "She's one of the most sought-after research subjects in the history of the DPI. It's like we got ourselves a free bonus. Take her."

The other men surged into the room, flanking her. Brigit flipped up her hand, as if to blast them with her power, fingers lightly resting on her thumb. She even imagined she could feel it rising up in her, but then she stopped herself. Her power was gone, and she was defenseless.

They gripped her upper arms and tugged her through the open door, into the atrium. She resisted enough to give them a hard time, but not enough to give away the only powers she had left. Might as well save that knowledge and take them by surprise with it when the time was right. They were making her furious, though, and it was hard to control the urge to vamp up and rip their throats out.

But that would get her executed for certain. These men wanted to wipe out her kind. To use Utana to—*Utana. Could he help her? Would he even bother to try?*

She closed her eyes. *I'm caught, Utana. I'm caught. They know who I am. They're taking me— somewhere— I don't know where and I can't—*

There was a crash from above, which she recognized as his bedroom door flying open, and the men went still, all eyes turning upward to see Utana standing at the railing, naked and magnificent. He was holding his door guard by the neck in one outstretched arm, dangling him slightly above floor level.

"You dare put your hands on my woman?"

"Not now, Utana. The woman isn't who she

claims to be. She's a spy." Then Scarface tilted his head to one side. "But you already knew that, didn't you?"

Utana's eyebrows went up. "A spy, a slave, a dancer. It makes no difference. She is my property while she is here, and therefore she poses no threat. Release her."

"Take her out of here," Nash muttered to his men. Then he looked up at Utana. "I'm afraid this isn't up for discussion, my king. She is a criminal my government has been seeking for years, and you are far too weak to be—"

Utana shifted his eyes, and in a flash of laser beam light, the palace's front door was blasted to smithereens. He dropped the man he'd been holding. The guard released one brief shout as he plummeted to the floor, where he landed hard, and fell silent.

The other men released Brigit instantly, turning their guns on Utana, taking aim, firing at him over the sound of her screaming "No!" while she lunged at her nearest captor. His shot blasted the hardwood railing, sending splinters flying in all directions, and then she was shoving his barrel toward the floor and simultaneously kicking the other man squarely in the cojones.

"I said hold your fire!" Scarface barked, and paused to eye his henchmen. One was doubled over in pain, while the other one's weapon lay on the floor neatly pinned there by the woman's foot. Brigit quickly flipped the gun up into the air with her toes, then neatly caught it, worked the action and aimed it at Nash.

He narrowed his eyes on her. "You just revealed more about yourself, half-breed."

"Quarter-breed, actually." She dared a quick look up at the second-floor railing. "Utana!"

He wasn't there.

"Dammit, if you assholes killed him, I'll—"

"I am here."

He was halfway down the stairs, wearing only a burgundy satin kimono, knotted at the waist, and carrying a bulging pillowcase by its neck. "I thank you for your assistance, Nashmun. But I believe my time here has come to an end."

There were others now, a half dozen or so, coming from everywhere all at once, all in suits, all bearing handguns, all closing in warily around them.

"If they try to stop me leaving with my woman, you, Nashmun, will find yourself in more pieces than your front door. We go now. Goodbye."

Nash bowed his head, backing away slowly. "If I could just have a word with you, before you go, my king. If you would just allow me to tell you how very close we are to achieving our mutual goal—"

"I do not require your assistance to do that which is demanded of me by the gods." He paused, frowning. "I did survive the Great Flood without your help, after all."

Nash lowered his head. "All right. Go, then."

Too easy. Brigit sent the words to Utana. *Watch our backs on the way out.*

Then, together, they walked to the front door, picking their way through the splinters of wood and stepping out into the covered walkway.

The men followed, muttering to themselves. With her back to them, Brigit called up her vampire side, lowering her head to hide her face—the glowing eyes, the pale, tight skin and the fangs—but she opened her senses to hear the words they spoke in whispers and feel their mortal thoughts.

"Should we follow them, boss?"

"No." *There's no need.* "Back inside, everyone. Beckwith, get a contractor on the phone to see about this door."

"Yes, sir."

She felt them retreating, felt no further blasts of thought from them and let her fangs retract, her eyes go dull and mortal, losing their vampiric glow. They'd reached the end of the sidewalk, and she crossed the street, instinctively wanting to put as much distance as possible between herself and that houseful of gun-wielding DPI men. Then she turned right, following the shoulder of the road and wondering if her car would still be where she'd left it, two miles up.

A hand on her shoulder was a physical reminder of the hulk walking along at her side, not that she'd forgotten his presence for even a single second.

"You are…uninjured?" he asked.

"They didn't hurt me." She lifted her eyes to his. "I wasn't sure you'd help me. Thank you."

"You are my—"

He stopped himself there, but she knew exactly where he'd been going with the thought. He finished lamely with the word *friend.* But he'd been about to say "woman." No doubt about it.

She could not hold his gaze. "I'm not your friend, Utana. You need to stop thinking that way. I'm not your friend. I'm going to have to kill you, sooner or later."

"You are not going to kill me."

She shrugged. "Well, I'm sure as hell going to try."

"I do not believe you will."

She rolled her eyes, then glanced behind her.

"They will follow us?" he asked.

"No, I don't think so. I heard Nash thinking it wasn't necessary. I just wish I knew why the hell he thinks that."

"I do not know."

They walked on in silence for a time, and then, because she was curious, she asked, "Why are you so sure I won't try to kill you?"

He looked at her. His eyes were so dark and deep,

that melted dark chocolate-bar color, with black velvet lashes that made him look almost like a little boy—unless you widened your scope to see the rest of him. The wide jaw, the muscular body. God, that body. But his eyes were the essence of innocence, and even love.

So deceiving, those eyes.

"You stopped them from killing me just now," he said. "You knocked their weapons down and kicked them, and screamed at them like a woman gone wild. You risked your very life to save mine. Why would you do such a thing?"

She lowered her head, watching her sock-covered feet move, one in front of the other, over the dusty gravel along the road's shoulder. The hems of the too-big jeans dragged in the dust.

"Brigit?" he asked.

"I needed your help to get out of there."

He shook his head. "It was more than that, and you know it. Do not lie to me, Brigit. Tell me—why did you help me?"

"I've been asking myself the same question, Utana. And the only answer I can come up with is that…I acted on instinct. On pure instinct. I mean, for crying out loud, we had sex last night. It's normal that I would feel…something."

"I also feel…something."

"I didn't mean it like that. Like—like you're saying it. It's not that I feel something for you, it's that I felt compelled to protect you. And I suppose that's natural, too, given that I...took a little sip from your..." She made the mistake of looking at his shoulder and then his neck as she spoke to him. "Your great big, corded, hard, salty neck."

He shot her a look.

She averted her eyes, cleared her throat. "I imagine it's a lot like the way the vampires feel about the Chosen—you know, humans with the Belladonna Antigen? I've explained to you about the connection between them, the bond?"

"Yes. And how the vahmpeers are compelled to protect and watch over such humans. I understand."

She nodded, and then she paused. "That's *it*. That's *exactly* it."

"It?"

She stopped walking, gripping his forearm. "Utana, I heard Lillian and Nash talking outside your room earlier. Nash said they were setting a trap for the vahmpeers—er, vampires." God, she was spending way too much time in his kingness's company. "I went into that office off the atrium to see what I could find out. And I found a list, names and addresses—"

"Wait. You are speaking too fastly. I do not know 'addresses.'"

"An address is...the place where you live. Each street has a name, each house has a number."

"I see. All right. Go on."

"These names were all the names of humans who possess the Belladonna Antigen. They were the names of the Chosen. And beside each one was a symbol to tell whether or not that person was 'in custody.'"

Utana blinked, his magnificent intelligence processing her words rapidly. "Nashmun is taking all of these Chosens captive. Just as he thought to keep me captive. And you, as well."

"Yes. That has to be the way they're baiting this trap of theirs. They're going to use the Chosen to lure the vampires out of hiding."

He frowned at her. "If they are afraid, the Chosen humans, they can call out to the vahmpeers?"

"No. Most of them don't even know of their connection to the Undead."

"Then how will the vahmpeers know they are in danger?"

"Just as you would know, if I were in danger. Or in pain. You would feel it, wouldn't you, Utana?"

He nodded slowly. "Even before I had met you, when I was with your brother, James, on the boat and you were crying out for his help, I felt you—even then." He stared into her eyes. "I would feel your call even if I were across the sea, Brigit. Your soul and mine—"

"Stop it. Just stop it right now."

He stopped talking. She was tingling, all warm and gooey inside, and hating herself for it.

"The vahmpeers," he said, returning to the safer topic, "will feel the call of the Chosens if they are in fear or in pain."

"Yes," she said. She sought his eyes, found them, locked on. "Utana, I have a very bad feeling that Nash and his men are going to do something terrible to those innocent people. Something so bad that their cries of fear and pain will be powerful enough to summon every vampire still alive."

"And then the vahmpeers will all arrive to attend to them. At the same place, at the same time."

"And Nash can wipe them out."

"Or order me to do so for him." Utana said it slowly, thoughtfully.

"I'm sure that was his plan. Now he'll have to do it on his own."

Utana nodded slowly. "Do you know where is this place, where the Chosens have been takened?"

She had to lower her head to keep from smiling at his childlike use of modern English. "Yes, I do. But I cannot tell you where it is."

"You must tell me, Brigit. Otherwise, how will I help you to set free them?"

"You want to help me free the Chosen?"

He nodded, holding her gaze. "I am not a king who ever allowed innocents to suffer, nor to be used as pawns in kingly games of war. Such a practice is disgraceful, and worthy of beheading."

"And if all the vampires arrive at the same place,

at the same time? Will you use the opportunity to finish what you've set out to do, Utana? Will you kill them all?"

He lowered his head. "I promise I will not kill any of the vahmpeers until all of the Chosens are safe."

"Not good enough." She faced front and began walking again.

13

Soon enough she spotted her car right where she'd left it, in a conveniently located pull-off near a riverbank. The spot was intended for anglers in need of a place to leave their vehicles while they walked the river, fishing. But the season for fly-fishing had long since passed, and it didn't look as if another vehicle had been near the place. The tire marks in the gravel were the ones she'd put there herself when she'd left the car a few days earlier.

She hurried to it, her keen eyes scanning it for nicks or dings and finding none.

Utana came right along beside her, reaching for the passenger door. But she held up a hand, and said, "Wait. Don't touch it yet."

Utana frowned, and she knew it was hard for him to take orders. Well, if he were going to ride with her, he'd better get used to it. They weren't in his den of fake devotees anymore. And yet she softened her barked command. "It could be dangerous," she explained.

He nodded, took two backward steps and stood with his arms crossed over his chest, watching her as she inspected her beloved baby.

"What must I promise, Brigit—what would be… good enough, as you say, to make you tell me where the Chosens are imprisoned?" Utana asked.

She was momentarily confused as she moved slowly around her car, bending over to peer beneath the wheel wells, dropping down on all fours to inspect the undercarriage. Without pulling her head from beneath the car, she said, "I want you to promise me you won't kill them. Not any of them. Ever."

He was silent, so she came out from under the car and rose up to look at him. He was standing a few feet from the hood. His head was tipped back, his eyes searching the sky. "How can I promise you that I will disobey the dictates of the gods?"

She rolled her eyes and crouched down again. "I don't believe the gods want you to murder innocent beings, Utana. And if they do, then they aren't gods at all. They're demons."

"Brigit, take care, lest they unleash their wrath upon you as they did me."

She popped up again. "No, you know what? I'm right about this, and you need to listen to me. Your gods, they must be good ones, to inspire such devotion. And yet you're going around claiming that they've ordered the genocide of an entire species. I would think they'd be furious with you for that."

He dropped his head and met her eyes, a frown marring his brow.

"What if it wasn't them?" Brigit asked.

He looked at her over the top of the car, blinking as if she were speaking words he had yet to learn. "What meaning has such a question? If not the gods, then who? Who sentenced me to centuries of living death and slowly growing madness?"

"Maybe no one did," she said. "Maybe it was just an unforeseen side effect of an immortal being beheaded and cremated. Did you ever think of that? Maybe if that desert witch hadn't burned your body to try to free your soul five thousand years ago, you might have revived, healed, reattached your severed head and been fine?"

He considered it. She saw the wheels turning behind his eyes. "But the gods allowed it. They allowed my suffering."

"The gods allow all kinds of misery, Utana. Innocent children get terrible diseases, or die of starvation or in senseless wars. Surely that doesn't mean the gods are punishing them. It might just be that… shit happens, Utana."

She got slowly to her feet, moving closer to him. Maybe the healing touch of her hands had had some impact after all. She'd never seen him thinking this deeply about the possibility that he had been wrong.

"Or maybe," she went on, "just maybe, all of this is part of some greater plan. Maybe you didn't remain conscious all those years so that you could murder the children you created. Instead, maybe you were allowed to live on so that you could see the beautiful race that sprang from you. The wonderful, powerful, miraculous family that you fathered. Maybe the gods thought you deserved that chance, and that the centuries of suffering would be worth it to you."

He shook his head slowly, turning away from her, as if her words were too much for him to process.

Sensing a powerful wavering in his stubborn beliefs, she hurried around the car and stood close to him, her legs almost touching his. Lifting a hand to his cheek, she made him look down and into her eyes. "Maybe it was the only way for you to be here now, Utana. With *me*."

She hadn't planned that part. It had sort of burbled up out of her, along with an inexplicable rush of hot tears that welled up in her eyes despite her rapid blinking.

His hand rose to push her hair away from her face, and his eyes plumbed hers so desperately that she could literally feel the yearning in him. The longing for her answers to make sense, to be believable to him. And she realized in that moment, for the first time, that he wanted another way out of this. He wanted her to be right—or anyone to be right, besides him.

But would he tell her that? No, of course not, the stubborn jerk.

"I will consider your words, my beautiful Brigit."

"I need you to do more than that," she whispered. "I need you to promise me that you will not kill my people."

"I will consider your words," he repeated. "And this much I will promise. I will never harm you. You have rendered me incapable of that." He lifted his eyes to the heavens, as if awaiting a bolt of lightning to come down and take him out. When it didn't, he seemed more emboldened. "And I find I wish to make yet another concession. I will not use this trap set by Nashmun and his people to kill the vahmpeers. I will…I will make a truce with them until this matter is settled and the Chosens are safe."

She searched his face, seeing relief there. Just putting off the task seemed to take a load off his mind. "How do I know you won't turn the beam from your eyes upon them the moment the Chosen are free?"

He took a step back from her, made a fist and thumped it hard against his chest, right over his heart. "I vow to you, Brigit, I will aid your people in rescuing the Chosens. And I will do no harm to them. When the task is complete, we shall go our separate ways, your people and me. And only when we meet again will I resume the sad mission my gods require of me. If, indeed, I determine that it is their command. I swear these things on the name of Inanna, who will strike me down should I break my vow to you. For you are so like her, you must surely be beloved of her."

She was taken aback by that. "I'm…like Inanna? A goddess?"

He smiled only slightly, but the amusement in his eyes was impossible not to see. "So very like her. Warrior goddess, enchantress, her temper equaled only by her beauty."

Brigit looked into his eyes and knew he wouldn't swear on Inanna unless he meant it. "I believe you."

His eyes held hers, his hand gently moving through her hair. "You should always believe me, Brigit," he said softly. "For to look upon your face, or into your eyes, and speak lies to you would be impossible for me." Their bodies seemed to tug at one another until suddenly they were pressed together and he was bending to kiss her. His mouth caught her lips, moving over them. He kissed her long and slow and tenderly. And she melted inside.

When he lifted his head at last, she said, "All right. We'll do this together." Her heart felt lighter, and she wondered if she could do it, could put aside what he had done, what he still might do, to her people. Could she forget about all of that just for a little while during this…this truce?

She'd certainly managed to forget it last night. And whenever he kissed her. Or touched her. Or looked into her eyes.

"Tell me now, Brigit. What do you seek upon your…car?" He nodded at her T-Bird.

"Tracking devices or explosives, or anything they might have put on it, if they noticed it parked here and were suspicious." Seeing his puzzled frown, she explained. "Tracking devices would enable them to follow us, to find us wherever we go."

"Amazing."

"Explosives would just blow us to bits—like a beam from your eye."

"Ah, I see. And have you found any of these things?"

"No, I don't see anything." She moved away from him again and took her keys from the hidden magnetic box underneath the rear license plate. Then she hit the button to open the hood. Quickly she moved to the front of the car and leaned in, looking over the spotless engine and again seeing nothing amiss.

She closed the hood, nodding. "I think it's safe. I don't feel as if anyone has tampered with it, and I don't see any evidence that they have, so…"

"So then we go."

"Yes. We go." She got behind the wheel. Reaching across, she first slid the passenger seat all the way back, then opened his door from the inside. Utana got in. Then she quickly started up the car, pulled a U-turn and drove on.

It was a huge relief to Utana to have put his merciless, cold-blooded mission aside for a time. He had no intention of breaking his word to Brigit, and was in fact grateful that he had a reason to hold off on carrying out the dictates of the gods.

The blood that already stained his hands was a burden that was rapidly becoming too heavy to bear. He had killed many. Granted, he had come to believe that at least one of Brigit's claims was utterly true: that his sanity had been eroded by five thousand years of living death. He'd been buried alive, trapped with the ashen remnants of his physical body inside a limestone statue, unable to see or to feel, but conscious.

And only later, thousands of maddening years later, when the statue had been unearthed by modern man, had he discovered that he could still *hear*.

And he'd heard so much.

People had come and gone in the various museums where the statue had eventually ended up on display. He'd heard their conversations, their arguments, their whispered confessions to one another. He'd been moved from nation to nation, had listened to people speaking in tongues he had never heard before. And he had absorbed the languages, one and all, learned them, listened and tried to make sense of every word and line that was spoken. Gods knew he'd had little else to fill the void of time.

But the nights, oh, the endless, soundless nights. Those were the worst times of all, with their echoes of all the silent years before the statue had been unearthed. For at night the museums were devoid of visitors, enshrouded in deathly silence, with no possible way to measure or sense the passage of time. And no way to know when the words would return, or if they would return at all.

Sometimes the occasional click-clack of what he later realized were the security guard's slow, measured steps would remind him that he was not alone in the universe. Other times, nothing would.

During those endless times madness had taken him over, though he hadn't realized it then, when the only thoughts in his mind had been prayers. He'd begged his gods to release him from the pit, his black prison of eternal darkness. He'd promised over and over that he would do whatever they asked of him, if only they would grant him the unthinkable bliss of release.

And so they had.

He had emerged enraged, wild. Senseless, really. Only moments after he had been reawakened, he had heard the one called Lucy relating the words of someone else, someone who had written, perhaps upon one of the ancient tablets of his own time, that he had been cursed by the gods for sharing his immortal gift with King Gilgamesh long ago. And later he'd absorbed the information contained on the tiny device in her bag—in a book called *The Truth*—which claimed the vahmpeers were little more than soulless beasts with an insatiable thirst for the blood of man, beasts that killed at will without remorse. He had learned that this race of blood drinkers had sprung from Gilgamesh himself. Gilgamesh, whose immortality had been bestowed upon him by Utana, in direct opposition to what he knew the gods had commanded.

He had come to believe that only by undoing the sin he'd committed then—the sin of sharing immortality with King Gilgamesh, who'd shared it with others, who'd shared it with others, on down through the ages, creating a race of immortal night-walkers—only by undoing that sin, could he ever be pardoned. And so, from the moment of his resurrection, he'd held only one goal in mind: to kill the vahmpeers and thereby redeem himself in the eyes of his gods.

What he had since learned about the vahmpeer race made him very sorry that he had acted in haste. And now he wondered, what if Brigit were right, and it was all a mistake? What if he had misunderstood what the gods required of him? What if ev-

erything he had done to the vahmpeers had been
for no reason whatsoever?

Had he slaughtered innocents?

Had he murdered his own children due to nothing more than a mistake?

Had he annihilated Brigit's friends and beloved
ones…for nothing?

The notion churned in his belly, clawed at his
heart. How, for the love of the gods, could he live
with himself if that turned out to be true?

And yet, he prayed that it was. For even though
he could not undo the harm he'd already wrought,
at least he would not have to wreak any more. And
in truth, he was unsure whether he were capable
of any more killing. Even if the gods insisted upon
it, he might very well be unequal to the task. To
murder the people Brigit so loved, when he felt
compelled to protect them instead—he did not
know if he could do it. And therefore he might be
doomed to return to his living death—perhaps at
any moment, should the gods realize how shaky his
resolve had become.

He tried to soothe himself by watching the scen-
ery as they drove along what Brigit told him was
a "highway," and by marveling at all they passed.
A great city, with buildings as tall as ziggurat pyr-
amids and monuments that stabbed into the sky.
How they made them to stand so tall was beyond
him. The ziggurats had been wider at the base, nar-

rowing in steps toward the *cella* at the very top, where the gods resided. Some of these buildings they passed by were the same width at the bottom as at the top. How did they not tip over?

After that they drove through countryside. Rolling meadows, forests and breathtaking mountains.

"Your land is so green," he said at length, needing to distract himself from the dire thoughts in his mind.

"It's beautiful, isn't it? We do have desert, far to the west. But here on the East Coast, it's very green and lush. Those are called the Blue Ridge Mountains," she said, pointing at the rising peaks around them.

"Ah. Blue Ridge. It is a good name."

"Yes, it fits them."

"And this road," he said. "Has it no end? How did your people ever manage to build such a fine, smooth road for such distances as we have traveled already?"

She glanced sideways at him, her eyes amused. "We've only gone about sixty miles, Utana."

He did not know how far a mile was, nor did he care in that moment. He was struck breathless by the smile in her eyes and teasing curve of her lips. Her sky-blue eyes crinkled at the corners when she smiled, and they sparkled when they were unhindered by fear and worry and anger.

"We have many, many people and lots of great

big machines. There are roads like this one almost everywhere in our nation."

"Amazing. And what of these…lines that have been painted upon their surface?" he asked, pointing.

Brigit explained traffic laws, lanes and passing rules, and the meanings of the various signs to him for the next twenty minutes, until he thought he understood most of it. It was a good way to pass the time, and eventually he said, "I will try it."

She blinked at him. "Try…what?"

He tapped the steering wheel with his forefinger.

"You want to drive?" She shook her head. "No. Look, this is a serious mission we're on here, Utana. We've got lives depending upon us. Hundreds of innocent lives. This is no time for me to be giving you driving lessons."

He frowned at her. "Would we not still be moving in the same direction?"

"Well, yes, but that's beside the point."

"How it is beside the point? We keep moving forward, we lose no time—if I go too slowly, you will tell me. If I cannot go fast enough, you will retake the helm. Let us find food, and when we resume the journey, I wish to try…drive."

She closed her eyes very briefly, then leaned over and reached past him to open the glove compartment. She pulled out the car's manual and dropped it into his lap. "Read that, and then put your hands

on the car and absorb its vibes or whatever it is you
do to inhale information like air. And then I'll let
you drive after we eat breakfast. Very briefly. *Very*
briefly, Utana. In a parking lot, where there's lots
of room."

"But…that would slow down our pace."

"It won't matter. It'll be daylight soon. We can't
meet with the vamps until nightfall anyway. And we
won't waste more than five minutes. Maybe ten."

He went silent, staring at her. "You are taking
me to meet with the vahmpeers?"

She looked at him, then away again. "I think
it's the best thing to do. If we can convince them
to accept the truce you offer, we can come up with
a plan to free the Chosen without putting the vampires at risk."

His throat was dry. The notion of facing the people
he might very well have so deeply wronged—
or might very well soon have to kill—made his
stomach rebel and his chest feel tight.

"Utana, you're going to have to make your peace
with them sooner or later."

"Am I?" he asked.

She nodded. "I love them. I *love* them, Utana.
Haven't you figured that out yet?"

He nodded, awash with yet a new layer of guilt.
To distract himself, he placed his hands on the
owner's manual of her precious vehicle—yes, he
knew she adored this machine—and closed his eyes

to absorb its contents. He did not need to do the same with the machine itself, for he already had. It was likely, he thought, that he knew more about the car than its proud owner did.

Brigit was grateful that Utana had stuffed the suit he'd so detested into the pillowcase along with several of his preferred robes. Her belly-dancing outfit was in there, too, she noticed, as she dug through the makeshift rucksack.

She insisted he take the time to exchange his regal robes for more ordinary clothing before they got out for breakfast, and then she forced her eyes to stay on the road while he struggled to change in the tiny passenger seat. At least he looked passably normal when they walked into the Denny's at 6:00 a.m.

Two hours on the road and they were barely a half hour from where they had begun. But she'd deemed it necessary to head in the opposite direction for a time, and to change course several more times, before finally heading toward her ultimate destination: Maine, where her family were holed up, along a route that would take them past St. Dymphna's Psychiatric Hospital for a look-see.

She was nervous as hell about him meeting her family again. They were going to be furious with her for not killing him. But when she explained, they would have to understand. He'd been ill. What he had done was no more his fault than the uncontrollable tics of a mortal with Tourette's syndrome.

They would understand. They would forgive her. And eventually they would forgive *him,* too.

Yes. There was no question about that. What else could they do? They were her family. They loved her.

Setting all of that aside, she walked beside Utana into the restaurant, where the air was thick with the succulent scents of bacon and maple syrup and fresh coffee. Her stomach growled.

The place wasn't crowded, but there were more customers than she would have expected at this early hour. No one gave them a second look as the hostess led them through the place to their booth. Scratch that. No one gave *her* a second look. *Everyone* looked at Utana. Not because he was odd to them, but because he was so big, and so freakishly good-looking. Men watched him with wariness in their eyes, maybe sensing the innate danger in him. Women watched him with blatant admiration.

They slid into a booth, and the hostess laid their menus and silverware, rolled up in napkins, on the table and said their waitress would be with them shortly, before scurrying away.

Brigit picked up a menu, opened it and felt her stomach rumble.

A waitress was on them almost instantly.

"Coffee?" she asked, full carafe in hand.

"God, yes." Brigit turned her cup over, then

glanced at Utana, who was taking in the place with fascinated interest. He was looking at everything, the people, the tables, the food, the kitchens, and he was sensing and smelling and feeling it all, she knew. His first time in a restaurant—well, except for the one he'd demolished in Bangor.

He'd come a long way. What a strange journey this must be for him. She reached across the table and turned his cup upright, as well. "Him, too. You'll like this, Utana. Trust me."

He nodded, meeting her eyes as the waitress filled his cup, as well.

The woman dumped a handful of tiny plastic half-and-half containers on the table and said, "Be back in a minute to take your order."

Then she was gone.

Utana stared at the black liquid in his cup. Raising it, he sniffed and then wrinkled his nose. Then he tasted it, just a sip, and grimaced.

Brigit bit back a grin and told her heart to stop twitching spasmodically every time he did something so damned adorable. "Watch me," she said.

He did, and she peeled the paper seals off of two of the tiny creamers and poured them into her cup. He did the same. She took two tiny white packets of sugar from the rectangular dish stuffed full of them and added them, as well. He followed her lead, avoiding the blue and pink packets, and using only the white, as she had. But he tasted the sugar first, on his fingertip, and his eyes grew huge.

"This…it's sweet."

"Yes. That's the point." She picked up her spoon and stirred her coffee.

Watching her every move, Utana did the same.

Setting the spoon aside, Brigit lifted her cup and took a sip. Then she closed her eyes. "Mmm. I needed that."

Setting his spoon aside, too, Utana took a sip of his own. And then he grimaced again, wrinkling his nose.

"You don't like it?"

"It is bitter. Perhaps more…" He took another white packet and read the label. "Soo-gar," he said.

She shook her head. "Sugar," she corrected, but he ignored her, pouring five more packets into his cup, stirring and tasting after each one, before finally nodding.

"Ahh. Now it tastes good."

"Oooohkay."

"Mmm. Yes. Good." He drained the cup and set it down. "Where is the food?"

"They will prepare it in the kitchen, which is back there," she said, pointing toward the doors beyond the counter. "And then they'll bring it to us, but not until we tell the waitress—that's the lady who was just here—what we want." She opened his menu and placed it back in front of him. "Here. These are our choices."

He looked at the images of the food and nodded. "They look...so real."

"Very convincing, aren't they?"

"There is so much. What is good?"

"All of it, Utana. Trust me on that."

He looked skeptical, probably doubting the wisdom of her taste buds, after the coffee.

Pursing his lips, he nodded. "Then I will ask for all of it."

Her brows rose, and she peered over the top of her menu at him, but he was still engrossed in his. "How about this? Since I've had just about everything they serve here, why don't you let me order for both of us? Would that be okay?"

He smiled at her. "That will be very...okay with me. But keep in your mind that I am very hungry, Brigit, and that my capacity for food is far greater than yours."

She nodded. "Understood."

St. Dymphna Psychiatric Hospital
Mount Bliss, Virginia

Roxy's shift had begun early. 7:00 a.m. But that was all right. She'd been spending almost all of her time at the hospital, just to stay on top of things. She'd fallen a little bit in love with some of the patients. Particularly little Melinda Hubbard, a girl who, she had decided, was not only one of the Chosen but also a powerful psychic.

The girl's mother, Jane, was neither. Her sole purpose in life was to protect her little girl. Roxy respected that, even if the woman had taken a huge misstep in bringing the kid here. Who the hell could blame her for trusting her own government?

Roxy was enjoying a cup of coffee and working a jigsaw puzzle with Melinda, while her mother showered. The rooms weren't bad, actually. The workers here had gone out of their way to make the place look less like a hospital and more like a hotel. Each room had a little round table and a couple of chairs. TV sets were mounted high on the walls. The railings had been removed from the beds, and nightstands with clock radios and pretty lamps and doilies had been set up. Really, they were pretty nice. You know, if you could get past the knowledge that you were being held prisoner, anyway.

Roxy thought most of the inmates were starting to figure out the prisoner thing. There was an air of restlessness permeating the place. People had asked to leave and been told no. People had asked to go outdoors and likewise been denied. It wasn't sitting well.

Jane emerged from the bathroom, a thick towel around her head.

Her back toward the hidden camera Roxy had pointed out in the front corner of the room, she whispered, "I don't know how much longer I can stand being here, Roxy."

"It won't be much longer." Roxy picked up the remote and cranked up the volume on the TV set, just in case. "Senator MacBride ought to be making her report soon. This place is going to be shut down in short order, you mark my words."

"You did well getting her out here," Jane said. "I'll always be grateful for your help."

"Yeah, well, we haven't been sprung yet."

Roxy lifted the remote to turn the volume down again, then froze, her eyes glued to the screen as an announcer gave the grim news that Senator Marlene MacBride had been found dead in her Washington, D.C., apartment that morning. Cameras jostled for a shot of a body bag being carried from a posh-looking building to a waiting ambulance.

"Oh, my God," Jane muttered.

The reporter went on. "No cause of death has yet been released to the public, pending autopsy, but a source close to the senator claims she was murdered by a vampire. Senator MacBride had recently been named head of the newly formed Committee on U.S.-Vampire Relations, and sources claim her initial report would have strongly favored funding what's been called 'A full-on, no-holds-barred effort to contain and monitor the Undead.'"

"That's not what she was going to report at all," Roxy whispered. "She came here. She knew…"

The little girl looked up at her, her huge eyes far too knowing.

"Don't be scared, Melinda," Jane said, hugging her daughter close. "We're going to be all right."

"I know we are, Mommy. That lady senator wasn't supposed to help us anyway. Someone else is. A guy. A really big guy. He'll be here soon." She sighed and lowered her head. "And then he's gonna die. Just like that lady senator did, and that makes me feel really sad."

14

An hour later, after watching Utana down three full breakfasts and a handful of sides, Brigit returned with him to the parking lot. Much to her dismay, he went straight to the driver's door and started to get in. But he didn't get very far, because he was simply too big, given the way she had the seat adjusted.

"Guess you don't fit. Sorry about that," she said, not sounding sorry at all.

He sent her a knowing look. Too knowing. Then he crouched until he found the buttons for the electronic seat adjustments, and after a few false starts managed to get the seat moving in the direction he needed it to: backward. And then he slid behind the wheel, fitting just fine.

"I never should have let you read the manual," she muttered, but she got into the passenger seat and, reluctantly, handed him the keys. "Here you go. Now, go very slowly. This car cost me a small fortune, and I love it. A lot."

"I will…use care."

"You'd better."

She instructed him as, step by step, he depressed the clutch, started the engine, slid the shift into first gear, released the clutch while pressing the accelerator and promptly stalled. But only once. The second time he managed to take off quite smoothly, and the car only jerked a little as he shifted into second, then third. Soon he was driving in smooth circles around the empty far end of the parking lot.

It amazed Brigit how quickly he picked up the rhythm of shifting, of using the clutch and gas pedals in smooth synchronization. After about ten laps he nodded, smiling at her, and brought the car to a stop, remembering to use the clutch so that it didn't buck and stall.

As he shut off the engine and turned toward her, he was beaming like a kid on Christmas morning. "I like this…driving. I wish to do more."

"It takes most people at least a few days to learn to drive a stick," she told him. "You're some kind of a genius, aren't you?"

"I do not know…geneeus."

"Genius. It means a person who is far more intelligent than most."

"Ah." He shrugged. "Immortality bestows much…

intelligence. Consider how a newly born one cannot easily direct his hands to do what he wishes."

She nodded. "Right, newborns have no hand-eye coordination."

"But as they grow older, it becomes natural." He shrugged. "Is it not reasonable, then, that the longer one lives, the more...graceful...one would become?"

"Without the bad parts of aging, I suppose that makes perfect sense." She got out, and he did, too, trading sides so Brigit was behind the wheel again.

"And I would guess," she went on, "that the ability to absorb knowledge and an understanding of how things work just by touching them must help, too."

"Yes."

"Did that come with the immortality?" she asked, as she restarted the car.

"No. I was that way from childness."

"Childhood," she corrected.

"Ah."

"So you've always been able to read a book just by touching it?"

"We had not books. We had tablets. But yes."

"That's amazing." She looked at him sideways as she steered back into traffic, heading toward the on-ramp to take them to the highway again. "Will you tell me about your childhood, Utana?"

His brows rose as she glanced his way. He was

surprised, she thought, by her interest. "I barely remember it. I lived some…" And there he paused, thinking. Brigit had no doubt he was translating his way of counting a lifetime into hers. "Nine hundred…years after the Great Flood. The earliest memories, they…"

"Fade," she said, as he searched for the right word.

"Yes."

"Do you remember your parents?"

"My father was more tribal chieftain than king. There were no palaces, no great city-states, yet. Not then. I remember our people moving, following the rains."

"Nomads."

"Yes. The…pictures in my mind are…thin. Dusty. Without color. So much time. So much time…"

"And what about your…adult life?" she asked softly. "You were a king. You must have had a…a queen?"

"I had…a harem. Slave girls to serve my needs. I treated them well. Had I not, the gods would not have chosen me."

"So…no queen? You know, one woman more special to you than all the rest? One who ruled by your side?"

"To share power—especially with a woman—it was not the way of my time," he said.

She sensed he was trying to explain something he knew she wouldn't necessarily approve of. "I understand that times were different then," she assured him.

"So different. So very different it is as if nothing remained the same."

She nodded slowly. He must feel alienated and foreign, even still. "And what about the flood? Did you really build an ark and put all of the animals of the world…?"

"I merely interpreted the signs and moved my household—my women, my sons and daughters, my servants and my herds—to the highest place I could find. There I built a ship, to enable us to sail forth in search of other lands that had escaped the flood, other survivors. But we never did sail far enough to find any. One of your years we remained on the mountaintop, while the waters raged below. Eventually they began to recede, and we returned to the valleys."

"Then why were you rewarded with immortality?"

He shrugged. "Why was I sent the signs so that I could survive while others did not?"

"I don't know." She found herself fascinated by his story, but even so, she was trying to find loopholes without looking as though that was what she was doing. She wanted to convince this man that religion was not a good enough reason for genocide.

Then again, it was one of the main reasons why

anyone had ever committed such an atrocity or gone to war in the history of mankind.

"What were these signs, Utana?"

He shrugged. "The sun was blotted by the moon. I had seen it before, and always it foretold disaster. Too, I noted the animals vanishing from the desert."

"And didn't anyone else see those things, too?"

"All who cared to look."

"Then the gods didn't send the signs just to you. They sent the signs to everyone, hoping someone would listen and move and survive. Yes?"

He blinked at her.

She could only look at him in brief glimpses, because she was driving. "I mean, anyone could have interpreted them as a warning. You just happened to be the only one who did." Then she frowned. "Or were you? Were there others who moved to higher ground before the floods came, Utana?"

"I do not know. How can I, when I was the first to go?"

"Well, when you returned to the valleys, were there others there?"

He nodded. "From other lands. None of my own tribe."

"So you're not the only flood survivor. Maybe you're just the only one who was also a priest king and therefore sort of famous."

"Then why was I the only one given the gift of immortality?"

Shrugging, she said, "Maybe the gods wanted you to start a new race. Or maybe it was just something you ate. Or maybe you were already immortal, even before the flood, and you just didn't know it yet."

His eyes widened, and she sensed his shock and thought that she had probably pushed him far enough for one day. But then his expression twisted into one of pain, and he bared his teeth, squeezing his eyes tight.

Alarmed, she veered to the right before jerking her attention back to the road and correcting their course. "What is it? What's wrong? Is it what I said, because I wasn't trying to—"

"Fear. I feel fear." He closed his eyes and pressed his hands to his head. "And it is not from the vahmpeers. It is…mortal." He lifted his head and speared her with a look. "It is the Chosens. They are near, and they are fearful."

"You're right," she said. "I can feel them, too."

Brigit looked at her GPS. "I got so caught up in your story that I wasn't paying attention. We're getting close to the place where they're being held, Utana. I'm sorry. I should have warned you."

"You have decided not to take me to your people first?" he asked.

Did she detect hopefulness in his tone? "No," she said. "I just thought we could take a look. It's sort of on the way."

* * *

It was not an ideal time for "reconnaissance," as Brigit called it, Utana thought, as they sat in her car outside a building as large as any temple. But it was not a temple. That much was clear. It was a beautiful structure made of small red bricks, with arches of gray stone surrounding the windows and doors. It sat within a large grassy field and was enclosed by a fence, with a gate that opened in the front. The gate was of a different material, however. Black iron, not silver like the rest. To the left, beyond the fence, was a small woodlot. To the right, a large area with a surface like the road on which they drove, where many cars were stored.

In front, a circular drive wrapped around a tall statue of a woman, perhaps some modern goddess, bearing an oil lamp that contained an actual flame. Sentries were posted at the front entrance, one man on either side of the door. They wore green suits of clothing, the pattern blotchy, and they held weapons in their hands. Rifles. Tiny caps adorned their heads.

"They are soldiers?" he asked, not needing Brigit's nod to confirm it.

"Yes. Probably have no more clue what's going on inside than we do. Maybe less."

"It is not a soldier's job to know, only to obey without question. So it was in my time, at least."

"That much hasn't changed," Brigit said softly.

She started up the car, began to pull away, but he put a hand over hers on the steering wheel.

"What?" she asked.

"We cannot leave. The Chosens are inside that building."

"I know. But we can't rescue them right now, and there's no point in us being discovered out here casing the place. They'll throw us inside with the others if they catch us. And then what good will we be to them?"

She continued driving.

"We should stay here. We should return to that place after darkfall and free the captive Chosens."

"We know where they are," she said. "And we know Nash isn't going to kill them right away. Not until after he uses them to lure every vampire left alive to their death, at least."

Her jaw was set in a familiar way, speaking to him of her stubbornness, as she drove. But she was going slowly, as if she, too, were reluctant to leave. "Our priority is to get to my people, to warn them that this is a trap and to convince them to let you help. Then we'll make a plan and rescue the Chosen. It's the only logical way to do this, Utana."

He could tell by the way her voice trembled as she spoke that she was feeling the same pull he was. She, too, wanted to spring into action at once, to rescue the prisoners immediately. Leaving them behind was painful and difficult for her, as it was for him.

"Go that way," he said, pointing to a road just past the property that turned left. "Drive around to the rear, that we might observe the portals and sentries there."

"All right," she said, nodding. "No harm in that." And she turned left, driving slowly, watchful, lest they be discovered.

There were no entrances to the building along the right side. Just that large strip of pavement and the numerous vehicles parked there. He saw that the fence encircled the entire building.

"I wonder if that fence is electrified," Brigit said as they drove on.

Utana knew about electricity. He'd felt its jolting power when he'd touched the gate at the mansion. He felt for the prisoners within, and the fear and unease he could still sense made *him* feel uneasy too. Nervous and restless.

They turned left again, now driving along the back side of the building. The lawn stretched out far behind it. At the building's base, panels of glass angled outward. They began at a man's height above ground level and then angled outward, slanting all the way down to the ground itself. Above, there was a fire escape.

"Odd, the windows there," Utana said, pointing.

"They look like skylights—they must be there to let sunlight filter down into the basement."

He understood. A basement—the subterranean

level of a building—would naturally be devoid of light. These rooflike windows would solve that problem. They also revealed that the basement must be slightly larger than the above-ground part of the building.

And yet still he saw no entrance to the building.

They turned left again, but this road, leading them to the one where they had started, ran alongside the woodlot, blocking their view of the building.

Soon enough they were driving past the front again, resuming their journey toward her beloved vahmpeers.

"If we tell your people about this place," he said, choosing his words with care, "will they not feel compelled to come here? To try to help? And would that not be exactly what Nashmun wishes for them to do?"

He saw her brow crinkle in the center as she considered his words. The tiny lines that formed on the bridge of her nose distracted him from his train of thought, but only briefly.

"They'll know anyway. If Nash does something to hurt or traumatize the Chosen, my people will feel it. Already, you can feel it, and so can I. No matter how far away the vampires are, they'll know. If it gets any worse… Maybe they're already sensing the Chosen's unrest. And they'll come, no matter what." She sighed, then nodded firmly. "No.

It's better if I tell them it's a trap. At least that way they'll be forewarned."

"But still, they will come. Yes?"

She shot him a brief look. "Yes."

"Would you not wish to prevent them coming here at all, if you could?"

"Well, yes, but I don't see how—"

"I will tell you how. We get the Chosens out. We do this before their distress becomes any…louder," he said, for lack of a better word. He knew she would understand his meaning.

"Alone?"

"I believe we are two of the most powerful people in your world today, Brigit. I believe there is no force in existence that we two, together, cannot overcome."

She blinked and lowered her head, as if his words had elicited some strong emotion within her. "Well, we were. Now…*you* are. And I…"

"You are far more than you know, Brigit Poe." As he said it, he reached out with one hand to push her blond locks behind one ear, the better to see her face.

Her cheeks warmed, pinkened, at his touch.

"Will you give me back my power, then?" she asked.

He considered his answer for a long moment. The building they had been examining was far behind them now. The countryside rolled out before them as they continued to drive northward. Hills of lush green rose higher toward bluish mountain peaks that stabbed into the sky.

Would she return to her original plan to kill him if he told her the truth?

He looked around him, accustomed to finding a means of escape before entering any dangerous situation. It was the soldier in him, he supposed. A king must lead armies, and he had learned to lead them well.

As he weighed his chances, he felt a smile tugging at his lips. She would not blast him to bits—at least not while he resided inside her precious car. He was safe—for the moment.

"I asked you a question, Utana. Will you give me back my power?"

"I already—"

Brigit halted the car so dramatically that he stopped in midsentence. She pressed her temples, closed her eyes tight.

"Brigit?" They were in the center of the road, and not entirely within the boundaries of the correct lane. "Brigit, are you all right? What is it?"

She blinked her eyes open and stared directly forward. "It's J.W.," she whispered.

Utana tore his concerned eyes from hers and looked instead to where she was focused. Brigit's twin brother, James of the Vahmpeers—the very man who had raised Utana from ashes—stood far ahead in front of the car. And as Utana looked on, he strode closer, down the center of their lane, and stopped there, placing one hand on the vehicle's hood. His broad shoulders blocked out the afternoon sun, and the gathering winds tossed his golden hair like ocean waves. But it was his eyes that held Utana's attention. His eyes carried the message of his fury. Could he have blasted Utana with a beam from them, he surely would have done so.

And now that he was here, perhaps his sister would feel the same. It was a very good thing, Utana thought, that he had not had time to complete the words he had begun to speak to her.

A horn blasted behind them, and Brigit jumped, then shook herself free of her momentary shock and began easing the car forward. J.W. backed out of the way, walking to the shoulder, where his own vehicle, an old pickup truck, was parked. Brigit drove past it, then pulled onto the shoulder a solid fifty yards ahead. She wanted there to be some distance between J.W. and Utana. For J.W.'s sake.

As she reached for her door handle, she felt Utana's hand on her upper arm. Warm. Strong but gentle. When she looked at him, there was a question in his ebony eyes.

"I don't know what he wants. Probably he was on his way to check out St. Dymphna's, like we were just doing ourselves. Or maybe they sent him to find out why I haven't done what I was sent to do."

Utana held her eyes. "To destroy my body, and return my soul to a dark and timeless prison."

"Yeah. That." She had to avert her eyes when she said it. "Don't worry. I'll talk to him, okay? Just wait here. I'll be right back."

His eyes asked her not to go, but it wasn't as if she had a choice here. He was her brother. She opened her mouth to say something more, but then closed it again, not even sure what words were so eager to escape. She gave Utana a reassuring smile instead. "I'll be right back. Promise."

He said nothing, just held her eyes, making it very hard for her to turn away, to open her door and exit the vehicle. She did it, though, and then walked back toward her brother's truck. Two-tone, red on top, cream on the bottom. It was an older model, late seventies, but rather than a restored classic, it bore the look of a tired-out ride. A little attention, though, and it could be something special.

She patted its hood as she approached her brother, who was standing in front of the bumper. "She needs tires, J.W. And there's some rust starting up around the gas cap. You don't get on that soon, it'll be too deep, and you'll have to—"

"What the hell do you think you're doing?" he asked, firmly cutting her off in mid chatter.

Brigit lowered her eyes, nodding slowly. "Not even going to say hi? Just straight to the condemnation?"

"What are you doing, Brigit? Why is that monster still alive? And why the hell—"

"He's not a monster. He's a man, J.W. And I think he—"

"Not a monster?" J.W. gaped at her, seemed to have to fight for the ability to speak again. "Are you forgetting how many of our people he murdered?"

"Not for a minute," she whispered. "And neither is he. It's eating him up inside. But the man was half out of his mind when he did what he did. He'd been trapped in a living death for thousands of years, resurrected into a world he didn't understand, shown a race he created and told by others that he would be returned to the eternal prison you pulled him out of, unless he destroyed it. He believed he was told these things by the gods themselves. He *believed* it, J.W."

"I don't give a damn what he believed."

"He'd been lied to, both by Folsom's piece of shit book full of propaganda and by that DPI bastard, Nash Gravenham-Bail."

"Who the hell is—"

"Scarface," she snapped. "Remember? I had him prisoner, thinking he was one of the vigilantes? As we made our way to the yacht, he managed to get Utana's attention. He fed him a pile of bull, and Utana let him go. Remember, J.W.?"

"It's James," he said.

You would think by now he would have given up on that constant refrain, she thought.

"And yes, I remember," he added.

"He was DPI, J.W. He was laying the groundwork to use Utana against us. And it almost worked."

"It did work, sis. He blew away dozens of us. And you were supposed to kill him, Brigit. You were supposed to kill him before he could kill any more of us."

"Well, I haven't, so deal."

They stood there, face-to-face in a stare-down that Brigit eventually lost when J.W. said, "He took my power. And he hurt my Lucy."

"That was an accident, and you know it."

"Yeah, I do. He was trying to kill me, and she got in the way. That doesn't exactly make it all right, Bridge."

She had to look away. "The first thing he asked me when I found him was whether Lucy was all right. He was mortified for having hurt her. He likes her."

"I don't fucking care if he likes her!" He tipped his head back, shoved both hands through his hair in frustration, then looked her in the eye again. "Brigit, what's going on with you? Has he brainwashed you, put some kind of mind control vibe on your brain, or what?"

She paced away from him, pretending to examine the truck but actually searching for words instead. She ran her hands down the side panels. The paint was still good under all the dirt. Just a little touch up, a little sanding and body putty, fresh paint and maybe a layer of clear coat, and it could be a classic.

Traffic flew past, sending mini-blasts of air at her over and over.

When she circled back around to the nose of the truck, J.W. met her eyes again. "What are you going to do?" he asked her softly.

"I think he deserves another chance, J.W."

He lowered his head, shaking it slowly. "That's not your call. You were sent to take him out, Brigit. If you won't do it, the elders are just going to send someone else. You know that."

She released a puff of air that could have been a laugh, had she let it mature. "They won't succeed. He's too strong. I've been looking for a vulnerability, a weakness, all this time, and I haven't found one yet."

Her brother's brows rose, a spark of hope coming to life in his eyes. "Is that why you're with him? Looking for a weakness?"

"That *was* why. In the beginning."

"And now?"

She nodded toward the stretch of road behind them, the direction from whence she and Utana had come. "You knew the Chosen have been vanishing for a while now. We've all suspected the government was rounding them up. Utana and I have learned where they're being held."

"We already know," James told her. "They're at St. Dymphna."

"Well, aren't you all just way ahead of us, then? I suppose you also know they're nothing more than bait for a great big DPI vampire trap?"

Her brother blinked, his eyes telling her that he hadn't known that at all.

"They're going to do something to them, J.W. They're going to hurt them, scare them, something to put them into a state of anguish or pain or fear."

"So the vampires will feel their need and come to their aid," he said, putting the pieces together at last.

"Now you're getting it. They figure they'll lure out every vampire left alive, so they must be planning to really put the screws to the captives. And then they intend to kill you all."

"How?" J.W. asked.

"They intended to use Utana to do it." She put her hands on J.W.'s shoulders and stared forcibly into his eyes. "But he refused. He came with me instead."

"Yeah. To do what? Blast us all on his own timeline?"

Throwing her hands in the air, Brigit turned away in exasperation. "I wanted to come to you all, to warn you. He didn't want to do that. He wanted to rescue the Chosen on our own, to keep everyone else far from danger."

"Oh, so he's looking out for us now." J.W. threw his own hands in the air and walked in a small circle. "Am I supposed to believe he's decided to thumb his nose at the supposed dictates of his gods and not kill us after all?"

She shrugged. "Not yet."

Her brother's eyes widened, brows arching high. "Are you kidding me? He hasn't decided yet, and you're *still* taking his side?"

"Believe me, the second he seems inclined to harm a hair on any of your heads, I'll take him out." She didn't tell her brother that she no longer had any idea just how she would manage to do that, now that her powers were gone. She wasn't going to give him any more reason to hate Utana than he already had. He didn't know the man—not like she did.

"Great. That's just great."

"Now that you're here, we have a far better chance, though," she said. "The three of us can free the Chosen before the DPI does whatever horrible thing they have planned for them."

Her brother looked at her, searching her eyes as if for some explanation that would make him understand the change in her. But she knew he wouldn't find one. She didn't even know what had changed in her, so how could he? All she knew was that returning Utana to an endless existence of being buried alive was beyond her. She couldn't do it, couldn't kill him, knowing that would be the result. Nor could she allow him to harm her people. She was being torn to pieces by the conflict that would only be resolved if Utana chose to betray his gods for her, and her people chose to forgive the man who had decimated them.

Odds didn't look very good for either event.

With a frustrated, furious sigh, J.W. shook his head. "No. I don't want any help from that murderer. And if you're with him, Brigit, then I don't want any help from *you,* either. And you can trust me when I tell you, our family will feel the same way."

"No." Brigit felt hot tears burning in her eyes. "Don't say shit like that, J.W., not to me."

"You need to choose—right now. You either come with me now, or you take off with him and let us handle our own problems. Make your choice, Brigit. Us or him?"

"I want you to talk to him," she said. "Just talk to him. Please, James."

"No." As he said it, he looked past her toward her car. And then his eyes narrowed, and he went on, "Looks like he's made the choice for you. Though it pisses me off to think he had to."

"What the hell are you talking abou—" She turned as she spoke, then stopped when she saw her car speeding away without her.

15

"I take it you taught him to drive?"

Brigit nodded, still staring into the empty space, now that the T-Bird was out of sight.

"Bad idea. I guess you're stuck with me now, sis." J.W. slammed her shoulder from behind as only a brother would do. "Only question is, would you rather storm the castle, just the two of us, or head back to face Rhiannon and explain to her just exactly why it is you went soft?"

She glared at her brother and said, "Neither." Stomping to the passenger door of his pickup, she yanked it open and said, "Get in and start driving, J.W. We're going after him."

"We'll never catch up," he argued, but he went around the truck and climbed in. "He's got way more horsepower than we do."

"Horsepower, yes. Gas? Not so much." She climbed in and shut the door, as her brother started the engine and pulled the truck into motion. "We've been on E for the past twenty miles. I was about to stop for gas when he started picking up vibes from the Chosen."

"And I take it you didn't teach him the finer points of pumping gas while you were supposed to be blowing him away?"

"No, I never quite got around to that."

"What *did* you get around to?"

She felt her brother's eyes on her, heard the question he was really asking. If she looked him in the eye just then he would see the answer she wasn't ready to give. So she stared straight ahead and said, "He'll run out in another ten miles, give or take. If we hurry, he'll still be with the car."

J.W. sighed, and she supposed her nonanswer was all the answer he needed. He was her twin, after all. The person closest to her in all the world.

And his lack of faith in her had been like a blade to her heart. She wasn't sure she could ever forgive him, even when he finally came around to realizing that she was right. He'd put a rift between them, and she didn't think he even realized it.

But this wasn't the time to address it. Not now.

Utana drove Brigit's car, his skills increasing exponentially with each passing mile. The process was not difficult for him, and that wasn't something he was particularly proud of. It wasn't as if he were somehow responsible for the superior intellect with which he'd been born. Nor for the gift of immortality given him by the gods, nor for the centuries upon centuries of life that had enhanced his mind even further. None of it was his doing.

Driving this machine, however, filled him with pleasure. If there had not been so many problems on his mind, the experience would have been one of pure bliss, he thought. Much like the experience of possessing Brigit's beautiful body had been, although not nearly as powerful. In that case, even the worries plaguing him had been unable to interfere.

They were interfering now.

His pleasure in the power of the automobile, its instantaneous response to his every command, was diminished by the questions tormenting him.

And there were many.

Utana had tuned in to the mind of his beautiful Brigit while she'd spoken with her brother. Her twin. He had heard the words they exchanged, yes. But, too, he had felt the emotions. James's anger. Brigit's heartache.

Her brother, the person she loved most in all the world, had bade her choose—between him and his family and Utana himself.

Utana had opted not to force such a difficult choice upon her. And perhaps that was only partly an unselfish act on his part. It was true that he did wish to spare her a difficult decision. Partly, though, he feared which choice she would have made. Surely she would not alienate her family any further by consorting with *him*. Not when protecting her family had been her reason for remaining with him all along.

She hadn't killed him. Perhaps it would have been better for them both if she had. Truly, his feelings for her were mixed up in his mind—and heart—and he knew not how to make sense of them, nor sort them out.

He knew one thing, however. He had not lied when he told Brigit he could not murder her. He knew that without any doubt, and if the gods insisted that her life be taken, then he was doomed to return to the living death he'd suffered.

Nor did he want to take the lives of those she loved. And if he were honest, he no longer believed himself capable of doing so—of causing her that kind of pain. So if the gods instructed him to spare her, but to immolate the rest—well, he did not think he could do that, either.

Hell, he wasn't sure he was able, now, to take any of their lives. The vahmpeers. The race he had unintentionally created. And perhaps his mind would be easier if he just admitted as much to himself and gave up struggling with the decision. For deep down, he knew, the decision was already made.

Blinking slowly as he drove, he heard himself whisper, "Yes. The decision is already made. I cannot kill them. I *cannot*." He looked at the distant horizon. "And I *will* not."

Drawing a deep breath that expanded his chest and filled his lungs, then releasing it slowly in a long, long sigh, he realized that he felt a sense of relief. As if the weight of the very world had been lifted from his shoulders. A weight that dangled now, menacing and ominous, overhead. He knew the decision he had finally made was the right one. But he feared that in the making of it, he had doomed himself to return to an inescapable and unbearable hell.

"Only when I die," he told himself. "And so I will simply find a way to remain alive. For as long as I possibly can."

A smile tugged at his lips as that heavy weight dangling above him seemed to evaporate and float away. Temporarily, at least.

And then the car spat and bucked a little. It sputtered and coughed, and then its engine died entirely. He depressed the clutch to let it coast off onto the side of the road as Brigit had done when she had stopped to talk to her brother, seeing now the logic in doing so.

But once he brought the vehicle to a safe halt, out of the way of other cars that might come speeding past, he could not start the engine again, no matter what he did.

In only a moment, he knew the reason, felt it through his hands on the steering wheel. The liquid called gasoline, on which the vehicle fed, had run dry. It needed more.

Utana got out, feeling lighter, despite the setback of being on foot. It was good, having made this choice. He was almost eager to tell Brigit about it. But he knew, too, that his troubles would not end there.

Her people—*his* people—would not easily forgive him for what he had done. Perhaps he could make it right, however, by rescuing the Chosens and protecting the vahmpeers from the trap being set for them. Surely Brigit had told James about that by now. Surely the vahmpeers would not attempt to go there tonight. They would wish to take time to form a plan.

Therefore, *he* would go tonight. He would free the Chosens. And when it was done, he would seek the forgiveness of the Undead.

And after that, regardless of the results his effort reaped, he would try to live this life with as much pleasure and bliss as he could manage, knowing that when it was over, the wrath of the gods might very well await him.

"So be it, then," he said softly. "So be it."

He walked away from the car, leaving it there, keys inside. Then he trudged off the highway and across a weed-strewn lot, heading back in the direction he'd come, but trying to do so off the beaten path and out of sight.

When he reached his destination, the hospital called St. Dymphna, where the Chosens were being held, he went into the woodlot to the building's left. He crouched amid the trees, concealed by the vines that had twined themselves around the fence. Making himself as comfortable as was possible, he waited, and he watched, and he listened. And most importantly, he *felt*.

This, he thought, was going to be easy.

Brigit stood beside the T-Bird, turning in a slow circle as the wind blew her hair into a tangled mess. "Where the hell is he?"

"Probably gone back to Scarface to report in," J.W. said. "He was probably working for him all along, Bridge. Just playing you, so that you'd lead him to the rest of us."

"You're wrong." She knew better.

Didn't she?

"I am? That's what you were doing, though, right? Bringing Utana, the guy who's supposed to annihilate us, straight to our door?"

She closed her eyes, lowered her head. "You keep pushing me, bro, and I'm going to have to knock you on your ass."

He moved closer to where she stood. "Let me take you home, Brigit. Just let me take you home."

"We don't have a home. Or are you forgetting that just about every safe house in vampiredom has been torched by vigilantes?"

"Home is where your family is, sis. They're all waiting for you. And they'll forgive you for not blasting him into a thousand pieces. Hell, they'll probably be relieved to find out you have a heart after all, even if you did choose a damn poor time to start using it."

"Fuck you, J.W."

"James. I keep telling you, it's James."

She sent him a look. Then she pursed her lips and shook her head. "We can't go all the way back to Maine. The Chosen don't have time, and I don't think Utana does, either."

"Scarface won't kill him until he has what he wants from him. No worries on that score," her brother said. He opened the T-Bird's door, reached in to remove the keys, then closed it and hit the lock button.

"He won't go back to Gravenham-Bail, anyway," Brigit insisted. "He'll try to free the Chosen all on his own, and he's going to get into trouble if he does. He has no idea the kind of security or the weapons the DPI will have waiting for him in that place."

J.W. shrugged, turning to face her. "Maybe that's not a bad thing, Bridge. Maybe they'll manage to do the job for us that you couldn't bring yourself to do. Maybe they'll send him back to the grave, where he belongs."

She slapped him. She slapped him so hard that he

rocked backward, catching himself against her precious car and probably scuffing up the paint. And then she stood there, her eyes beginning to glow with vampiric fervor and rage. Her fangs had elongated automatically with her anger, and her heart was pounding in her chest. There was an urge inside her to tear her brother apart. She'd never felt that way before—not about him. Her twin. And it frightened her.

"My God," J.W. said, staring at her as if seeing her for the very first time. "You love him."

"You don't know shit about what I feel. Or who or what he is, for that matter. But I'll tell you one thing—*James*. You wouldn't exist without him. None of us would. He's our creator, and neither you nor anyone else has the right to judge the man. Much less return him to an endless existence of darkness, of paralysis, of sensory deprivation. It's a living death—the most cruel and inhuman punishment anyone could imagine. No one deserves that. *No one!*"

She turned and stomped back toward his truck. "I'm going to the nearest gas station to get a can of high test and a funnel. You can ride along with me or wait on your ass here. I could care less either way."

"And then?" he asked, hurrying after her. He caught up just as she reached for the driver's door and gave her a shove she wasn't expecting. Then, as she stumbled out of the way, he climbed behind the wheel.

She raced around to get in the other side. "And then I'm going after Utana, to try to keep him from getting himself killed," she said, as she got in.

J.W. started the truck and put it into gear. In a moody silence, her brother drove to the nearest gas station. Neither of them spoke a word the entire time. He went inside to buy the gas can, then returned to fill it up and stow it in the truck bed. She waited in the cab. She was angry. Furious, far more so than she had ever been with him before.

As he started the engine and pulled onto the highway again, she said, "I do not like being this angry with you, J.W."

His jaw twitched. He didn't meet her eyes. "I don't like it, either."

"I'm sorry I hit you," she said.

He was silent for a long moment as she watched his face, saw the struggle there, and the way his Adam's apple swelled and receded like a wave as he swallowed. "I'm sorry I said what I did. And that I forgot for a minute that…you're my sister. My twin. And that we're the only two of our kind. And that no matter what else happens…we're supposed to stick together."

She felt hot tears stinging her eyes and thought how stupid it was to cry like a girl over something she should have known was coming. She and J.W. always had each other's backs.

"So?" she asked.

"So let's go find Utana. And then we'll bring him to meet the family—the elders. Let him have his day in court, so to speak. He's got a lot to answer for, but maybe—"

"We can't take him to Maine, J.W. We have to get the Chosen out of government hands before the DPI and Scarface do something awful to them. You know they'll want to make them scream—the louder the better—to lure the vampires to come to their aid."

"I know. But we don't have to go to Maine."

She lifted her brows and stared at him. "I don't understand."

"Everyone was worried about you. And feeling the energy of the Chosen, too. They're already here—in Virginia. At the plantation."

Utana crouched in a woodlot just beyond the chain-link fence that surrounded the place they called St. Dymphna. He hadn't yet learned who this particular saint was, but he understood what saints were in general: enlightened beings who no longer lived, favored by the god of this time. Demigods, in a way. Humans prayed to them, and they were said to intercede on behalf of the faithful.

If this Dymphna were looking down on what was being done in her name—and he presumed this saint was female, as the statue in front of the hospital named for her was a woman—he thought she would surely send bolts of lightning down upon the place. Which must mean she wasn't watching. Or maybe the gods of this world were false. He'd seen no evidence of their existence so far. In his day, the gods had been everywhere. Interacting with man in every moment of every day of his lifetime. The Anunaki were involved in every aspect of life. The singular god of today seemed all but invisible. Present in name only, like a figurehead. As if there were no more life to him than to the statues that represented his saints.

In Utana's time, even the statues contained the living essence of the Anunaki. They were fed and washed and clothed, those statues. The people of today seemed to care little about serving their god. Or maybe he simply had yet to see it, he thought. For surely no race would neglect its deities so.

As he crouched and observed, he admired again the beauty of the building. Many of the buildings today were plain and cold, large smooth rectangles lacking imagination or design. But others were breathtaking, in this time. Oh, not as spectacular as the ones from his beloved Sumer. The temples, the statues, the ziggurats. But nice. This one spoke of age—relatively speaking. It was, he sensed, more than a century old, and built to last a good deal longer.

The doors in the front were arched on top and

possessed inserts of the glass that was so prevalent in the architecture of this time. Utana had yet to see a building without it. More importantly, those doors were guarded by soldiers.

Here, on this side of the tall fence, red-green vines had twined themselves around and through the links, providing him with cover. The woodlot was vacant and had been left untended. Its uneven rows of trees were littered in between with weeds and shrubby brush that offered camouflage, as well. He was very well hidden. It was a good vantage point from which to observe, and he couldn't help but think that, had he been in charge of this place, he would have sent men to clear this lot. Truly, Nashmun had overlooked a vital aspect of his strategy.

In front of the building, there was nearly nothing of the earth. A concrete walkway bordered the curving drive. In the center of that curve, between the building and the road, stood the fountain with the woman carrying the oil lamp. Little birds, carved of stone as she was, perched on her arms. She was beautiful. And in front of the outer gate there was a large square of chiseled stone, with the words *St. Dymphna Psychiatric Hospital* carved into its face.

He crouched there in the woods, his position giving him a good view of the front and left side of the building. There were no guards on the side.

No entry, either, other than the windows and a side door that looked impenetrable. The windows on the lowest floors were barred. The rest were not.

He watched for a while, then moved farther along the fence to give himself a view of the back. Manicured lawns spread like green carpet behind the place. There were flower gardens and shrubs, and footpaths that wound among them. Small tables stood here and there, and Utana deduced it was meant to be a place of peace and rest for the patients who normally lived in this building. Safely enclosed in the mesh fence, they could enjoy being outside.

And there, angling to the ground from the building's rear, were those glass panes Brigit had called "skylights" stretching over the basement.

He saw no sign that the gardenlike back lawn had been recently used. Nor had it been tended well. Leaves littered the tables, benches and footpaths. The grass was shaggy, not neatly trimmed as modern man seemed to prefer it.

His haunches were growing sore from crouching, and the modern pants he wore were uncomfortable in this position. Utana straightened, thinking on how he would get inside, whether it would be better to try to enter covertly, or whether it might be best to simply blast the front doors open and obliterate anyone who tried to stop him.

He rather preferred the former. He was tired of violence, of killing.

"Hello, my friend."

Startled, Utana turned quickly.

Nashmun stood facing him, looking him up and down, and Utana regretted allowing himself to be so caught up in his reconnaissance that he failed to sense his former vizier's approach.

"How did you find me?" he asked.

"I knew you'd come here. Brigit was snooping in my computer, so I was fairly certain she had found out about this place. And about the people who've taken refuge here."

Utana blinked. "The Chosens within the walls of this place are prisoners, not refugees."

"No doubt that's what she wants you to believe. I am well aware of who she is, you know."

Utana averted his eyes. "She is a dancer."

"She is the most sought-after subject in all of the world, Utana. She is a mongrel, part vampire, part human. And we need to bring her in. To study her. For the good of all mankind."

Utana felt his blood heat at the notion. "You will stay far from her, Nashmun. Or I will kill you."

Nash blinked twice, then nodded as if in understanding. "She has confused you. I understand, Utana. It happens to the best of us. She's very beautiful, after all, and you're a man, like any other."

"I am unlike any other."

"You know what I mean." Nash clapped Utana on the shoulder. "Where beautiful women are concerned, we're all pretty much alike, aren't we?" He was smiling as if there were no enmity between them. "Come with me, will you? Let's talk a while."

"There is nothing I want to hear from you."

"No? Well, perhaps there's something you'd like to hear from *them,* then." He nodded toward the asylum as he spoke. "The Chosen. Come on, I'll take you on a tour of the place, introduce you to some of the refugees. Let them tell you in their own words why they're here. How does that sound?"

Suspicion buzzed loudly in Utana's brain, and he examined the man's face, his eyes, tried even to hear his thoughts, in search of an explanation. "What trick is this you are attempting now?"

"No trick, Utana. I simply want you to know the truth, so that you'll reconsider completing your mission, and help me wipe out the scourge of vampires from the planet once and for all. It is your destiny, you know."

"Only the gods can say what is my destiny."

"Well, they're not very talkative in this day and age, my friend, so you might just have to figure it out for yourself. Come inside with me. Listen to what the Chosen have to say."

After a long moment, Utana nodded. He'd wanted to get inside. What better way than by invitation?

"What the hell is he doing with that SOB?" James whispered.

Brigit stood on the road beside James's truck,

feeling as if her heart had just been hit with a sledgehammer as she watched Utana walking side by side with Nash Gravenham-Bail of the DPI into the St. Dymphna Psychiatric Hospital.

When they'd pulled onto the shoulder out front, James had opened the pickup's hood to make it look like an ordinary bit of engine trouble, rather than like a pair of quarter-blood vampires spying on the DPI's baited trap. Brigit had left her car a mile away, gassed up and locked tight, outside a Dunkin' Donuts. She had fully expected to find Utana here. But she had thought he would be casing the joint, planning his attempt to rescue the Chosen. Not consorting with the enemy.

"Bridge?" J.W. put a hand on her forearm to get her attention.

She blinked the stupid hot tears from her eyes and shook her head. "I don't know. I don't know what's going on here."

"But you know who that is, right?"

"I know who he is. That's Scarface."

"He was there when they shot Lucy."

"I know, J.W."

"Well, what the hell is Utana doing with him, then?"

She blinked away the blur from her vision. "He picked Utana up outside Bangor a few days ago. Convinced him that he was some kind of diplomat, acting on behalf of the president. I followed them to a small airport, where they took off in a private jet. He took Utana to a D.C. mansion where they let Middle Eastern royalty stay when they're in town. Treated him like a king."

"Shit, they're going all out."

"I convinced Utana that they were bullshitting him. Or...I thought I had. He left with me. But now, I don't know. I just... I don't know what the hell is going on, J.W."

"Well, I do." He slammed the hood of the truck down, grabbed his sister's arm and led her to the passenger side. "He's still working with the bastard. Leaving that mansion with you was part of the plan. You bring him home to the family and that scar-faced DPI scum follows right behind him, leading them straight to us."

"Nash was having me arrested when we left. Utana...he saved me."

"Why did he have to?"

She blinked twice, then averted her eyes.

"He took your power, didn't he, sis? The same way he took mine. He did, didn't he?"

Lowering her head, she nodded just once. "Only because he was afraid I'd try to kill him with it."

"So if he's so damn reformed, why hasn't he given it back?"

"I...he will. We were just discussing it, in fact, when you showed up and interrupted."

He stared at her for a long moment, then heaved

a deep sigh. "Look, I can see that he's got you tied up in knots, Bridge. Maybe he's even worked some kind of mental manipulation on your mind, but I'll tell you now, you're not seeing things clearly here. You're too close to this to see it, but it's obvious from the outside."

"No."

"He tricked you into leading him to us. Or almost did. He's still working with the DPI. You just saw him with your own eyes, walking along practically arm in arm with that bastard." He took her shoulders in his hands and gave a gentle shake. "He's still planning to wipe us out, Brigit. Don't you see that?"

Her tears spilled over then, and she was furious—with herself, with her brother and with Utana most of all, for making her want to believe in him so very badly that she couldn't listen to logic or reason anymore.

"Shit." J.W. looked straight up. "I was right. You're in love with him, aren't you?"

She didn't answer. J.W. lowered his head to meet her eyes, and she imagined he saw the reply shining from them.

"Dammit, Bridge, I'm sorry." He folded her into his arms and held her against him. "I'm so sorry. I know it hurts. And it clouds your vision. You can't see straight. There's a reason why they say love is blind. You've gotta trust me now, okay? I'm your brother. You don't have any reason to doubt my motives or question where my loyalties lie. Trust me, okay?"

"I...I trust you."

"Okay." Releasing her, he opened the truck door. "Get in. I'm gonna take you home. Or at least to what we're calling home for the moment. You need to be around your family. You need to heal and get your head to stop spinning."

"But...but what if you're wrong?"

He made a face as if she were an idiot, then softened it with love. "Go on, get in."

Brigit got in.

16

Utana walked beside Nashmun through the sterile, colorless halls of the building he had been watching. There were people in every room, ordinary-looking people, none of whom seemed to be in overt pain, although he still felt their fear and growing uncertainty, their questions.

"Many of the people here didn't even know of their potential connection to the Undead," Nashmun was saying, strolling at a casual pace, nodding and smiling at staffers and wary-eyed patients alike as they passed. "Until we told them, of course. Bringing them here allows us to protect them."

"And why do they need protecting?"

"Well, vampires have a bond with these people. They can sense something in their blood from miles away, pinpoint it, home in on them. They tend to act like guardian angels. But only at first, of course.

Their goal is to keep them safe until they reach the prime age for transformation."

"Trans-formation?"

"Yes. That is the ultimate goal, after all. Vampires can't reproduce—well, with a few obvious exceptions, some of whom you've met already. But aside from Brigit Poe and her twin brother, James, and their mother, Amber Lily, who's half and half, we don't know of any offspring born of the Undead. The only way they can propagate the species is by changing innocent, unsuspecting humans into vampires. And humans with the right blood antigen—a rare one known as the Belladonna Antigen—are the only ones who can be changed successfully." He shrugged. "Those who aren't changed are…well, to put it bluntly, eaten. The antigen makes their blood extremely potent. They're the vampires' favorite meal."

Utana suppressed a shudder and strove to keep his face impassive. Nashmun was watching him closely, seeking his reactions, as they walked along the corridors, passing closed door after closed door. "And this is what you've told these Chosens?" Utana asked.

"Not initially, no. Our goal was to protect them, not to frighten them. But they were beginning to be afraid of us, to ask questions, to want to leave the safety of this place. So this morning we assembled them all in the big conference room downstairs and explained it to them. Just as I've now explained it to you."

"I see." This must be why he'd felt the surge of painful fear, he thought.

"Do you? Do you understand what I've told you, Utana? These innocent people would have been transformed into…into bloodsucking night-walkers—against their will—by those monsters. If they objected, they would have been devoured. That's why your gods commanded you to destroy the vampires."

Utana nodded as if in understanding, even while his mind raced with questions. He was no longer so certain that his gods had commanded him to annihilate the vahmpeers. He'd read that they had in the book he'd stolen from James's mate, Lucy, when they'd been on the boat together. But the book had been written by a man, not by the gods. It was man's interpretation of what had been recorded on a stone tablet from Utana's own time. And yet, he realized, that stone tablet, too, had been written by a man.

Just a man.

And men were flawed, their understanding of the Anunaki and their ways limited and often in-complete. So it had been in his own time, and so, he had seen, it remained today.

"What becomes of these Chosens," he asked,

"should they not be…made into vahmpeers, nor imbibed by them?"

"What do you mean?"

"I have been told that they weaken, grow sick, die before their time."

"It's bull. Something the vamps spread around to try to justify their crimes against humanity. But it's not true."

Utana studied the people wandering the halls, apparently without restraint. He paused to peer through the glass in one of the many closed doors they had passed and into the room beyond.

"No need to do that, my friend. We can go inside." Nash reached past him, tapped twice on the door and waited for a friendly "Come in" to push it open and lead the way in.

"Hello, Jane," he said, with a nod at the pretty blonde mother who sat in a rocking chair, gazing out the window. And then he nodded at the little girl who sat on the floor surrounded by open books with pictures in them and colored sticks she was using to scribble on the pages. "Hello, Melinda. What are you coloring today?"

Melinda looked up, wide-eyed. Utana focused on the child intently, his mind probing hers, listening to her thoughts, which flowed unguarded and innocent.

I don't like this man. The little girl's thoughts

clearly referred to Nashmun. *He's ugly and scary, and his smiles are only pretend.*

But even while thinking those things, the little girl obediently held up the book to show a picture of a raven, which she had filled with orange, yellow and purple shades.

The coloring sticks were amazing, and Utana found himself wanting to sit down beside the child, take them up and join her in her artistic endeavors.

"That's very nice," Nashmun said.

You didn't even look at it, you big old liar, the little girl thought.

Utana smiled at her insight, her honesty, and crouched down low. "You might be a great artist one day," he told her.

She met his eyes. "Gosh, you're big."

He could not restrain a smile. "And you're little."

His smile is real. I think he's a good guy. I wonder if he's...the one.

Nashmun was speaking to the mother. Jane. "This is my friend Utana. He's concerned, wants to be sure everyone here is comfortable and feels safe."

The mother's eyes shifted toward Utana, but he only afforded her a brief nod before returning his focus to the daughter, though he kept listening.

"We have everything we need. But frankly, Mr. Gravenham-Bail, we'd like to know when it will be safe for us to leave here."

Utana tried very hard to direct his thoughts toward the child, but he wasn't sure she would be able to hear them, even while Nashmun made conversation with the mother. *Are they being good to you here?* Utana asked the child.

They won't let us go home, the little girl thought. *I want to go home. I want my room and my dolls and my closet full of pretty clothes, and my own bed. That's what I want.*

"As you can see, Utana, we've converted all the rooms into miniature apartments for our guests. They have televisions," Nashmun said, waving toward the box mounted to a pole in a corner, "and window seats. There's a little table for private meals, although we also serve meals in the cafeteria. It's everyone's choice whether to eat with the group there, or bring their meals back to their rooms to enjoy them in privacy."

"And are they allowed outside?" Utana asked, standing upright once more. "The grounds in the back are quite…enchanting."

We never get to go outside! Melinda mentally huffed.

"We're working on that. As soon as we are sure it's secure for them to—"

"Surely it would be secure by day, Nashmun. Those from whom you claim to be protecting them cannot walk in sunlight."

"That's what I've been saying," Jane said.

"If this woman wished to leave this place, right now, with me, would you allow it, Nashmun?"

"Of course," Nash said softly.

The woman's face lit with hope, and the little girl could barely contain her excitement. "Does that mean we're going home, Mommy? Right now? With the nice one?"

"You are absolutely free to go, Jane. If you want to put yourself at risk of being torn from your child forever and put *her* at risk of being made into a forever-seven-year-old blood drinker. Never to grow up. Never to see sunlight—"

The little girl's face was twisting into a more horrified grimace with every word Nash spoke, until Utana shot his hand out, gripped the man's forearm and squeezed hard enough to silence him.

"Do not be afraid, little one," Utana said, crouching low again, reaching out a hand to smooth her beautiful blond curls. Gods, she reminded him of Brigit with that hair. "I will not let harm befall you, I promise. Nothing bad will happen to you," he told her softly.

Yes, it will. But it won't be any boogie monster that gets us, it will be him. Just like he did that nice lady senator. He killed her. I know it.

"I'm the head of the government agency in charge of overseeing your safety," Nashmun said and put a hand on the woman's shoulder. "Jane, do you really think the U.S. government would have funded this place, this project, if they didn't honestly feel that those of you with the Belladonna Antigen were in need of protection?"

Jane looked from one man to the other. Utana could see her struggling to hold back the words she wanted to say. In the end she simply nodded, no doubt pretending to believe Nashmun's transparent lies.

"It won't be for much longer," Nashmun told her. "I promise you."

"How much longer?" Jane asked softly.

"Another week, at the most. All right?"

She nodded, but her daughter stomped a foot. "No! I wanna go home now!"

"A week isn't long at all, sweetie," her mother said, kneeling down to wrap the little girl in her arms, as the child's eyes welled up with tears.

Utana nodded. "I have seen enough."

"All right. I'll escort you back downstairs, then," Nashmun said.

Looking at the little girl, who was resting her head on her mother's shoulder, Utana thought, *Do not worry, little one. I will return you to your home very soon now.*

Melinda lifted her head and turned it, wide blue eyes blinking up at him, trusting him, as Utana reluctantly followed Nashmun out of the room.

As he went, he heard her call after him, her mind

as pure and honest as the wind, *I don't want you to die, but you will if you help us. I saw it.*

The warning brought him up short, even as the door swung closed behind him. He didn't fear death. He would welcome it, in fact, if it truly were death. But to be returned to the state from which James of the Vahmpeers had awakened him…? That prospect filled him with dread.

But his black-hearted vizier was moving on, and Utana forced himself into motion again, following.

It was not lost upon him that the little girl had warned him against helping her, even though she must believe he might be her only hope.

What a beautiful, honest child.

"This way," Nashmun said, leading him toward the box they called an "elevator," which Utana disliked. They'd ridden up in it, and he had felt sick to his stomach. But the journey had been brief, at least.

He stepped inside, and the thick doors slid magically closed.

"You see?" Nashmun said, smiling up at him. "They're being treated very, very well here. And as soon as they've served their purpose…"

Suddenly Utana felt a jab in his thigh. He looked down to see a needle there, and even as he realized what was happening, his head began to swim, his vision to dim, his knees to weaken.

"As soon as they've served their purpose," Nashmun said again, as Utana sank to the floor, "that purpose being to serve as bait for our trap—they'll be eliminated, just like the vampires who flock here to rescue them will have been. Every last one of them. And then we'll know exactly how to destroy them in every other nation where they exist, until the vampire scourge is wiped out of existence forever."

"The Plantation" had once been an extremely productive tobacco farm, bordered by a wide and placid river that kept any danger of frost at bay during all but the coldest of nights.

It had been owned by vampires for three generations and was one of the few such places that had not yet been destroyed by mortal vigilantes intent on burning every vampire alive. It helped that it was isolated. The nearest town was a tiny one, and people there minded their own business.

Oh, sooner or later, it would be discovered, but for now, it was safe. And the house was like something out of *Gone with the Wind*. Tall columns, a wide veranda, a broad curving staircase and a fireplace that took up half of a huge living room wall.

That was where her family awaited her that evening, just after dusk.

Brigit had never before feared her honorary aunt, Rhiannon. Then again, she'd never had reason. She'd been Rhiannon's protégé, learning at her feet how to be strong, powerful, ruthless. How to appreciate, cherish and use her gift. How to call up and manage her inner vampire.

And she'd gone against everything Rhiannon had taught her where Utana was concerned.

Now, as she walked beside her brother through the sprawling living room of the plantation house in the wildest wilds of Virginia, she felt a shiver race up her spine and knew, as she had never known before, how Rhiannon's enemies, or even strangers, felt upon meeting the imposing bitch-queen for the first time.

At the bottom of the stairs she stopped, unable to convince her feet to go any farther.

Her brother's warm hand on the small of her back did nothing to bolster her courage. In fact, she braced herself against it, as if afraid he might push her, when all she wanted to do was turn and run away.

"She loves you, Brigit. That hasn't changed," J.W. said softly.

"I failed her." She tried to swallow away the constriction in her throat that made her voice emerge tight and raspy, but it didn't ease. "I failed all of you."

"It's not over yet, Bridge."

"It is for me." She sniffled and fought back tears. "I'm in love with him, J.W. I'm in love with the enemy."

Upstairs, a door flew open, and in a heartbeat Rhiannon flew down the staircase, a blur of motion, and stood there before Brigit, regal and beautiful as always, though Brigit could have sworn, as she dared to meet the vampiress's eyes, that she saw worry there.

"Are you going to say hello or just stand there staring all night?"

Brigit nodded, unable to hold Rhiannon's steady, probing stare. "Hello, Rhiannon. It's good to see you." And then another vampiress descended more slowly, stopped halfway and held out her arms.

Moving past her aunt, Brigit rushed up the stairs and straight into the arms of her mother.

She was vaguely aware of Lucy moving past the two of them, welcoming J.W. back into her passionate embrace, and of others gathering in the living room below. Roland. Eric and Tamara. Her own father, Edge. And more. She wondered if all the surviving vampires were gathered here, in this place.

Sniffling, Brigit lifted her head from her mother's shoulder at length. *Those* eyes she could hold. "I'm so sorry, Mom. I've messed up everything. I didn't kill him when I had the chance, and now he's taken my power from me, and I—"

"Shhhh. Let's take it one step at a time, shall we?" her mother asked softly. Turning her, keeping one arm around her shoulders, Amber Lily walked beside her down the stairs. "You're here and you're safe, that's the most important thing."

"And you're wrong. So woefully wrong," Rhiannon added. She'd poured thick red liquid into a wineglass, and now she swirled it thoughtfully.

Sniffling, Brigit turned to face her. "About what?"

"About being without power. You still have it." She wrinkled her nose. "I can smell it on you." She crossed the room, her long dress skimming just above the floor so it almost appeared that she floated when she moved. She made her way to a Victorian-style love seat and sank onto its burgundy brocade. Pandora, Rhiannon's black panther, trotted down from upstairs and settled at her feet, lifting her head briefly in greeting, only to close her eyes again as soon as her mistress's hand stroked her jet-black fur.

"He took my ability away, Aunt Rhi. The power you're sensing in me now is…" Lifting her eyes to meet her brother's she said, "It's yours, J.W. He gave me the power he took from you."

"Why would he do that?" J.W. asked, looking puzzled.

Brigit sighed, moving farther into the room, greeting the others with her eyes, accepting a hug from her father before settling into a comfortable chair near the darkened, cold fireplace. She rubbed her arms, shivering.

Rhiannon flung a hand toward the hearth, and

the logs stacked there burst into flames. "I can tell you why," she said. "He must have needed healing. He's only concerned with his own well-being, after all. Isn't that the entire reason he wishes to annihilate us? To avoid what he thinks is the gods' punishment?"

"That's unfair, Aunt Rhi," J.W. said. He turned, keeping one arm around his beautiful Lucy's waist, and they walked to the sofa to sit together, every possible part of them touching. "Given what that punishment entailed..."

"Either he suffers or we die," Rhiannon snapped. "His choice to make, or so he believes. And the suffering was his to endure. No fault of ours."

"But, Rhiannon—" Lucy began.

"No, she's right." All eyes were on Brigit as she interrupted. "He gave me J.W.'s power because he was injured. Grabbed hold of an electrified fence at the DPI mansion where they were keeping him. Making him think he was an honored guest, when he was, in fact, a prisoner. And all the time reinforcing what he believed about having to destroy the race he created or return to a living death."

Rhiannon averted her eyes. "Hell."

"I thought I could convince him that it was a mistake. That the gods would never want him to wipe out an innocent race. I believed that his mind was damaged by all those years of living death."

"Well, that is likely true," Rhiannon said, staring thoughtfully into her wineglass.

"So I tried to heal it."

Every eye turned her way, and Brigit went on. "When he asked me to heal him from the electrocution, I also placed my hands on his head, and tried to direct that healing light into his mind. And I thought it had worked. He was beginning to believe me—to change his mind about hurting any of you, ever. I know he was. Or…I thought he was. Until…"

"Until?" Rhiannon asked.

Brigit closed her eyes, but the tears burning beneath her lids seeped out anyway.

"Until he ditched her," J.W. explained. "And we went after him and saw him with the scar-faced bastard we now know is DPI."

"Where?" Rhiannon demanded.

"At St. Dymphna—the former mental hospital where they're holding the Chosen," Brigit said, able to speak again at last. "But Aunt Rhi, it's a trap. The DPI has been rounding up the Chosen and taking them there for only one reason. To use them as bait to lure all of you there so they can wipe you all from existence in one final blow—an ambush attack."

Lifting her brows, Rhiannon said, "A blow to be dealt us by Utanapishtim, no doubt."

Brigit looked at the floor. "That was the plan." Blinking her eyes dry, squaring her shoulders, she lifted her head again. "But we were coming here to warn you. Utana wanted to help us rescue the Chosen. He gave me his word that he would not harm any of you."

"And then he ran back to report to his friends at the DPI," Rhiannon said. She drew a deep breath, then blew it out again. "Nonetheless, all is not lost. Not yet, at least."

"How the hell is all not lost?" Brigit looked around the room at the rest of them. "They're going to do some bad-ass shit to those innocent people they've got locked up in that loony bin. Soon. Anytime now, maybe even tonight. They're gonna make them suffer enough so you'll hear their cries and go charging to the rescue. And they'll be waiting to wipe you out when you get there. How the hell is all not lost?"

Rhiannon met Brigit's eyes. "There is something you do not yet know. We have someone inside the hospital."

Brigit frowned, looking from one face to the next, and seeing surprise in most of them. "Who?" she asked, returning her gaze to Rhiannon.

"The oldest living member of the Chosen caste. Her name is Roxanne—Roxy. She was to have been rounded up with the rest, but unlike the others, she knows what she is, what we are. She's a trusted friend and confidante of Reaper, who is one of us. And smart—for a mortal. So she eluded them, forged some documents and managed to place herself on staff as a nurse there. She's been in touch with Reaper, but only twice. It's risky for her to try to communicate. She's being watched—they all are—her phones tapped. But we know more than we would have without her. So far, the Chosen are safe and well."

Blinking slowly as she digested that information, Brigit felt the first glimmer of hope in her chest. "Can we ask her if she knows where Utana is?"

"If we can safely contact her, yes. Though I do not know why you still doubt that he is our enemy."

"I know how much you want to believe in him, sis," J.W. said. "But come on, you can't keep denying the truth."

"Why do you want to believe in him?" Rhiannon asked. She looked at Brigit, narrowing her eyes.

At the same time Amber Lily came around the chair in which her daughter sat, crouched in front of her, looked into her eyes and searched her very soul. "Oh, no," she whispered at length. "Oh, my poor baby."

"It's fine. Mom, I'm fine. I just—"

"You love him," her mother whispered.

"You love him?" Rhiannon gasped.

Brigit lowered her head, her face burning. "I'm sorry. I didn't mean for it to happen."

Rhiannon threw her hands in the air, then

dropped her head back against the settee. "By the wings of Isis, child, haven't I taught you better?"

Then her head came up again, and she frowned, pressing her fingers to her temples. She seemed for a long moment, as if she were listening to something only she could hear. And when her eyes refocused on the here and now, she pursed her lips.

"Reaper has heard again from his mortal pet, Roxy. Very briefly. She reports seeing a very large, foreign-looking man, who was first being shown around the hospital as if he were some VIP by Gravenham-Bail, your friend Scarface. And later, being pushed through the lower floors on a gurney, unconscious."

Brigit shot to her feet. "I knew he wasn't on their side."

"Don't jump to conclusions, Brigit," J.W. warned, getting up as well, putting a hand on her shoulder. "It might be another trick."

"How?" Brigit demanded. "Unless Scarface knew somehow about our informant and expected her to pass this information to us?"

"If that's the case, Roxy's in danger," Lucy said softly.

"And if it's not, then Utana is," Brigit replied. She looked at her mother, her father. "I have to go back. I have to get him out of there."

"Brigit, I cannot allow it," Rhiannon decreed.

Brigit looked at her beloved aunt and found it difficult to believe the words she heard coming from her own lips. "You can't stop me, Aunt Rhi. I'm going. Believe me, I'm going."

There was a long, drawn-out silence as the two women stared each other down. Finally Rhiannon nodded. "You're far too much like me for your own good, Brigit. Fine. Do what you feel you must. But before you do, you need to restore your brother's power to him. We'll need you both armed with the healing power for the battle that lies ahead. I only wish you could have your destructive power back, as well."

Brigit blinked hard. "I...didn't even know that was possible. I can restore J.W.'s power to him? And not lose it myself?"

"I'm a high priestess of Isis, a daughter of Pharaoh," Rhiannon, formerly Rianikki, reminded her. "There is nothing that is not possible for me."

17

An hour later, even though she was itching to be on her way to find Utana, to discover for herself whose side he was truly on, Brigit lay upon a bed of pillows on the floor. J.W. was stretched out beside her, and there was a ring of glowing candles surrounding them, flames dancing so close she could feel their heat on her face.

Rhiannon knelt just above their heads. Her face always changed during these rites of hers. Whenever she performed magic, her expressive features turned placid, utterly tranquil. Even her eyes beamed with nothing but pure love, the kind the mystics called Namaste. Rhiannon called this expression "the eyes of spirit." It was, she had taught Brigit, the state of being in which the very essence of God or Goddess, or both, flowed through the priestess. That gaze sought, found and drew forth the deity within any other individual participating in the ritual. Brigit felt it, and not for the first time. J.W., though, might not have experienced this rush before. It was something too otherworldly to be described through words. It wasn't experienced through the five known senses. It was something else altogether, something that had to be lived in order to be known.

The room seemed to fade and her vision to become unfocused. Thoughts ceased their zipping in and out of her brain, and it, too, became quiet. Her breathing deepened, slowed, becoming such a rhythmic flow that she could no longer completely distinguish between inhale and exhale. It was all just like ocean waves, washing in, washing out, overlapping. Gentle, cleansing, calming.

Brigit felt herself expand to fill the entire room and then move beyond it, as her spiritual self floated free of her physical shell. Rhiannon was speaking softly, but her words were only a distant song, which made sense somehow, though the words themselves were lost. It was just a pretty noise now.

Gosh, Brigit felt so big. She wondered, as she always did, how she was ever going to squeeze all of herself back into that tiny little body. But she knew the self she was experiencing now was her true self. That part of her that was also part of… well, of *everything*. There was no separation between her body and the pillows. Or the floor beneath them. Or the ground beneath that. Or the planet. Or the stars. Or the entire universe. That was how big she was.

There was no separation between her and her twin brother. Or between her and Rhiannon, who always seemed so much more than Brigit felt herself to be. But not really.

Rhiannon was telling her to look for her power. She was telling J.W. to look for it, too. Brigit couldn't make out the words, just felt the energy of the instructions. So she felt around until she found her power, and she gasped when she did. It seemed bright, pulsing, a ball of energy that was not unlike a star. She imagined herself cupping it in her hands, even though part of her was sure it would burn, which was silly. She was pure spirit. She couldn't burn.

She felt as if her brother's hands were cupping the star, too, even though neither she nor J.W. had hands anymore. And then J.W. stepped away from her—at least, that was what it felt like, and she sensed, rather than saw, that he now held a beaming, pulsing star cradled within his own palms, even while she still held one in hers. The star had divided, becoming two, neither one less than the original had been.

Rhiannon's voice was calling them back into their bodies now. Guiding them.

But Brigit wasn't ready. She wanted to see Utana. And the moment she thought of him, she *did* see him. She saw him first as a spirit as big as she felt right then, but all crammed into a tiny container— the statue where his ashes had been held, she realized. Smaller than a body. Far more constricting, because a body was able to experience life on the physical plane. To hone the focus down to this one, vivid, beautiful lifetime in order to relish every instant, every breath, every sensation, every morsel. And yet he'd been unable to experience life in that way. To exist in that way. Or in any way, besides in darkness.

She saw, then, the explosion of force when he'd been released by her own brother's extraordinary power. J.W. had revivified Utana in order to save the vampire race. But the prophecy he'd believed was telling him to do so had been misinterpreted. Utana was instead the means of their destruction.

And he'd exploded forth from oblivion in a flash that seemed as if it must have been second only to the Big Bang itself. The moment of creation.

Sensation had bombarded Utana like needles shot from a cannon and embedding themselves in every inch of his skin. Every touch had stabbed his nerve endings. Every pinprick of light had been blinding. The most subtle of smells had been overwhelming, and the slightest sound deafening, almost too painful to bear. He'd wanted only release.

"He was out of his mind," Brigit whispered. Or

she tried to. What came out sounded like babble to her. "He didn't even know how to be human anymore."

Rhiannon's voice called to her, the words still unintelligible but their meaning clear: come back.

Brigit tried to say "not yet," but again only a slurred, meaningless noise emerged. But she ignored that, seeking Utana again, searching, trying to experience him as he was now.

Peaceful. Silent. Asleep, resting, dreaming...of her. She saw a vision, of the two of them entwined, not entirely in physical form. The top halves of them seemed normal—torsos, arms, heads and faces, eyes locked on one another. Lips melded in an endless kiss. But the bottom halves of their bodies were smoke and glitter, green and gold, or those were the closest colors she could name. In truth, they were colors that didn't exist in this world. Colors humans could not perceive. The colors of pure spirit.

"Come back to me, little one," Rhiannon called. "You're floating too far away. Come back."

Brigit felt the most incredible sensation in her heart. It seemed to be expanding, so big it might burst, as her spirit settled at last into its temporal home. She felt tiny again, but reassured that the larger part of her was still there, and that she was still a part of it. A very small part of it, but still... She opened her eyes, and the room slowly came back into focus.

"I really do love him," she whispered. "And what's more, he loves me back." Blinking, she whispered, "I felt it. I saw it. It's real."

Utana came awake to pain, hot, searing pain, and the stench of his own burning flesh. An anguished scream was driven from the depths of his soul as his eyes flew open wide. Through a red haze of agony and wisps of smoke rising up from his own skin, his vision swam, cleared, swam again. Men were around him. Nashmun, his so-called vizier, stood only an arm's length away, holding a red-hot poker in his fist. And smiling. The scar on his face made the grin look demonic.

Utana lunged toward him, but his arms were brought up short, wrenching his shoulders as iron rang against iron. Chains. He was in chains. Upright, with shackles at his wrists and ankles, and a foot of iron chain from each embedded in the stone-like wall at his back.

"What meaning is this, Nashmun!" he demanded, his mastery of the language faltering under duress.

His vizier's smile died, and his eyes went as cold as twin granite stones. "It means you should have done what you were told to do to begin with, Utana. You were resurrected for a reason, after all. We brought you back to do a job."

Utana's eyes narrowed. He called on his inner power, intending to send its deadly beam to this man and end his reign of terror once and for all time. Nashmun was not worthy to live.

Nothing happened.

"It's the drug. The liquid we injected into you," Nashmun told him, gloating and pleased. "It will inhibit your powers for as long as I need them inhibited. You can't hurt me, Utana. You're helpless."

"I am never helpless."

"You are now. And we are not going to give you a choice. You're going to do the job we brought you back to do," Nashmun told him again.

"Why you say you raised me?" Utana licked his lips and tried to clear his mind of the fog that kept overwhelming him. "You did not. James of the Vahmpeers, he is the one. He awakened me." He thought of James—Brigit's beloved brother—who had raised him from ash. He had insisted Utana must save his people. Instead, Utana had tried to annihilate them. How James must hate him for that.

"James Poe, the male half of the mongrel twins, did exactly what we wanted him to do," Nashmun said. "Don't you see, Utana? We've been planning all of this for years. Every single detail. We found the prophecy, the real one, not the bits and pieces you and your demon offspring have been playing at deciphering. We found it first. We translated it. All of it. And we saw our opportunity to rid the world of this unnatural, demonic plague once and for all. All it took was a little editing, a little chipping away of those clay tablets. A character here, a sentence there. The vampires read that prophecy exactly the way we wanted them to. James brought you back because we made him think that's what he was supposed to do."

Brigit had suspected as much, hadn't she? And James's beautiful mate, the genius Lucy. Truly the women had been far wiser about all of this than the men had been. The men should have left it all to them to begin with.

As the thought of Brigit came into Utana's mind, she filled it. Her image, her face, her eyes, all swam there in his inner sight, rippling before him like a blissful mirage in the desert. Beautiful, alluring, and he wanted to reach for her, to touch her. He thought he could smell her skin, taste her kiss, but only for a moment. And then she vanished, like the vision she was.

Had she been right about all of it? Had the gods ever truly decreed that he must wipe out the vahmpeers? Had his long sentence of living death truly been a punishment for creating the Undead race? Or was all of that yet another tentacle of this DPI beast's many-armed plot?

"What sayed the tablet—the true one?" he asked, even though he had little hope the betrayer would tell him.

"Nothing much. And certainly nothing I'm going to share with you. Not yet, anyway. Maybe just before I kill you. But not yet. First, I need you to do your job."

"You wish me to murder the vahmpeers."

"That's right."

"What sayed the tablet? Did the gods truly decree that I must do this? Or did you only make it seem so?"

"It doesn't matter. You're going to do it. You're not going to have a choice."

Utana strained at his chains, but it was useless. Someone approached, a small, nervous man in white. He jabbed Utana in the thigh with another needle, and immediately he felt his head beginning to fill with mists, his eyes to grow heavy.

"Why…you wake me to burn me, to taunt me, then make me sleep more?"

"I only needed you to scream in pain, Utana. And you did. I don't need you anymore right now. You just rest. Oh, and just so you know, if you get your strength back and try to break those chains, I'll know. We've installed sensors to detect if you break free." He moved closer as Utana's head fell to one side, his neck suddenly too weak to hold it upright. "That's a good king. You just sleep now. I imagine your favorite mongrel belly dancer will be here within the hour."

Alarm and sudden understanding brought Utana's head up again, but only briefly. He imagined Brigit in his mind, knew she would have heard his anguished shout, felt his pain. And he knew, too, that she would come to him. Just as Nashmun wanted her to do. He tried to shout a mental warning at her, but he had no idea if the message was received. His own mind went dark even as he tried to call out to her. And then he knew no more.

"Did you feel that?"

Brigit gasped the question as her arm snapped around her own middle, hand clasping her waist.

The vampires were gathered around a circular table, studying two sets of blueprints of the same building. One set, dated 1911, was labeled *St. Dymphna Asylum.* The other, dated 1986, was for St. Dymphna Psychiatric Hospital. There had been modifications, expansions, made in between. The place was currently serving as a prison for the Chosen. Though that was certainly not what the DPI were calling it.

They all looked up, though, at Brigit's exclamation. J.W. hurried around the table to her side. "What is it, sis?"

Her brows bunched together, eyes closed, she said, "It burns!"

Her brother tugged her hand away, examining the flesh between her midriff-baring T-shirt and her low-riding jeans. Then he went still, raising his eyes to her face. "There's nothing there."

"It's not my pain." The heat began to ease. Brigit relaxed, opened her eyes, met her brother's gaze. "It's Utana. He's hurt."

"He has my power. If he's hurt, he'll heal himself."

"He's with those people, James. The DPI. Gravenham-Bail."

"He works for them, remember?"

She shook her head. "Then why did he just scream in pain as if something—or someone—was burning his flesh? God, it felt like a branding iron."

From beyond her brother, Damien—the vampire once known as Gilgamesh, king of ancient Sumer—whispered, "I did not feel the pain. But I heard him cry out." And then he looked past J.W. to Brigit. "I was made by him. I was the first. For me to hear his cry is natural, inevitable. For you to feel his pain—that's something else entirely, Brigit."

"By the gods, have you shared blood with him?" Rhiannon gasped.

Brigit met her aunt's critical eyes and did not flinch. "I drank from him. I drank in his power, and it made me stronger. That strength will benefit us all."

"Not if you use it to help our enemy, it won't."

"Rhiannon, they're going to try to force him to kill us. All of us," Brigit insisted. "Do you understand that?"

"I didn't see anyone *forcing him* to raze Haven Island with his eyes, burning alive every vampire in his path."

Brigit glared at Rhiannon. "Why don't you try being buried alive for a few thousand years, Aunt Rhi? See what it does to your temper, not to mention your sanity. He believed what they wanted him to believe. Just like we did when we raised him. *They're* the enemy. Not Utana."

"We've all agreed on a plan, Brigit," J.W. said softly. "We'll go in and get the Chosen out of that place before the DPI makes their move. Before they're expecting us. We'll take them by surprise. If we go rushing back there now, though, before we're ready, we'll blow any chance we have of saving the captives."

She blinked at her brother. "But he's in pain."

"He's not our priority." He said it coldly, without inflection, as if Utana's anguish was not even worth consideration.

"But perhaps he *is* yours," Rhiannon said, as she came across the room and stood nose to nose with Brigit. The other vampires in the room watched silently as Rhiannon uttered but one word. "Choose."

"I'll get him away from them. Bring him in. If you talk to him, you'll see—"

"Choose, Brigit."

"He can help us."

"We do not want or need any help from that monster. If you bring him within reach of any vampire, I will tear him apart with my own two hands." Rhiannon paused there, turning away while blinking rapidly, angrily. "And you with him, if you try to stand in the way." Her voice had thickened, deepened.

"Rhiannon!" Brigit's mother shouted.

"He has murdered our people," Rhiannon went on. "He intends to murder the rest. You cannot be with him and remain with us, Brigit. And so the time has come, my little rebel, for you to choose. Him? Or us?" She turned away, as if putting Brigit from her life.

Brigit's heart twisted into such a tight, hard knot that she could hardly bear it. Tears of anger and rage welled up in her eyes. Besides her own mother, Rhiannon was the woman she loved most in the world, but she'd turned her back to Brigit now, both literally and figuratively. Brigit looked around the room at every vampire there. No one spoke nor moved to defend her. All of them were waiting to see what choice she would make.

Her eyes met J.W.'s, but he said nothing. Even her own twin, her other half, refused to support her. Blinking back tears, she clenched her teeth, stiffened her spine and lifted her chin. "You're wrong about him. About me, too. You're very, very wrong. And I will prove it to you." She moved to pick up her jacket and the little backpack she used because she wouldn't be caught dead with an actual purse, then turned to face them again.

No one had moved, but Lucy clutched J.W.'s arm, staring at him so hard that Brigit knew she was talking to him with her mind. Yelling at him, maybe. Her parents were hugging one another, her mother crying softly and thinking at her, *I understand, my love. You have to go see for yourself. I'll be here for you, when you return.*

"I will prove it to you," Brigit said again. "I'll show you that he's good. That he's one of us. But I shouldn't have to. I guess you're just all so used to thinking of me as the bad twin that you can't wrap your narrow minds around the fact that I'm the one who's supposed to save us. Not your saintly J.W. No. The good twin fucked everything up, remember? The prophecy was talking about me—not him. I'm the one who's supposed to fix this. And that's what I'm going to do. But I swear on the dust of the dead, it'll be a cold day in hell before I forgive you for not trusting me." She looked at her brother. "Any of you."

And then, without another second's hesitation, she slammed out of the house. Moments later her tires spat gravel and left rubber as she shoved the car into gear and sped away. Hot tears were flooding down her cheeks, and they made her angry.

She clutched the steering wheel with one hand and pounded it with the other. "Dammit, why do I care?"

This was wrong. It was wrong, and so damned unfair. J.W. was the one who'd walked out on his family, denied his vampiric side, tried to live as a mortal for his entire adult life. Not her. She'd stayed; she'd been loyal. She'd embraced her fangs and developed her powers. She'd done the lessons, learned the history, studied at Rhiannon's feet. She was the one who'd stood by them.

Even though they'd condemned her power as evil, warned her not to wield it, made her feel like something less, while elevating J.W. to the status of a Christ figure. And yet, when the chips were down, they'd wanted her to use her unworthy power after all. To kill for them. They'd wanted her to entomb a living man, a beautiful man, the father of their race, for all time. And then had the nerve to turn on her when she'd refused.

"I hate them," she muttered. "I hate them all."

Even if Utana were the monster they believed him to be, doing such a thing to him would be wrong. But he wasn't. He *wasn't*. She knew him. Utana was no monster. He was a man, and she loved him.

But even as she drove on, sobbing, she heard herself whisper, "Oh, God, what if I'm wrong?"

* * *

Midnight. The late-summer hum of insects was more present than the buzz of traffic. It was quiet outside the asylum walls tonight. "Too quiet," Brigit whispered, and tried to laugh at her use of the clichéd movie line, but she failed to work up even a smile. She was worried.

She crouched in the trees outside the chain-link fence, peering in at the place. She felt Utana's energy and knew he'd been in this very same spot not so long ago.

The hospital seemed harmless, ordinary. Hard to believe the Chosen were all being held inside. She was fairly sure that was where Utana was, too. In that brief blast of agony she'd felt emanating from him, she'd also received a block of other impressions. The unmistakable feeling of a room below ground. A basement. The smell of concrete and paint, and perhaps propane fumes. The antiseptic atmosphere of a hospital. The rippling waves of energy coming from hundreds of humans, flowing down from above. The cold feel of iron at his wrists and ankles. The jangling of chains. The aura of the scar-faced Gravenham-Bail nearby, his smugness, and his feelings of triumph, of victory at hand, of hatred for those he was about to destroy. The thrill of pleasure that notion gave the man sang from his soul like a choir of demons. He was truly evil.

From Utana came feelings of confusion followed by anger, and then a rush of fear like a layer of ice, flash freezing all the rest. Fear...not for himself but for her. And then nothing.

She was going to hurt that DPI bastard. She was going to hurt him bad.

Brigit unzipped her large duffel. Weapons filled it: guns, knives, even a small crossbow. She'd kept the stash in the trunk of her car ever since this insanity began, intending to use it to fight back against the vigilantes who'd decided to destroy the vampire race by burning their homes while they slept by day.

But that, too, had been no more than a DPI brainstorm. Gravenham-Bail himself had instigated that movement, feeding the flames of fear until they blossomed into violence.

She selected a few choice weapons, then zipped the bag again and tucked it beneath a stand of brush, making a mental note of the exact location, should she return here later.

She eyed the chain-link fence, certain it was electrified, then spotted a limb high overhead. Hunkering low, she jumped, sprang high, caught the limb easily. Then she swung like a trapeze artist. Once, twice, each time gaining more momentum, more distance. On the third swing she pulled her knees to her chest and cleared the fence. In a second she'd landed in a low crouch and was staring at the giant of a building.

She blinked in the darkness, looking around, staying low and still. But there was no movement, no indication that she'd been seen. She darted nearer the hospital and began making her way along the side, her back to the brick wall as she moved as silently as she could along the wide bed of white gravel that encircled the place. Here and there a rosebush or shrub blocked her path. She hopped over them rather than step away from the building and expose her silhouette against the night sky. Inch by inch she moved, a silent child of the night.

Just the way Aunt Rhiannon had taught her.

When she reached the front corner, she peered around, then ducked quickly back. Two guards stood, as always, at the front door. She needed them to leave their posts, and, moreover, she needed that door opened for her.

Lowering herself to all fours, she crept around the corner, then crawled toward the door, until only a single shrub stood between her and the guards. She stared at them from behind the branches, homing in on their minds, listening to their thoughts.

They doubled the security tonight, one guard thought. *That's never happened before. Must be expecting trouble. Wish they'd tell us more. I hate this need-to-know shit.*

And the other one: *I should get off early, go home*

*a few hours before she expects me, see if I can catch
her in the act. I know something's going on. I know
it.*

Brigit focused her eyes on the radio attached to
the second man's belt. And then on his mind. She'd
rarely tried to control the minds of mortals. But she
needed to do so now.

It was dark, which meant it was safe to vamp
up, bringing out the Undead part of her. Her fangs
elongated. Her eyesight sharpened, and the blood-
lust was like a hunger pang. But her mental powers
were heightened, too. She focused her thoughts.

They're calling you.

Guard number two picked up his radio. It was
dead silent, but still, frowning, he listened.

Get inside, Brigit thought at the men as urgently
as she could. *We need you in here ASAP!*

"Shit," said the first. "This must be it." He drew
his sidearm.

The second clipped the radio to his belt, drew
his own handgun and then hit the buttons on the
security panel and opened the door.

Brigit, still on all fours, sprang over the shrub the
way Pandora might have done. She hit the ground
on two feet, knees bent, and sprang again, this time
landing on the top step, barely managing to grip the
door just before it fell closed.

She stood there, her back to the wall, holding the

door open by a hairsbreadth, just enough to keep the locks from engaging, while the guards started to make their way through the building. And then, quick as a heartbeat, she slipped inside.

And heard the click of a hammer being drawn back as the cold steel barrel of a gun was pressed to her head.

"Welcome to St. Dymphna, Brigit. We've been expecting you."

18

Utana roused, but slowly. It felt as if his eyelids had been sealed shut, and his head—by the gods, his head pounded like a band of lilis drums. His knees had sunk down onto the hard, cold floor, his arms still stretched overhead and aching from being held so long in that position. His hands were numb.

And yet none of those things compared with his awareness of Brigit. She was near, and the realization filled him with an instant wave of joy and relief, which was immediately overwhelmed by horror. If she was here, she was in danger.

And even as he realized that, the door to his prison opened and she was brought in. Chained, as he was, at ankles and wrists, men holding her on either side. Utana rose and lunged toward her as the men shoved her inside and she fell to her knees, but his chains brought him up short.

She seemed unharmed, and fury rose from her like steam from a boiling pot as she lifted her head and turned their way. For the first time Utana saw the blindfold around her eyes.

"Well? Aren't you going to say hello to your boyfriend?" Nashmun said to her.

Brigit looked toward Utana, as if sensing him there. Her nostrils twitched as if she were sniffing the air.

"I am here," Utana said. "And more sorry than I can tell you that these pigs have you now."

"We would have had her sooner or later, anyway, Utana," Nashmun said. "Don't feel too badly. Besides, you're going to be able to make her stay with us a whole lot less unpleasant."

"No," Brigit whispered, her head swiveling to follow Nashmun's voice.

The man smiled, a grim, evil smile. "You see? She's figured it out already. But I suppose I'll have to explain it to you, Utana." He nudged Brigit with the toe of his shoe and leaned closer, as if sharing a secret with her. "He's a little slow, since we had to drug him. You know, to keep him from blowing us all to hell and gone." Then he shrugged and went on. "Tonight the Chosen are going to begin suffering untold agonies. Their cries will summon the vampires here. And when they arrive, you, Utana, are going to kill them."

"I have already told you, I will not."

"Yes, you will. Say it. Say, 'I'll do whatever you say.'"

"Never."

Nashmun nodded to one of his henchmen, who had come to join him, standing over Brigit, who was still kneeling on the floor. He drew a blade from his belt, then, bending, clasped her face hard in his hand.

"Leave her!" Utana shouted.

But the blade moved closer. Brigit flinched as its cold steel touched her cheek. Utana surged, yanking uselessly at the chains that held him, even trying yet again to drum up the power from within to blast the bastard into the next life. But it was not to be found. No beam emerged from his eyes. He could only watch in agony as the blade drew a bloody path from high on Brigit's cheekbone all the way to her chin, in a close imitation of the scar Nashmun bore upon his own evil face.

Brigit clenched her jaw, refusing to cry out. But Utana howled his rage. The blade moved away from her. The henchman wiped it against his shirtsleeve, first one side and then the other. And the cut in Brigit's cheek trickled blood, scarlet rivulets running down her beautiful face.

"I will kill you for this!" Utana promised. "You," he said with a nod at the henchman. "And then you," he added to Nashmun. "But for you it will be slow."

"It'll be slow for your mongrel pet here, too, Utana," Nashmun replied. "Slow and excruciating. Oh, wait, that's a pretty big word for you, isn't it? It means it's going to hurt like hell. And I promise you, I will make you watch me skin her alive if you do not do exactly what I tell you."

Utana drew a shuddering breath.

"I'll leave you two to think it over," Nashmun said. "The night is waning, so we're going to have to wait to begin the fun. It's nearly dawn. But tonight…" He laughed and rubbed his hands together. "Tonight we're going to wipe out every remaining vampire in this country and fulfill my life's work. Nice, huh?"

And with that he jerked his head toward the door. His henchmen left the room, with Nashmun following right behind.

Brigit lifted her head, brought her chained hands together and pushed the useless blindfold from her face. She blinked her vision into focus and saw Utana there, chained to the wall. Above him was the sloping glass of the skylights they'd seen from outside, darkened now, and opaque.

She lowered her eyes to the man again, happier to see him than she'd ever been to see anyone in her entire life.

Then she gasped at the sight of the deep, ugly burn on his abdomen, just above the hip bone. The sight of it made her wince in remembered agony. She'd felt that burn.

Lifting her gaze from his side, she met his beautiful onyx eyes, and she saw the anguish there. For her. She knew it was all for her.

But despite everything else, her dominant emotion was one of relief. She pulled herself to her feet and ran to him, pressing her body to his, running her manacled hands up and down his chest as she inhaled his scent. She tried to smile, but it hurt her wounded cheek. "I knew you weren't plotting against us with that scar-faced bastard."

He tried to embrace her, but the chains stopped his progress. "Is there someone who does not know this?"

Raising her head, looking into his eyes, she nodded. "My family. My brother, J.W.—excuse me, *James.*" She poured on the sarcasm. "They all believe you returned here to help Gravenham-Bail plot our destruction."

"All...except for you."

She nodded. "All except for me." Tilting her head to one side, she asked, "But why haven't you blasted them by now? Was Scarface telling the truth about that? They drugged you?"

"I have tried to raise my energy, to send the beam from my eyes to destroy them. They have...done something to my power. Taken it with their...inject-shun."

"No, Utana. They don't have the know-how to take your power from you, only block it for a while." She stepped away from him regretfully, looking him up and down first, almost unable to look anywhere else, she was so glad to see him again. Still, she forced her eyes away and scanned the room around him. She spotted a hypodermic needle on the floor and bent to pick it up, her chains jangling. There were still droplets clinging to the inside. "Is this what they stuck you with?" she asked, holding it up.

He nodded.

"It's a drug. They have all kinds, you know. The DPI has been experimenting on captive vampires for decades. They have a tranquilizer that works to weaken them, to inhibit their powers. I imagine this is some variation of that same drug, only probably a hell of a lot stronger, to make it work on someone as powerful as you."

"Can it…?"

He was worried that he'd lost his power forever, she realized, and hastened to reassure him that wasn't the case. "It'll wear off. I doubt even *they* know how long that might take." She glanced at the door. "You can bet your ass they won't take any chances on any of them being in the line of fire when that happens, though. But then again, they can't keep doping you, can they? They need you up and running at full strength if they expect you to blast any vampires tonight."

He lowered his head, his jaw clenching.

"Don't look like that." She lifted her chained

hands to touch his face. She couldn't seem to stop touching him. "It's not as if you're really going to do it."

He couldn't reach her, and she knew he wanted to touch her as badly as she did him. It must be so frustrating. She moved to his side, and immediately he pushed his hand through her hair, stroking it gently. "I cannot stand by and watch them harm you."

"They *can't* harm me. What the hell are they going to do? Cut me some more? Look, Utana. Look at my face." She turned her cheek toward him. "It's already healing. It'll be as good as new by the time they come back here."

"And yet you felt the pain of his blade."

"I will gladly feel pain if it means my people get to live."

He tugged her shoulder, so that she moved closer to him, and then she leaned against his body, resting her head on his broad, powerful chest. It rumbled beneath her ears when he spoke again.

"I have thought long on the things you told me, Brigit. About how no man can truly know the minds of the gods. About how the words inscribed in the tablets of old are no more than man's imagination, his attempts to understand that which is not meant for him to understand."

"I knew you would. You're one of the most intelligent men I've ever met. I knew you wouldn't just dismiss my opinions without thinking them over."

"I know the gods. They are not cruel without cause. I *did* disobey them, but the Anunaki as I know them would never punish an entire race for one man's crime. It makes more sense to believe that man misunderstood what befell me, then recorded his misunderstanding as if it were the truth."

"Because you were immortal, you could not die," she said softly. "If someone had come along after that beheading and put your head back on your body, maybe you would have healed and lived again. Like I said before, maybe it was because of what the desert witch did. Maybe burning your body as she did, believing that she was helping you, she actually doomed you to all those years of suffering. And maybe annihilating my people wouldn't make one bit of difference to your state of being, Utana."

"There is no way to know for certain," he said. "All the same, my Brigit, and whether your words are true or not, I had decided before I returned to this place that I could not and would not raise my hand against your people again. Regardless of the consequences to me. I told my gods as much."

She lifted her head from his chest, staring up into his eyes. "Why?"

"Because bringing you pain is more than I can bear to do."

He lowered his head until his lips brushed across hers. "Never," he whispered against her mouth, "has a great king been brought so low by one so slight. My heart, little Brigit, you hold in your hands. The mighty heart of an immortal king is more fragile than a butterfly's wings in your grasp. No arrow, no weapon, could pierce its stonelike shell. And yet at your touch, at your kiss, it quivers like a frightened lamb. I find there is nothing I will not do if you only ask it. These things I admit to you with great trepidation."

"Shut up and kiss me, King."

His lips pulled into a semblance of a smile, and he lowered his head and kissed her deeply and thoroughly. It killed her that he couldn't wrap his arms around her, but she twisted hers around his neck and kissed him back all the same. Passion rose up like heated mercury, filling her and spilling out. He obviously felt it, too, because he was as aroused as hell, and there was not a damn thing they could do about it.

Breathless, she lay against him and held him.

"I am sorry it has come to this, my love," he told her.

"Don't be sorry. This—" she said, touching his waist with her manacled hand "—this feeling between us…it's good. It's really, *really* good." She blinked back tears. "The best thing I've ever known. The best thing in my life."

"In mine, as well. Now and always."

Straightening, Brigit said, "All we have to do is figure a way out of this mess."

"If you can get the Chosens out by day, while the vahmpeers rest, so that there is nothing left to lure them to here, I can take care of the rest, my beautiful Brigit."

She saw him staring intently across the room and turned to see what he was looking at. A row of massive white tanks lined the far side of the basement room, the boiler sitting a safe distance from them.

What was he thinking?

"How the hell am I going to do that?" she asked.

"With your power."

She frowned at him, and he smiled softly. "I have learned much from you, Brigit. Now it is time for me to give you some knowledge in exchange. And it is knowledge you have been needing for all of your young life."

"I don't know what you're talking about, Utana."

"Your power. I began to tell you this before your brother arrived to interrupt me. Your power to… ''splode' things," he said, using her own childhood term and smiling. "You already have it. I gave it back to you when we were still in the palace house with Nashmun."

She frowned. "No. No, you gave me James's power. The power of healing."

Utana stared into her eyes, willing her to understand something, she thought, and yet she didn't.

"Are you saying I can use the power of healing to get us out of this mess?"

"I'm saying that you can use your power of ''sploding' to get us out of this mess."

She blinked rapidly. "But I don't have it."

"Yes, you do. Your power and your brother's are one and the same."

She felt her eyes widen, her brows rise. A hum filled her head as she felt her reality beginning to tilt on its axis. "Our powers are opposites."

"They are but opposite ends of the same stick," he said.

"I don't…I don't understand."

"Brigit, when you call up that beam of light… of…energy…"

He was taking his time, she knew. Searching for the right words to make her understand what he was trying to tell her.

"When you channel it through your body and out through your eyes, it comes to you from the very same source that your brother's power of healing comes to him. It is no more than your intention and focus that determines what the power can do."

She actually staggered backward a few steps, blinking almost sightlessly at Utana. "That can't be true."

"It *is* true, Brigit. You are no more the bad twin

than James is the good one. You never have been.
You are both channels for an energy that is neither
good nor bad, but simply *is*."

Brigit felt as if her head was swimming. She was
actually dizzy, and her eyes were watering with
tears at the enormity of what he was telling her.

"Try," he said. "Prove to yourself it is so. But…
quietly, if you can."

Blinking, still stunned, she was determined to
put Utana's revelation to the test, though nearly certain it would fail. "What if they're watching? Listening?"

"Already I have determined there are no such
devices in this room, as there were in my former
bedchamber," he said. "Go ahead, try it. Direct the
healing beam out through your eyes, instead of your
hands. Keep the beam narrow and tight, and only
emit a little, lest you alert them."

Nodding, nervous, Brigit held her wrists up in
front of her and focused her eyes on the clasp that
locked the iron manacles around them. She opened
her channels, as she had before. The energy flooded
into her, both from above and from below. It met
and melded in her center, and then she mentally
guided it upward, to her eyes. The beam shot from
her killer gaze just as it had before—but milder. It
emerged soft and yellow-gold, then turned orange
and then red as she poured more force into it. And
still she kept it tight and thin, controlling the stream

in a way she had never been able to do before. Sparks rained from the iron bracelets, and then they fell to the floor at her feet.

She was breathing heavily, rapidly, staring at her bared wrists and the iron on the floor at her feet. "This isn't possible."

"It's more than possible. It's true."

"But...but this changes everything." He nodded at her as she shifted her gaze back to his eyes again. "It changes my entire life. Everything I ever thought I was is...it's different now."

"I am sorry I did not tell you sooner. I only realized in the mansion after I was injured, when you asked for your brother's power instead of your own, that you did not know they were one and the same. And to tell you then would have allowed you to kill me."

Tears were brimming in her eyes now, hot and acidic. She quickly divested herself of her leg irons, burning her foot a little in the process, and then she flung herself against Utana, wrapped her arms around his neck and kissed his face. "Thank you. You can't know what this means to me."

He smiled into her eyes. "Finally I have given you something besides grief and anger."

"More than you know." She let go of him, then stepped back and aimed her deadly stare at the chains that held him.

"Wait, Brigit!"

He barked the warning so suddenly that it made her jump. She shot him a questioning look.

"Nashmun told me there were…sen-sores within my chains. He said he would know if I broke them free."

"Who cares if he knows? We'll be long gone by then. I'll blast them, and we'll get the hell out of here."

"And then what will we have gained? He will still have the Chosens to torture, to use as a lure for the vahmpeers. No. We must not alert him. We must let him believe we are contained here. I will stay, to keep that illusion intact. Perhaps he will not return to this room until he is ready to use me—in case the…inject-shun has worn off and my powers have returned. You must go."

"Go…where?"

"Up," he said. He nodded toward the tanks, and she looked farther this time, seeing the furnace and the wide ductwork leading up to the hospital above. "You must go up into the higher levels of this tower. Up to where the Chosens are held. And you must remove them. Return for me only when they are safe."

"But what if—"

"Perhaps you will not even need to return for me. Perhaps this…drug will wear away as you have predicted and my strength will return. Either way, we must not alert Nashmun that you are free until the Chosens are safe."

"Utana, I don't want to leave you here!"

"I know." He smiled, lowering his head and kissing the top of hers. "I know, but your people must be saved. Please, do as I say, Brigit. It is my way of making amends to those I have wronged. Please?"

She lifted her eyes to his, tears streaming now. "If anything happens to you, Utana, I don't think I can—"

"I feel...love for you, my Brigit. A love more powerful than armies or kingdoms or the gods themselves. Know that. Know it well."

Tears streaming, she pressed her face against his. "I love you, too, Utana. Never thought I'd be saying that at all, much less to you, but it's true. I love you."

He kissed her. She tasted the salt of her tears on his lips—perhaps mingled with some of his own. For a long, long time he kissed her, and when he lifted his head at last, she saw him blinking quickly to dry his eyes. No doubt in his time kings didn't cry.

"Now," he said softly, his voice thick and hoarse, "I will tell you all I observed when I walked among the Chosens."

19

As quietly as she could, Brigit made her way up through the air-conditioning ducts of the hospital. According to Utana, the Chosen were being housed on the fourth floor. Nash's headquarters seemed to be located on the first. There were "nurses" staffing the fourth level, but Utana had observed that they were deceptive, dressed in clothing that indicated they were something they were not. He had not entirely understood this, but Brigit did. Whatever else they were, they were first and foremost DPI operatives. Guards. And yes, some of them were probably nurses, too, just as that bitch Lillian was both an M.D. and DPI. But their job was to keep the Chosen from escaping. They might be going out of their way to make their captives feel more like guests, to keep them complacent and compliant. To make them want to stay where they were until they were no longer of any use. But Brigit knew the DPI, knew how they operated. And she didn't doubt that if anyone tried to leave this place, those Florence Nightingale pretenders would show their true colors. Figuratively speaking, they had claws and fangs that made vampires look like pussycats.

And once they had no more use for the Chosen— well, she didn't even want to speculate on what Nash Gravenham-Bail and his ilk had planned for them then.

Utana had given Brigit a thorough briefing on the layout of the place, and she also remembered it pretty well from what she'd seen on the blueprints she'd studied with her family. There was, as they'd observed when they drove past, a fire escape at the back of the building, its lowest level still some ten feet above the ground, like a catwalk just above those sloping skylights that provided the ceiling over Utana's current prison.

The catwalk extended the length of the hospital, and there was a retractable ladder attached to one end of it—the end nearest the parking lot.

The fire escape, she had decided, would be the means of exit for the Chosen. The only access point from the fourth floor would be through the windows at the back of the cafeteria, Utana told her.

He added, too, that there was a nurses' desk only a few yards from the elevators, situated in the center of a wide hallway that extended to both right and left behind it. Patient rooms lined that hallway in both directions. There was one room at the very end of the right-hand extension that he had disliked, though he hadn't known why. He'd felt, he said, "bad energy" that seemed to come from it.

Brigit had no doubt that the staff on the fourth floor had a quick and easy means of alerting Scarface if something seemed suspicious. She was going to be extremely careful. And she was going to have one hell of a time making her way up four stories by way of the ductwork. Much less doing so in relative silence.

And yet she did it.

It took a long time, crab-walking up the vertical sections. At each floor she encountered a four-way junction, where horizontal pipes shot off, while the main shaft kept going up, higher and higher. At the fourth such junction she was, she reckoned, at the fourth floor, and she took the left-hand turn, crawling on hands and knees, wincing every time the large ducts bent noisily under her weight.

She lay on her belly, hoping to eliminate or at least minimize the sound, and slid onward. It worked pretty well. Eventually she came to a register grate that looked down on the floor below.

A corridor. Not much to see there. A few people walking this way and that. Nurses. Even patients. No one looked sinister or particularly frightened. Silently, she slid over the grate, imagining herself as a giant python, and kept going, following the hallways. She took the first Y that veered off to the side, hoping to get a look into the rooms themselves. And the next time she paused over a grate she was indeed looking down into one of the patient rooms. She sighed in relief. She'd found her way. And apparently she'd done so undetected. So far, so good.

The room below her seemed empty.

She jiggled the grate loose and, moments later, lowered herself through the opening, dangled from her hands and then dropped to the floor, landing in a low crouch. Silence. No one near. She rose slowly, taking her first eye-level look around—and seeing a little girl with blond hair and blue, blue eyes staring right at her.

The girl didn't look surprised to see a stranger come dropping out of her ceiling. She didn't look alarmed, either. She looked...knowing.

And then she looked pointedly up toward the corner where ceiling met wall, to the right of the door.

Brigit followed her gaze and spotted the camera there, then quickly moved farther out of range and met the little girl's eyes.

"Can they hear us, too?" she asked in a whisper.

The child moved to the small round table, reaching for a remote control among all the coloring books, crayons, plastic teacups. She aimed the device, and the television came on, the volume loud. Then she set the remote down.

"Now they can't," she said. "Did you come to get us out of here?"

"Yes, I did. But you need to be very quiet and not tell anyone until I say. All right?"

The girl nodded. "I knew you would come. That big man who came before—you know him, don't you?"

"Yes, I do. How do you know that?"

The girl shrugged. "I saw you in his head. He told me he was going to help us—you know, *with his quiet voice*." She whispered the final four words.

"Did he, now?"

"Uh-huh."

"I'm going to need some help. Can you help me?"

"Yes, and my mommy can, too. Do you want me to go get her?"

"Where is she?" Brigit asked.

"She just went down to the cafeteria to get us some lunch. She'll be right back."

"Then why don't we wait for her, okay?"

"Okay." The little girl sat down at the table and tapped her foot expectantly. She was surrounded by coloring books and crayons, most of which were worn down to the halfway point. She must be terribly sick of coloring.

"Oh, I am," she said softly. "If I have to color one more picture, I think I'll go nutso!"

Brigit frowned. "You just heard what I was thinking, didn't you?"

"You mean your quiet voice? Yes, I heard it. I hear lots of people's quiet voices. Mommy says not to tell people about that, but I trust you."

The door opened and a woman came in, then paused to stare at Brigit. Her eyes registered both surprise and alarm, which was much more the reaction Brigit would have expected from her child. Putting a finger to her lips seemed to do the trick. The woman hesitated in the doorway, then stepped the rest of the way inside, closing the door behind her.

"I'm here to get you out," Brigit told her, keeping her voice very low.

"Thank God," the woman said. "They're planning something—something bad."

"How do you know? Have you heard something?" Brigit was eager to get any information this woman might have gleaned.

"Mommy doesn't know. But I do. They're going to make us cry," the little girl filled in. "I heard their quiet voices talking about it. Some of them don't want to, but they have to. To get the vampires, they said."

"Well, no one's going to make you cry now, I guarantee you that." She turned to the mother. "Do you know a woman by the name of Roxy?"

The fear and trepidation in the mother's eyes evaporated beneath a quick smile. "Everyone knows Roxy. She's a nurse here."

The woman knew Roxy was on her side; Brigit read it in her face. No words were needed, and that was good, because the more they said aloud, the more chance they would be overheard.

The little girl was tugging on Brigit's blouse. "What, honey?"

"Roxy's not really a nurse," she whispered.

Brigit lifted her brows and shot the mother a look. "This is one gifted little girl you've got here."

"She's special. In a great many ways, although that's something we've been keeping to ourselves around here. Anyone different seems to attract a lot of…attention. I just want to get her the hell out of here. Now."

"Don't I know it." Brigit thinned her lips. "And I understand, believe me. I'm pretty different myself. You're doing right to keep her abilities to yourself."

"That's what Roxy said."

Brigit nodded. "Can you get her for me? Get her in here without raising any suspicion? If you do, I promise, you'll be the first two out of here."

"When?" the woman asked.

"Tonight. It has to be tonight."

The woman nodded, stretching out a hand for the little girl.

"Uh-uh," Brigit told her. "She stays with me."

It earned her a furious glare from the protective and obviously devoted mother, but she couldn't give in on this. "I'm sorry. But I don't know you, and I can't afford to risk that you might blow my cover. Too many lives depend on us succeeding. I promise, I'll keep her safe. You go get Roxy."

Sighing, the woman looked at her daughter. "You'll be okay for a few minutes, Melinda?"

She was asking more than the words said; Brigit knew it by the intensity in the woman's eyes.

The little girl seemed to understand that, too. "It's okay, Mommy. She's not one of the bad ones. She only thinks she is."

Her mother frowned, shooting Brigit a concerned look.

"I used to think I was bad. But someone very wise has made me think maybe I'm good after all."

"Oh, you are!" Melinda said. And then, to her still worried mother, "She's friends with the big guy."

"Oh." And briefly, a look of sadness came over her face. She nodded, searching Brigit's eyes and extending a hand. "I'm Jane, by the way."

"Brigit," she replied, accepting the woman's hand.

Nodding again, Jane hurried away. Brigit didn't like the little chill that rushed up her spine, though, at the look the woman had worn at the mention of Utana. What the hell was that about?

Five minutes later a flaming redhead whose personality matched her hair accompanied Jane back into the room.

The oldest living member of the Chosen caste was not what Brigit had expected. Guessing her age would have been impossible, but she was, by appearances, far from old. And far from ordinary, even among the Chosen. She wore white scrubs, like the rest of the DPI drones staffing this place. But she also had on rainbow-patterned Crocs over a pair of hot-pink socks. Her orange-red locks were fighting their way out of the bun that tried to hold them up in back, a few tendrils springing free, as lively as if they belonged to Medusa. She even wore an old-fashioned nurse's cap perched on top of that wild hair. Her eyes, heavily lined and smoky, were full of hell. She couldn't hide it and didn't try.

How she hadn't been found out by now was beyond Brigit's comprehension. But she liked the woman on sight.

The scent of the Belladonna Antigen, the zinging energy of it, snapped and crackled from her in a way that Brigit could not mistake, and in a far stronger, more vivacious way than from anyone else in this place. Indeed, it was different from the essence of any other member of the Chosen Brigit had ever met in her life, and she'd met many of them.

Roxy met Brigit's eyes and lifted her brows, alarmed at seeing a stranger. "And you are…?" she asked.

"Brigit Poe." She extended a hand.

Roxy gasped, a hand flying to her mouth to

cover her surprise, even as she shot a look behind her toward the closed door. Turning back to Brigit again, she whispered, "You're one of the twins."

"Yes."

The other woman clasped her hand at once but didn't shake it. Instead she closed both her hands around Brigit's and just held them there. "Hot damn and hallelujah. You don't even know how glad I am to see you here. I'm Roxy."

"I know. But I'm curious. Why are you staff here, rather than a patient?"

"I couldn't show up as one of the Chosen. At my comparatively advanced age, they'd have singled me out for special study. Removed me from the general population and stuck me in a lab somewhere to play guinea pig to their mad scientist. You know, much like they'll try to do to you if they catch on to who you really are. One of a kind. The DPI loves studying gems like us. And what good would I have been to the cause locked away in some lab?" She rolled her eyes expressively. "So just tell me what to do and let's get shut of this place. I've had chills chasing each other up and down my spine every second I've spent here. I think the bastards even followed me home last night."

"I need to know how many nurses are on duty at a time, and how often anyone checks in from other floors. When the shifts change, and how that goes down. Anything else you can think of that will help."

Smiling slowly, Roxy nodded. "You need to know the best time to start moving the so-called patients out of here."

"Yes."

"When are you doing it?"

"Tonight," Brigit said.

Roxy nodded. "It's about freakin' time. All right, here's the gist. Every two hours, they send up some of their goons to do a sweep of the floor. They check everywhere, believe you me. Under beds, in the closets and restrooms. On the hour in between those sweeps, the head nurse has to phone downstairs to report in. If it's not her voice on the phone, or if she fails to give them the correct password, they know something's wrong. And the password changes every day."

"We're going to need that password."

"I already know it. I listen in to that old crone every day, just in case. Today's is 'Run, Rabbit, Run.' But if it's not her voice on the phone, it won't matter. The routine is taking a dramatic change this evening, though."

"That doesn't bode well," Brigit said. "Tell me as much as you know, Roxy."

"First," Roxy said, "the guards will do their usual sweep of the floor. Then the routine changes. The entire fourth floor staff are all supposed to do a head count, ensure that every patient is in his or her own room, lock their doors and then head below to meet on the first floor. The doors to this floor will be sealed."

"And then what?" Brigit asked, breathless with fear.

"They won't tell us. All I know is that all patients are to be locked in their rooms by sundown and the nursing staff has to be off the floor."

"All right. All right." Brigit paced and thought. "If I wait until the staff is clear, then rush through here, unlocking all the rooms—"

"You can unlock them all with a switch at the nurses' desk. Though that might tip them off downstairs." Roxy glanced at her watch. "But you don't have time to worry about that right now, sweetie. The next sweep of the floor is about to begin. How in all hell did you manage get in here?"

Tipping her head, Brigit looked up. Roxy followed her eyes and saw the vent in the ceiling. "Now there's an idea," she said softly

"Everyone clanging around up there would draw notice. It was almost impossible for me to be quiet. More than a hundred people—there's no way. Besides, we're four floors up, with nothing but vertical ductwork in between. I'm thinking the fire escape is a better option," Brigit said.

"Then you'd best think of a way to deal with the fence. Sucker's electrified."

"I was afraid of that."

"You'll figure something out." Roxy bent low, interlacing the fingers of both hands and nodding at Brigit to step up. "Go on, get back where you came from until sundown. I'll meet you right here then."

Brigit accepted the boost and climbed into the duct, quickly righting the grate behind her.

The little girl moved to stand directly underneath, and she tipped her head up, blinking her eyes as if there were tears trying to get out. "Tell that big man to be very careful," she said.

Then her mother drew her away as the door opened and others entered the room. Brigit slid away from the vent, then lay there, motionless and silent, while men in military fatigues searched the room below her. Roxy was right. They didn't leave anything out. Except the vent where she hid.

But what the hell had Melinda meant about Utana being careful?

Had she foreseen something? Did she have the gift of prophecy on top of everything else?

Brigit's heart twisted into a knot of fear. She wasn't going to let anything happen to him. She refused. It wouldn't end that way.

When the search ended and the floor beneath her quieted once more, Brigit belly-slid her way to the main vertical shaft. Then she crab-walked down to the very bottom and reemerged into the basement where Utana was waiting, hanging there, suspended by his powerful arms, head hanging low, eyes closed. The skylights over his head were still opaque, and she realized they'd been blocked somehow, making it impossible to see outside, but she knew it was still daytime beyond the walls of this place.

Poor Utana. He was exhausted. And drugged to boot.

Brigit went to him and for a moment just looked at his beautiful face, his thick dark lashes, his heavy brows. She slid a hand over one cheek and kissed the other. "Utana?"

He stirred, lifting his head, opening his eyes. They softened when they touched hers, but only briefly. A frown quickly followed. "Why are you back here?"

"I can't move the Chosen until tonight. Just after sundown. But don't worry. I have help on the inside, and we're going to pull it off. But it's hours from now, and I thought...I thought I'd rather spend those hours here with you than curled up in a ventilation duct."

He nodded. "I am glad to hear it."

"I met the little girl. Melinda," she said, laying her head in the crook of his shoulder. "You made quite an impression on her."

"It is she who impressed me," he said. "She is special."

"Yes. And she seems to think you're in grave danger, Utana."

He lifted his brows, deliberately looking left and then right, at the chains on his wrists. "I am in chains," he said. "That may well seem grave."

"She's psychic, Utana. She *knows* things."

He lowered his head as she lifted hers and met her eyes. "My love, tonight we face battle, you and I. There is always risk involved, but we fight for the greater good. And we fight, more importantly, together."

"But, Utana, if anything happens to you, I—"

"I do not wish to spend these hours together talking about death." He lowered his head until his lips were nearly touching hers. "Come to me, woman. Make me forget the chains that hold me captive."

"I'm going to blast them and set you free."

"No. Your plan is in place. We must play it out, for good or bad. Trust me, my love, when my powers return to me, I will have no problem breaking these bonds."

She ran her hand over his, bumping over the iron that held him. "I love you, Utana. I don't care what my family says, or what you've done. I'll make them all understand somehow, but even if I can't—even if I have to choose between you and them—I'll choose you. I will always choose *you,* Utana."

He searched her eyes then, and she thought his

dampened. "I deserve not such devotion from such a pure and mighty heart."

"I'm sorry I tried to kill you."

He smiled. "How many women, do you suppose, find themselves making that particular apology to their men?"

"Is that what you are?" she asked him. "Are you my man, Utana?"

"I am yours alone." Closing the distance between his lips and hers, he kissed her.

Brigit devoured his kiss, her arms twining around his neck, her legs rising to anchor themselves around his hips. She didn't care that someone might burst in—she didn't care that her life might end tonight if this went badly. She didn't care that her entire family had turned against her—that not even J.W. had yet come to his senses.

She didn't worry about anything. She only focused on the feeling of Utana sliding himself inside her; of his skin, smooth and strong beneath her hands; of his mouth, which never left hers for even a single moment; of his hips, moving against her in a delicious and slow-building rhythm that drove her to a simmering, burning madness. And of the delicious release when that simmer became a full boil.

When it was over, he sank to his knees, arms held upright by the cruel chains. She curled around him and snuggled close, her head finding the natural cradle between his neck and shoulder. Just for these few hours, she thought, she would pretend that everything was all right. That their mission was over, and that they'd been successful. That her people were safe, and had forgiven both her and Utana, and that they loved her again.

Oh, if only it could be true. If only.

Reluctantly, she allowed herself to sink into sleep with that blissful yet, she feared, impossible dream wrapped around her like the warmest, softest blanket there could be.

20

Utana stared down at the woman who slept all curled around him. She'd positioned her body to be as close as humanly possible to his, every part touching, as if she couldn't stand to allow even air to pass between them.

She was beautiful, powerful and brave. Had this been a different time, a different age, and had he still been the king of his land, he would have made her his queen. The kind of queen she'd asked him about—the kind he had never considered. He knew now that was because he'd never known a woman who was as worthy as this one. Even the gods knew that his beautiful Brigit was worthy. One needed only to observe what she was going through to save her people, even when they had turned against her. To save *him,* even when she had no reason to believe in him at all. Her loyalty knew no bounds, and he admired that.

As he admired so much about her.

He allowed himself to rest for as long as he dared, relishing the feel of her in his arms. So deceptive, her size. She packed the power of a goddess into her tiny body.

But all too soon it was time. He felt the night's approach, knew it was only a bit more than an hour away, and she would need that time to free the Chosens. Gently, he stroked her hair, her face, with the whiskery growth upon his own, until her eyes fluttered open.

"It is time, my love."

She sat up straighter, stretching her arms wide, arching her back. Then she relaxed and smiled as she met his eyes. "I hate to leave you."

"I need to remain here. To ensure you have time to do what must be done."

"Has the drug worn off yet?"

"I don't know."

"Try 'sploding something," she suggested.

He looked around the basement room, his eyes falling on a wooden crate near the giant tanks on the far end. Focusing on it, he narrowed his eyes and called on the power.

"No!" Brigit clapped her hand over his eyes. Then, parting her fingers over one eyeball, she said, "Not that. Nothing that's anywhere near those tanks, Utana. They're filled with propane. Gas. It's highly flammable. You send a beam at those tanks and this whole place will explode."

He nodded, and she took her hand away from his eyes. She had confirmed for him what he had suspected. What he had hoped for.

But he could not reveal that to her. She would understand soon enough.

She picked up the length of chain holding his right arm. "Try this. Just don't burn it all the way through and set off their damned sensors."

Utana affixed his gaze to the chain, calling on the energy that he knew came not *from* him but rather, *through* him. He asked the gods to assist him. And he felt the power begin to move. The beam from his eyes shot out, but it was neither bright nor strong. It touched the chain but only warmed it. And in seconds, unable to sustain the power, he had to allow it to blink out.

Brigit touched the chain, nodded. "It got good and hot, Utana. You'll be yourself again in no time." Then she looked at the chains. "Let me free you."

"You know you cannot, Brigit." He bent closer to her and she rose to meet him as he kissed her lips. "Go now. Go free the Chosens. When they are safe, you and I will leave this place together. Go. And be careful, Lady Moonlight. Do not let harm come to you."

"You be careful, too. I'm going to be good and

pissed off if we don't have a chance to…to be…
you know."

"I know." He kissed her again.

"No, you don't," she told him. "Utana, we have
a saying in this time. When people go through the
hell we've gone through, and in the end, they find
triumph and peace, and are able to be together—
they are said to live happily ever after." She had to
pause, and he understood why. Could tell by the
thickening of her voice, the blinking of her eyes,
that tears were near for her. "I want my happily ever
after, Utana. I want it with you."

"It is a good saying. I wish to make it true for
you. I promise I will try."

"Do more than try," she said. "Make it so."

He nodded. "Go now," he told her. "Go before
it's too late."

And so, dashing the tears that spilled onto her
cheeks away with one hand, she went. He watched
her every step of the way, until she vanished from
his sight, and his heart felt as if it were already
dying at the notion that he might not ever lay eyes
upon his beautiful Brigit again.

"Nurse…um, Corona, is it?"

Roxy looked up from the nurses' desk, surprised.
It wasn't time for the evening inspection yet. "Yes?"

The man who stood at the desk was the scar-
faced bastard who seemed to be running the show

around here. Eyes the color of wet cement, and just as lifeless, just as cold.

"Yes, I thought so. I have a concern about the health of the little girl in 3-B. Miranda, isn't it?"

"Melinda."

"Right, right. She's having trouble breathing. Could you come take a look?"

Roxy was out of her chair and heading for the room immediately. "You should get a real doctor over here," she said quickly, thinking all the while that she wasn't anywhere near qualified to help a sick child. There were real nurses around this joint. Some of those DPI bitches were actually educated, degreed, registered nurses, and she was going to have to find a way to get one of them involved without giving herself away, if little Melinda was in trouble. She wasn't about to let anything happen to that precious, spunky little—

She stepped into Melinda's room, spotting the little girl in her mother's arms, huddled near the window on the far side, tears streaming down her face. "Honey, what's wrong?"

But before she could rush to the child's side, Roxy was quickly grabbed by men who'd been hiding on either side of the door. Her arms were pulled roughly behind her, and she was handcuffed.

"What the hell do you think you're—get your lousy hands off'a me, you pieces of—"

"Shut up, Roxy," the scar-faced man said. "We

know who you are. We've known for a while now."
Turning to the men who held her, he barked, "I
want this one and the girl taken to the secure area
for further study."

One of the men—the same one who'd handcuffed
Roxy—reached for little Melinda and jerked her to
him. She pushed him away, though, her skinny arms
stronger than they looked, and then she shrieked
and bit his hand. He let her go, and she buried
her face against her mother, hugging Jane's thigh
fiercely.

Scarface looked at Jane. "All right, fine. I'll tell
you a bit of information you are not yet supposed to
know. Every patient who is not in the secure room
is going to die. She, however, is special and needs
further study. As does our legendary Roxanne here.
Those are the choices."

"I won't go without my mommy!" Melinda
yelled. "You can't make me. I'll bite his hand right
off next time!"

Scarface's lips twitched, and Roxy thought the
snake-hearted fool was trying to hide a smile. "Take
the mother, too. She's not one of them, anyway, so
she's no threat."

If he thought she was no threat, Roxy mused, then
he'd never seen a mother bear protecting her cub.
Jane had an iron spine, and she loved her daughter
like nobody's business. Good. One more ally.

She heard a commotion and turned to look out

through the glass in the closed door. There were soldiers out there, a dozen of them, and they were herding all the patients toward the elevators.

She swung her head around, pinning Scarface with her eyes. "What's happening? Where are they taking everyone?"

He ignored her, but the look in his eyes told her more than words could. Wherever the Chosen were going, it would be their final journey before the one to the other side. He hadn't been kidding. He was going to kill them all.

And Brigit would return here anytime now, with her plan to free everyone, only to find no one left to free.

"This isn't what we were told was happening tonight," Roxy said, speaking rapidly, words spilling forth in her state of near panic. "We were supposed to lock all the patients in their rooms and then go to the first floor. You told us—"

"I told you what I wanted you to believe. Why on earth would I reveal the real plan to a vampire spy, Roxy? Or to any of the freakish humans who bear the vampire antigen? Do you think I'm stupid?"

"Pretty much, yeah."

He gave her a look that said he would prefer to smack her, but she only resumed gazing out into the hall, where she could see the elevator doors closing on the last load of the Chosen. Then Scarface reached past Roxy, opened the door and led the way as his two henchmen brought up the rear, herding the three captives into the hallway. "This way," he said, turning right, passing by the nurses' desk and heading all the way to the farthest end of the corridor. They marched past every empty patient room, all the way to the "secure room" at the end.

It was a white-padded room with no windows, no furniture. Nothing at all.

Scarface opened the door and stepped aside. The other men shoved the captives inside, then closed the door as the three of them stumbled and fell over each other.

Roxy jumped to her feet fast, hands still cuffed behind her, and lunged at the door, only to smash into it as it closed. She heard locks being turned from the other side. And then the men were gone, and they were alone.

"Why did he do this?" Jane muttered, hugging her daughter close. "Why keep us and not everyone else?"

Roxy looked at her, her eyes steady. "I imagine it's because we're different from the rest of the Chosen."

"The Chosen." Jane lowered her head.

"Those with the Belladonna Antigen. Like your Melinda. And me. And every other resident of this place."

The woman nodded. "That much I knew."

"But Melinda is special, even among the Chosen.

Her psychic abilities are...they're like nothing I've ever seen."

"I didn't think they knew. We tried to keep it to ourselves."

"There's not much they don't know."

"What about you?" Melinda asked. "How are you special, Roxy?"

"I'm the oldest. I dabble in a bit of witchcraft. And I'm really good friends with a lot of vampires."

The little girl's eyes widened when Roxy said that, and she moved closer to her mother.

Jane frowned, tilting her head to one side. "They told us that those with the antigen were especially vulnerable to...to vampire attack. They said they were bringing us here to protect us from them until the government got the situation under control."

"They lied," Roxy said. "And since it looks like we've got some time on our hands, I'm going to tell you all about the vampires I know. Besides, if anyone gets us out of this mess, it'll probably be them, and I don't want you two panicking when they do." She shifted her shoulders. "I hope they hurry, because this is damned uncomfortable." Then her eyes shifted to the little girl. "Sorry. *Darned* uncomfortable."

Melinda moved forward, smiling and held up one hand. In it was a tiny key.

"Where on earth did you get that?" her mother asked.

"I took it from the bad man—the one I bit."

"You're even more special than I thought," Roxy told her as she turned around, presenting her wrists.

The little girl inserted the key into the handcuffs, twisted it. One cuff popped open, and Roxy turned, brought her hands in front of her and used the key to open the other cuff. Free, she rubbed her wrists. "Thank you, Melinda."

"You're welcome. Now will you tell us about the vampires?"

"Oh, I'd be happy to. I've been dying to, in fact, but we had to be so careful about what we said before."

"Do you know lots of vampire stories?" Melinda asked.

"I know most of them. So many stories. So very many stories. You're going to enjoy this. Come on, sweetie, let's get cozy."

Brigit belly-slid through the ductwork until she was over the room where Roxy, Jane and little Melinda would be waiting to meet her. She was excited, primed for battle, alive like she'd never been before. But she was also afraid—and she'd never been afraid of fighting before. But then again, she'd never had so much to lose.

She peered down through the grate but saw no one below. The room seemed empty.

Frowning, she listened. Ahh, okay, there was

water running in the bathroom. They must be in there, then. Getting ready to make their escape.

Carefully, quietly, Brigit wriggled the grate loose, and then she lowered herself through the opening, dangling for only an instant before dropping to the floor.

The second her feet touched down, her upper arms were caught in iron hands by men who sprang on her from out of nowhere. A third quickly snapped a pair of odd-looking goggles over her eyes and yanked an adjustable strap tight behind her head, pulling her hair in the process.

She blinked, stunned. This, she realized, was not a blindfold. She could see through goggles. The glass lenses appeared clear. As the men held her arms, she struggled, while the third jerked the strap even tighter at the back of her head, until the rubber edges of the goggles bit into her face.

Through the lenses, she saw him. Nash Gravenham-Bail. He was clapping his hands slowly, smiling a grin of pure evil.

"It was a very nice effort, wasn't it, guys? Very nice." He stopped clapping and reached out, cupping her cheek. "You see, little Brigit, I've known who you were from the beginning. But when I saw Utana's reaction to you in that belly dance getup— you're very talented, by the way. Where did you ever learn to dance like that?"

"Fuck you."

He shrugged. "I doubt there'll be time, really. At any rate, from the moment I saw Utana's...well, let's be polite and call it fondness for you—I knew I could use you to keep him in line. I didn't plan on the two of you escaping, but...well, it's worked out quite beautifully all the same, hasn't it?"

He pulled a bulging sack from his shoulder. The pillowcase Utana had brought with him from the mansion, she realized. "I found this in your car. The costume's still in there. Put it on for us, won't you, Brigit? It'll be almost poetic."

"Go to hell, you scar-faced sonofa—"

One of the thugs clapped a hand over her mouth before she could finish. Talking slowly, Gravenham-Bail opened the pillowcase and tugged the silky, jangling belly-dance outfit from it.

"See, the guys here were hoping you'd say that. They're looking forward to putting it on for you. Oh, and I should probably mention that if you try to blast anyone with that rather unusual power of yours, you'll make your own head explode. The glass in those goggles is designed to reflect the beam right back at you. You're harmless. Impotent. Completely at my mercy."

"You think?" The words were muffled behind the hand at her mouth, but she said them all the same. Then she bent her elbows, using the men who held her as leverage. In a flash she lifted herself up, feet rising as her knees bent, and she kicked straight out to either side, catching the thugs squarely in the cojones.

They released her as they doubled over in pain, and then she lunged forward, intending to mow Nash over on her way out the door.

He stepped aside as if to let her pass but jabbed her with a needle on her way by.

She only made it four steps into the hallway before the weakness welled up within her. Her knees turned into liquid, and her vision swam.

Vaguely, as she sank to the floor, she was aware of Nash Gravenham-Bail coming to stand over her. "I was ready for that," he whispered. And then he crouched low and started peeling her clothes off as her body became too weak to fight and her head spun like an out-of-control merry-go-round. He was quick and clinical, stripping her and redressing her in the beautiful costume. He left her feet bare, and then nudged one of his soldiers, who was walking oddly.

"Toss her over your shoulder and let's get her outside. Are the Chosen ready yet?"

"Yes, sir."

"Good. And it's just about dark, too. The timing is coming together perfectly. Let's begin, then, shall we?"

Scarface led the way, marching not toward the elevators but along the hallway toward the back. She didn't know why. She hung all but helplessly over the soldier's shoulder as he strode along behind his boss. As they passed a door at the end of the hall, she got an odd tingly feeling and looked up.

Beyond the mesh in the safety glass she saw a padded room, with three figures inside. They were sitting on the floor, Roxy speaking, while Melinda and her mother looked on, mesmerized.

Aside from them, the fourth floor seemed abandoned.

It was not long before she knew why.

21

"Well, now, Utanapishtim, it seems your lady friend has abandoned you."

Utana tugged on the chains that held him, but they only rattled in response. More than an hour had passed since Brigit had left his side—maybe for the final time. He had not heard from her and had no clue what might be happening. But had the plan gone well, she would have informed him by now.

And he feared for her, for all of them. Night had fallen. And it was on this night, he knew, that Nashmun would set his evil plan into motion.

"Still weak, I see," his former vizier said.

"Too weak to do that which you intend to force me to do. You have defeated yourself in this battle, Nashmun. I cannot use my power to destroy the vahmpeers, no matter what you do to force me."

"Not yet. But as soon as the antidote kicks in,

you'll be fine." Nashmun walked up to him, driving another needle into his flank.

Big mistake, moving that close to his right hand, Utana thought. He grabbed Nashmun by his throat, lifting the scar-faced one off his feet into the air. "I will kill you here and now, and end this war."

Nashmun tried to speak, but only strangled grunts emerged. He clawed at Utana's hand on his neck, kicked his feet wildly in the air, and finally pointed urgently toward the ceiling up above and those sloping glass panels through which one could not see.

Before Utana's eyes, they began to move.

Startled, he watched as barriers that seemed to be contained within the glass itself slid away, rendering the skylights transparent at last. And beyond those windows Utana saw horror.

The yard behind the hospital, and the chain-link fence that surrounded it, were revealed to him. But the fence itself was barely visible. There were people, a hundred or more people, affixed to that fence. Some at ground level, some up higher. They were stacked two and three high, somehow bound to the fence's metallic links. And directly ahead, bound spread eagle to the fence, was his beloved Brigit.

"Release me," Nashmun rasped.

Utana relaxed his grip on Nashmun's throat, allowing him to breathe, but he did not let him go.

He stared, unable to take his eyes from Brigit. She was dressed in the costume in which she'd danced for him. Her hair was loose, her moonlight curls moving in the wind. Behind her, the sun had set. Beyond the distant blue mountains on the horizon, only a thin curve of fiery orange remained against the deepening sky. Nashmun spoke into the device attached to his wrist.

And suddenly, all the people affixed to the fence jerked like fish on a pike. Sparks showered around them, and Utana knew they were being jolted with electricity. Brigit's face pulled into a grimace of torment, and her scream of agony joined a chorus of them.

Then, as Nashmun moved his hand again, the torture stopped. And the people—the Chosens— went lax. Many of them were crying, many more shouting questions, demanding to be released.

Utana let go of Nashmun, who fell to the floor, gasping a few breaths and rubbing his neck with one hand.

"I will kill you if you harm her again," Utana said.

"*I* will kill *her*," the scar-faced betrayer promised, "unless you do exactly what I tell you from now on." He got to his feet, brushed himself off. "I'd rather keep her for research, but it's worth more to me to be rid of the vampire scourge. Now, here's what going down. In a little while—moments from now—it will be full dark. As soon as it is, we're going to jolt the hell out of those people out there."

Utana bared his teeth in anguish. "There is no

need to torture them further. They are innocents!" he shouted.

"Yes, in fact it *is* necessary. You see, the vampires will hear their cries, feel their pain and they will come here to save them. We've rigged the bonds so that the Undead will have to get inside the perimeter in order to set their precious Chosen kinfolk free. So they'll all be in there, all contained in one spot. When I give you the signal, you will blast them with that death ray of yours and they will all die."

Shaking his head fiercely, Utana said, "I cannot do what you ask, even if I wish it. You have drugged away my powers."

"That injection I just gave you was the antidote."

"I do not know antidote," Utana muttered in misery.

"Your powers have been restored, Utana," Nashmun explained. "But if you try to use them on me, we'll electrocute your lady over and over and over again. We won't stop until her hair catches fire and her eyeballs explode. It will be the most unbearable pain you can imagine. You will do as I say, Utana. Or they will suffer untold anguish. All of them. And your Brigit most of all."

Utana stared at Brigit. He didn't think she could see him, but he knew she would hear his thoughts.

My love, I am sorry. I am so sorry, I have failed you.

Her head came up straight, eyes searching the night for him. She looked toward him but not at him.

"Turn on the lights!" Nashmun shouted.

From somewhere out of sight, in another part of the room, one of his henchmen threw a switch, and the basement—the dungeon—was flooded with light. For a moment Brigit was invisible to Utana, but he knew she could see him.

I know what he's doing, Utana, but you cannot listen to him! Don't you do what says, my love. Don't you dare hurt my people to save me. Do you hear me? Don't do it, Utana!

Utana lowered his head, closed his eyes. *How can I bear to watch you suffer?*

It doesn't fucking matter how much I suffer! I'm immortal. I'll heal. If I die, my brother will bring me back. It will be fine.

"He won't do it, though," Nashmun said.

Stunned, Utana looked at him, his eyes flying wide in surprise.

"I've been working with their kind for a while now. You pick up a few things." Nashmun tapped his own forehead. "I can hear their thoughts. They're faint, garbled sometimes, but mostly I can piece them together. Her brother isn't going to save her. You see, not only has he turned his back on her—because of you, I might add—but even if he changes his mind, it won't matter. We'll take them both out, and if they revive—which we think they will, being immortal— they'll wake to find themselves entombed alive. So immortal or not, they're going to be out of commission. Imprisoned. Buried alive."

"No!"

"Yes, yes, yes. Buried alive. Just like you were, Utana."

The thought of Brigit suffering the anguish that had driven him to madness made Utana's heart bleed within him. "You do not need to harm them. You do not need to do any of this, Nashmun."

"No, I don't have to. But I'm going to. Unless you kill all the vampires. You take those blood-thirsty animals out for me, Utana, and I will let your woman go. And her brother, too. Then the three of you can go off together and live happily ever after."

Happily ever after. The words were the very ones Brigit had used. Such a beautiful saying—but befouled by coming from this evil man's lying lips.

"What do you say?"

Utana! Brigit was shouting at him mentally. *Utana, don't do it! I'll never forgive you if you do it!*

Know that I love you, Brigit. I love you as I have loved none before.

Baby, please, hold out. Don't do this. We'll get out of this somehow.

He's reading our thoughts, my lo—

"That's enough!" Nashmun nodded at his henchman, and the lights went out. Utana could once again see Brigit, but she could no longer see him. "Anymore communication and I jolt her. Understand?"

"You would rob me of even the chance to say goodbye?"

"You do what I say and you won't have to say goodbye." Nash looked toward the spot where the last rays of the sun sank at last below the horizon.

"Hit them again!" Nash shouted.

Immediately electricity surged through the fence, burning and jolting them all.

Utana closed his eyes, unable to watch the agony, but feeling it in every cell of his body. "I'll do it," he muttered. "Please, please, no more torture. Let them be. I'll do as you ask."

"Good. That's very good, Utana. Of course, we're going to have to give them another jolt, maybe two, to ensure the vampires come running to the rescue. But because you've agreed, I'll make them milder and shorter. They would be grateful to you if they knew."

Utana hung his head, his tears scalding his skin. He could not bear to see Brigit suffer. And there was only one way to ensure it would stop. Only one way.

Brigit's entire body was snapping with the remnants of the electric current that had been sent blazing through her when suddenly she heard Utana's voice in her head as clearly as if he were speaking aloud. As she sought him, lights came on in the angled skylights above the basement, revealing

Utana beyond them, still chained to that damned wall. He was directly opposite her, and she knew they were going to make him watch her suffer until he did what they said.

Damn that Gravenham-Bail and the DPI.

She talked, pled, cajoled, but in the end, Utana went silent, and she doubted it was by choice. He'd managed to warn her that Nash could hear her thoughts, and that was good to know, though it made for a terrible situation.

Then the lights inside went out and she couldn't see him anymore.

I love you, Utanapishtim. Ziasudra. And if I die tonight, my only regret will be that we didn't have more time together. And if I die a thousand years from now, my only regret will be exactly the same. I love you. I love you. I love you.

"Psst!"

Brigit went stiff, sensing a presence behind her, just outside the fence. And then feeling a rush of recognition. "J.W.," she whispered. "Oh, thank God, thank God."

"Easy." Reaching up a hand, he thrust his fingers through the links of the chain, weaving them through hers. "I would have left when you did, sis, but I thought I could talk sense into the others."

"And did you?"

"Of course I did. You know Rhiannon's temper. She would have come around if you'd given her a little more time. Everyone's on their way right behind me, waiting for me to find out what we should do next. But, listen, I want you to know, I would have come either way. Lucy and our parents, too."

"Would you?" she asked, her heart breaking.

"You're my sister. I'm on your side, even if you fall for the Devil himself."

Tears streaming, relief rushing through her, she nodded very slightly. "Gravenham-Bail can hear our thoughts."

"I gathered as much from the conversation I just overheard. That's why I'm whispering. Did Utana give you back your power? Can you blast a hole through the fence? Break the current?"

"They've got me goggled. I can't use my power. But you can."

"What do you mean?"

"J.W., our powers are the same. Mine and yours. Utana says they're just opposite aspects of the same force. I've always had the ability to heal. And you to destroy."

"Holy shit," he marveled, but only momentarily. "Then I'll blast it myself."

"No! Listen to me, if they know you're here, they'll force Utana to kill you all, and he might very well do it. He loves me so much...." Her whispers dissolved into sobs then.

"I know," J.W. whispered. "I know, Bridge, I

heard the entire thing. And I'm sorry. I...the guy really *does* love you. I was wrong about him. But I'm no more able to watch you suffer than he is."

"You need to wait—there's something else you have to do first. There are still people inside. Get them out. If we can't save anyone else, at least we can save them."

"People?"

"A woman named Roxy—she's the one who's been working from the inside to give the vampires information. The DPI must have found out what she was doing. And then there's a very special little girl, and her mother. You have to get them out of there alive, J.W. I promised."

"I'll get them."

"All hell's going to break loose here soon. You have to do it now."

"I don't want to leave you."

"J.W., she's a scared little girl. Seven years old. Named Melinda. They're on the fourth floor, all the way to the right down the corridor behind the nurses' station. Get them. Please." She nodded toward the skylights. "I'm scared to death that I know what Utana's going to do. Though I pray I'm wrong. You may only have minutes to get them out of there."

"All right. All right."

"Go, James. Now!"

And then he was gone.

Alone again, Brigit stared toward the now black glass beyond which her love, her soul mate, was being held. And she continued to send her thoughts to him, regardless of whether Gravenham-Bail could hear or not.

Don't hurt the one I love most, Utana. If you love me, you won't do the horrible thing you're thinking of. I'd rather die myself than have that happen. I can take pain. I can handle torture. But I cannot handle losing you—no more than I could stand to lose my family. I love you. I'll love you no matter what, but I'm begging you—

She went rigid as another bolt of electricity blazed through her body. A shower of sparks rained from the fence around her, and she screamed.

And then there was a burst of static, followed by a voice coming from loudspeakers mounted on top of the building. Gravenham-Bail's voice. "No more communication, Brigit. Next time, I'm going to have my men hose you down first. Believe me, it will intensify the, uh…sensations."

Fuck you, she thought viciously. *I can handle anything you can dish out, and when it's over, I'm going to make you suffer. And I'm going to make your friends and your family suffer, and I'm going to make everyone you care about suf—* "Aieeee!"

She forced herself to go silent in the wake of the latest jolt, not wanting her pain to distract her brother from his mission.

And then the others began to make themselves known to her. The vampires were near and drawing closer, enraged by what was being done to her, and to the others bound to the fence around her. Whatever was going to happen, it was going to happen soon—within seconds—and there wasn't a damn thing she could do about it.

Utana could not communicate openly with Brigit, nor with any of the race he'd created. But he could feel them. He opened his mind to them, to all of them, allowing their essences to fill him. He became aware of James, Brigit's beloved brother, entering the hospital building. Why, he didn't know, though he could tell that James was looking for something—some*one*. Utana also felt the approach of the vahmpeers. They were near. Very near. Within moments, he knew, those heroic creatures would be leaping the electrified barricade in order to save the Chosen, to save their beloved Brigit.

And he would be ordered to kill them. If he so much as hesitated, Brigit would suffer the wrath of Nashmun, and even more electricity would surge through her already pain-racked body. And he knew she could not withstand much more.

She hung limply now, her head down; that most recent blast had nearly done her in. Then, beyond the fence, Utana glimpsed motion.

The vahmpeers had arrived.

He closed his eyes, drew up the power within him, and let it build and build until it was humming in his head, vibrating throughout his entire body. He was barely able to contain it. Desperately, he sent one last thought to James.

It wasn't a thought Nashmun would be likely to interpret correctly. It was a number.

Ten.

"The vampires are leaping over the fence!" Nashmun shouted. "It's working. Just a few more seconds, Utana. On my signal. Hold… Hold…"

Nine.

"May the Anunaki show me mercy," Utana said in Sumerian.

Eight.

"Keep holding," Nashmun ordered.

Seven.

"I will do as you say," Utana said softly.

Six.

Utana continued drawing up the power. It rose from the ground beneath him, a glowing green light.

Five.

"Hold it, hold it…"

Four.

The power flowed down from the heavens, a golden yellow beam.

Nashmun lifted a hand. "On my word…"

Three.

"Wait for it…."

Two.

Get out of the building, James of the Vahmpeers. Do it now!

Nashmun's eyes went wide and shot to Utana's. "What the hell…?"

One.

Utana shifted his gaze, releasing the power from his eyes, and the beam burst forth with more strength than it had ever done before. The light blazed with the blinding flash of a sustained bolt of lightning. But it didn't shoot through the glass into the crowd of vahmpeers outside, who were rapidly freeing the Chosens from their fence of torture and death.

The beam flashed across the basement instead— to the propane tanks that lined the farthest wall.

James had left his sister and called up the vampire side of himself even as he ran straight for the building. As he vamped up, he poured on a burst of speed and jumped from the ground to the fire escape. Dashing up it, he knew he was moving almost too fast for human eyes to detect. And even if they could, everyone in Gravenham-Bail's command was too busy watching events unfold in the enclosed backyard to notice him.

He sped, leaping from level to level at top speed, arriving on the fourth floor in mere seconds and smashing out a window to get inside.

One quick glance showed him the nurses' station and the corridor he needed, and he went lunging down it to the final door on the right. He didn't even need Brigit's directions. He felt the pure song of the little girl's energy the moment he entered the building.

Without pause, he kicked the door open, and then he was inside, looking at three very startled females. That was about the time he heard, in his head, very loudly, Utana's voice, as the Ancient and Mighty One began what James quickly realized was a countdown, and he started to count for himself.

"I'm here to get you out!" J.W. shouted at them. "Come with me," he said.

The little girl was the first on her feet, the other two close behind, and James led the way down the stairs. He was down to the second-floor landing, with the little girl riding piggyback and clinging to his neck when his mental countdown got too low for comfort.

"Oh, hell." He had an inkling, and it wasn't a good one. Quickly James darted along the second-floor corridor, running. "This way—fast!" he shouted.

The women followed. He raced into the first room he saw and kicked the window. Safety glass. Dammit!

In his mind he heard Utana shouting, *Get out of the building, James of the Vahmpeers. Do it now!*

James called up the healing power, but this time he directed it with the intent to destroy, and aimed it at the glass in the window. A blast of light emerged from his eyes, and then the window was gone, annihilated. Without hesitation, he grabbed the two women and dragged them through the window.

One.

An arm around each woman, the little girl still clinging to his neck, James dove through the open window, even while hearing the deafening explosions that began below and then surged upward.

As they fell to the ground, landing in a tangle in the backyard, amid the vampires and the now freed captives, the explosion rocketed upward, blasting through the roof straight up into the night sky, briefly igniting the darkness, before it seemed to be sucked back in as the building imploded, collapsing in on itself.

James hustled his little group to their feet, running for the far end of the lawn as the building fell. He blasted through the fence, clearing the way, and everyone ran for cover.

Everyone except Brigit, who, freed by her family, fell to her knees on the grassy lawn and released an anguished cry in the shape of Utana's name.

22

As the vampires had been rushing to break the bonds and lower the captives from the fence, Brigit had heard Utana begin his countdown and begged the gods not to let him do what she feared he was about to.

She spotted James leaping out a second-story window with Roxy, Jane and Melinda all attached to him, and then her worst nightmare came true.

The last thing she felt from her beloved was the desperately sent thought, *Forever I will love you, Brigit of the Vahmpeers.*

And then her gaze was drawn to the darkened glass just in time to see a beam, an unmistakably familiar beam blasting from one end of the basement to the other.

"Utana, please, no!"

Everyone turned.

There was an instant when the room beyond

those skylights lit up from within, just a flash, and in that moment she could very clearly see Utana silhouetted in the light of the explosion he had wrought.

And then the explosion burst upward and the building came down. Someone was tearing at the bonds that held her, and she dropped from the fence onto the grass. She knew what he had done, even as she knew what the inevitable result would be. Clawing the goggles from her face, kneeling there in the grass while vampires and humans alike stampeded past her, on their way to safety, she wasn't aware of screaming his name over and over. She was aware only that her heart was shattered, blown to bits as surely as St. Dymphna's was.

Rising, pushing herself up from the ground, she lunged forward, arms reaching out as the building went down as if in slow motion.

Someone gripped her shoulders. Rhiannon, she thought, but she pulled free, sobbing the word "no" over and over again.

And then there was silence. Dust and smoke too thick to see through. And she stood staring at the clouds of dark ash where the building had been before.

The dust cleared slowly. And then there was the horrible aftermath. Six stories reduced to one pile of rubble that filled the basement and topped it like a small mountain. And beneath all of it, her one and only love was buried.

Again she felt Rhiannon's hands on her.

Again she shook them off. "We didn't deserve what he just did for us," she whispered. "None of us did."

And then the tears came, and she dropped to her knees. "Utana. Oh, God, Utana, I love you so much!" She fell face forward in the dirt, and her world went black. She felt it slipping from her, and hoped she would never again be forced to wake up to this brutal reality that was life. Never again.

"I would rather die with you than live without you, my love," she whispered. And her eyes closed on the world.

James raced to where his sister had fallen and knelt beside her.

Around him there was chaos, as the vampires worked to help the Chosen who remained, though there were few enough of those. Most had fled.

Others had been caught in the rain of shrapnel, but he didn't think there were any serious injuries. And as the vampires tended them, helped them, told them what little they absolutely needed to know and sent them on their way, the crowd became thinner.

Soon only vampires remained.

"There will be a response to this," Rhiannon said softly. "Officials, firefighters. Already they approach. We must leave this place."

"Not without Utana," James whispered.

"James, he's buried beneath tons of—"

"I can't leave him." He looked up from the prone form of his sister to meet Rhiannon's eyes. "Look at her, Aunt Rhi. She's devastated."

"I know."

"I've got to get him out of there. I've got to try to bring him back again. We owe him that much. He saved our entire race tonight. He saved my sister."

Sighing, Rhiannon nodded and looked at the devastated Brigit, unconscious now from pain too overwhelming to bear. "She was right, our little Brigit. None of us are worthy of him—our forebear. Creator of our race. Except, perhaps, for her."

"Get the others out of here," James said softly.

"The others aren't going anywhere," said a deep voice from behind him.

It was Edge, his own father. Around him, the other vampires had all gathered, even the very eldest among them, Damien Namtar who'd been known once as King Gilgamesh. He was the first man with whom Utana had shared the gift of the gods—the gift of immortality. He was the first true vampire.

He stood shoulder to shoulder with Roland de Courtemanche. Eric Marquand. With Dante and Donovan, and with the prince, Dracula himself.

"We'll hold off the emergency workers as they arrive," Edge went on. "Enthrall them, if necessary."

Dracula smiled sadly. "The glamour is, after all, one of my specialties."

"Go on, James," Rhiannon told him. "Get our forebear out of that rubble, so that we can wipe the dust of this place from our feet."

The vampires dissipated, Edge lifting Brigit in his arms and carrying her with him toward the road, to await the firefighters.

Alone in the backyard, at the rear of the destruction, James lifted his hands, focused his eyes and sent the beam of power he had once thought could be used only for healing into the rubble, clearing a path. He honed his senses to locate Utana's broken remains and blasted away debris, getting closer and closer.

He heard sirens out front, saw flashing lights beyond the wrecked building, but focused only on his grim task, trusting his family to hold up their end.

And finally he found Utana.

The man's body was broken so thoroughly that it seemed boneless as James used his vampiric strength to pick it up, wincing at the unnatural feel of it—crushed bones, flattened limbs.

He wondered if he would be able to raise the man again. Oh, he had done so before, but he believed now that he had been meant to. All of this had been part of destiny. And now that Utana's fate had been carried out, perhaps his job had ended. Perhaps, he'd been set free by his gods at last.

Lovingly, respectfully, James carried Utana out to join the others. They stood in a semicircle around the rubble. Around them, firefighters, police cars, a few ambulances, all stood still, lights ablaze, drivers sitting motionless and mesmerized in their seats. A few had already emerged and stood near their vehicles, as if frozen in time.

"One burst of motion," Dracula called, holding up his hands as waves of hypnotic force wafted over the rescue workers. "On my word, we leave here at top speed, all at once. We go in many directions, as a precaution. But we will gather once again at the plantation. Are we ready?"

They all nodded.

James wasn't as fast as the Undead. But he was fast enough. His father carried Brigit. And Dracula took Utana from his arms. "Fang up, J.W. You'll need all your power."

James nodded and invoked his vampiric side from within. His fangs emerged, and his eyes glowed.

Dracula raised a hand. "Now!"

And in an instant, in a blur, the vampires were gone.

In their wake, the human emergency workers blinked out of their stupor and refocused on the demolished hospital.

"God help whoever was inside," said one. "It doesn't look as if any of them survived."

The Virginia plantation was still a safe haven, though they would be forced to leave it behind soon, as they'd been forced to leave so many other places. Until then, however, it would do.

Brigit lay on a bed, staring sightlessly into space.

Her mother had bathed her, dressed her in a soft white nightgown, draped a blanket over her, upon their arrival. The other surviving vampires had gone in many directions, as Vlad had suggested. It had taken some time for them all to convene here, but they had finally done so, and not a moment too soon. The sun would soon be rising. The vampires must rest.

Stroking her daughter's cheek, Amber Lily leaned close and kissed her. And then the bedroom door opened and J.W. came inside.

"He's here," he said softly.

"Thank God," Amber Lily said. "She's not responding to anything. Where did they put him?"

"In the next room."

"Good." She leaned close to her daughter again. "Do you hear that, Brigit? They've brought Utana here. He's here, my love."

But there was no response. Brigit only stared sightlessly at the far wall.

Sighing, her mother battled tears.

"Go to bed, Mom. The sun's rising. I'll take care of her."

"Do you think it'll work?"

He nodded. "It has to."

The two embraced, and Amber Lily left the room.

J.W. bent closer to the bed and scooped Brigit into his arms. And then he carried her into the bedroom next door. He placed her in a chair, then dragged it up beside the bed.

Somewhere deep inside her mind, Brigit sensed that Utana was near. But dead. Lifeless. Or trapped, conscious, within a body that no longer lived. She couldn't bear the thought. J.W. sensed all of that moving through her mind.

"You have to come around now, Brigit," J.W. said. "I know it's painful to see him like this, much less to face the fact that it might not work, that his task in this world might finally be finished. But the faster we try to revive him, the easier it will be. And besides, if it isn't going to work, isn't it better to know?"

She blinked. Her vision swam into focus, narrowed in on her brother, then shifted to the man in the bed. She emitted a yelp at the sight of him, her hands flying to her mouth. Utana's body was destroyed. Utterly destroyed.

"He was ash when I found him the first time,"

J.W. told her. "Remember? I brought him back from that."

"It was his destiny." She reached out a trembling hand, laid it upon Utana's arm, then jerked it back when she found it cold. "What if his destiny is fulfilled? What if he's found peace at last? Can we really risk pulling him back from that? Do we have that right?"

J.W. knelt, then turned Brigit's chair to face him. He clasped her hands. "If it had been you who'd died, and he was alive and thought he had the power to bring you back, what would you want him to do?"

She held her brother's eyes. "I would want to be where he was. Wherever that might be."

"So you'd want him to try?"

"Yes."

"Even though he might fail?"

"Yes."

"Even if you were in…paradise?"

She shifted her gaze to the battered corpse in the bed. "Yes."

"And do you think he loves you every bit as much as you love him?"

Her eyes welled with tears. "He died for me. How can I doubt it?"

"Then you have to try to bring him back."

She shot him a look. "Me? James, you're the one who heals. You're the good twin. The healer. I'm the destroyer. I can't—"

"It has to be you, Brigit. I don't know how I know that, but I do. Now get to work. Go on. Drum up the energy, focus it through your hands, and lay them on your man."

Trembling, she looked again at Utana. Then, leaning forward, she closed her eyes and laid her hands on his chest. She opened her senses and felt the energy streaming down into her from somewhere above. She reached out with everything in her, and the power shot up into her body from somewhere below. The two beams of light, opposite and yet the same—twins, like she and her brother—met in her center, swirling in her solar plexus and pulsing there so strongly that she thought her body would burst with their combined power. But she mentally guided the melded beams up into her chest, into her heart and then split them and sent them barreling down her arms and into her hands.

The light burst forth from the centers of her palms with so much force that her body recoiled and Utana's sank into the bed.

"Heal," she whispered. "Heal, my love. Return to me. I will not live if you die. Accept the gift I would not have known I possessed if not for you. Heal, Utana. My one and only love. Mend your body and your mind. And come back to me. Return to your woman."

The light spilled out of her, from her hands, from her heart, seeming to bleed from her, and filled him.

She kept her eyes closed, but she felt the energy doing its work. She could hear the crackling sound of bones mending themselves, could sense the straightening of broken limbs, the plumping of flattened ones. His organs regenerated; his skull sealed over. All the cuts and scrapes in his flesh grew together, and then she felt his skin grow warmer and felt, in her own heart, the echoing beat of his.

Brigit opened her eyes to find Utana's, alive with light, staring up at her. And the wave of emotion that surged forth from her was enough, she thought, to drown them both. She opened her lips to speak his name, but no words emerged. And she heard her brother quietly leaving the room.

"You…brought me back."

"I…could not let you go."

"I was counting on it." He smiled, slowly and gently, and he reached for her. "Brigit. My love, my life from now on is at your side."

"You're damn straight it is."

He pulled her on top of him, his powerful arms wrapping tightly around her, and rolled her over in the bed as his mouth captured her lips and refused to let go. But at last he broke the kiss. "This is the beginning of our happily ever after, is it not?"

She smiled so hard she thought her face would break. "That's exactly what it is."

And she kissed him again.

Brigit did not know what the future held for

her people. But she knew what it held for her. A lifetime—or several—of absolute bliss, with the only man she had ever—or *could* ever—love. And that was enough for her.

That was enough…for anyone.

Epilogue

The remaining vampires—and there were painfully few—made their way to a village in the wilds of Romania. The village surrounded a castle where a few distant relatives lived, and where they would be made welcome, and kept protected and safe.

Who would believe a vampire village in Transylvania, anyway? It was too clichéd to be true. And anyway, they would be beyond the reach of the U.S. government, with all of its nosiness into things it did not, and could not, understand.

According to the newspapers and the surviving witnesses, heroic Nash Gravenham-Bail, the scarfaced agent of the DPI had sacrificed his own life to keep America safe. The vamps, the media claimed, turned to dust upon their deaths, which was why no remains were ever found.

The press bought that, because it was what the government told them, and for the most part the public bought into it along with them.

There was a lot of Monday-morning quarter-backing going on. Commentators and politicians blasting those in charge for the poor way in which this had been handled, regrets for the destruction of a race the world had never had the chance to truly know. A lot of mea culpas and heartfelt apologies. A lot of raging on the Sunday-afternoon news programs. But the party line was that no vampires had survived in the U.S. and that, as far as they knew, had never existed anywhere else. Maybe they didn't want it known that there were others in the world, or that the Chosen had been grievously mistreated, their civil rights violated, their lives unforgivably disrupted.

A generous settlement with a confidentiality clause attached, had been awarded by the government, and those with the Belladonna Antigen were promised that, so long as they never spoke of what had truly happened that night, they would never be watched nor studied again.

But the Chosen knew better.

They also knew, however, that they had a family of supernatural protectors who would spring into action if it was ever warranted again. A family of protectors forced to live in the shadows, in hiding, in secret.

At least for now…

* * * * *

**The more you run, the less you can hide
in the *Secrets of Shadow Falls* trilogy
from *New York Times* and
USA TODAY bestselling author**

MAGGIE SHAYNE

Available wherever
books are sold!

REQUEST YOUR
FREE BOOKS!

2 FREE NOVELS FROM THE
PARANORMAL ROMANCE COLLECTION
PLUS 2 FREE GIFTS!

YES! Please send me 2 FREE novels from the Paranormal Romance Collection and my 2 FREE gifts (gifts are worth about $10). After receiving them, if I don't wish to receive any more books, I can return the shipping statement marked "cancel." If I don't cancel, I will receive 4 brand-new novels every month and be billed just $21.42 in the U.S. or $23.46 in Canada. That's a saving of at least 21% off the cover price of all 4 books. It's quite a bargain! Shipping and handling is just 50¢ per book in the U.S. and 75¢ per book in Canada.* I understand that accepting the 2 free books and gifts places me under no obligation to buy anything. I can always return a shipment and cancel at any time. Even if I never buy another book, the two free books and gifts are mine to keep forever.

237/337 HDN FEL2

Name	(PLEASE PRINT)	

Address		Apt. #

City	State/Prov.	Zip/Postal Code

Signature (if under 18, a parent or guardian must sign)

Mail to the **Reader Service:**
IN U.S.A.: P.O. Box 1867, Buffalo, NY 14240-1867
IN CANADA: P.O. Box 609, Fort Erie, Ontario L2A 5X3

Not valid for current subscribers to the Paranormal Romance Collection or Harlequin® Nocturne™ books.

Want to try two free books from another line?
Call 1-800-873-8635 or visit www.ReaderService.com.

* Terms and prices subject to change without notice. Prices do not include applicable taxes. Sales tax applicable in N.Y. Canadian residents will be charged applicable taxes. Offer not valid in Quebec. This offer is limited to one order per household. All orders subject to credit approval. Credit or debit balances in a customer's account(s) may be offset by any other outstanding balance owed by or to the customer. Please allow 4 to 6 weeks for delivery. Offer available while quantities last.

Your Privacy—The Reader Service is committed to protecting your privacy. Our Privacy Policy is available online at www.ReaderService.com or upon request from the Reader Service.

We make a portion of our mailing list available to reputable third parties that offer products we believe may interest you. If you prefer that we not exchange your name with third parties, or if you wish to clarify or modify your communication preferences, please visit us at www.ReaderService.com/consumerschoice or write to us at Reader Service Preference Service, P.O. Box 9062, Buffalo, NY 14269. Include your complete name and address.

MAGGIE SHAYNE

32980	TWILIGHT PROPHECY	___ $7.99 U.S.	___ $9.99 CAN.
32906	PRINCE OF TWILIGHT	___ $7.99 U.S.	___ $9.99 CAN.
32875	BLUE TWILIGHT	___ $7.99 U.S.	___ $9.99 CAN.
32872	EDGE OF TWILIGHT	___ $7.99 U.S.	___ $9.99 CAN.
32871	TWILIGHT HUNGER	___ $7.99 U.S.	___ $9.99 CAN.
32808	KISS ME, KILL ME	___ $7.99 U.S.	___ $9.99 CAN.
32804	KILL ME AGAIN	___ $7.99 U.S.	___ $9.99 CAN.
32793	KILLING ME SOFTLY	___ $7.99 U.S.	___ $9.99 CAN.
32618	BLOODLINE	___ $7.99 U.S.	___ $8.99 CAN.
32498	ANGEL'S PAIN	___ $7.99 U.S.	___ $7.99 CAN.
32497	DEMON'S KISS	___ $7.99 U.S.	___ $9.50 CAN.
32244	COLDER THAN ICE	___ $5.99 U.S.	___ $6.99 CAN.
32243	THICKER THAN WATER	___ $5.99 U.S.	___ $6.99 CAN.
31267	TWILIGHT FULFILLED	___ $7.99 U.S.	___ $9.99 CAN.

(limited quantities available)

TOTAL AMOUNT	$ _____
POSTAGE & HANDLING	$ _____
($1.00 for 1 book, 50¢ for each additional)	
APPLICABLE TAXES*	$ _____
TOTAL PAYABLE	$ _____

(check or money order—please do not send cash)

To order, complete this form and send it, along with a check or money order for the total above, payable to MIRA Books, to: **In the U.S.:** 3010 Walden Avenue, P.O. Box 9077, Buffalo, NY 14269-9077; **In Canada:** P.O. Box 636, Fort Erie, Ontario, L2A 5X3.

Name: _____

Address: _____ City: _____

State/Prov.: _____ Zip/Postal Code: _____

Account Number (if applicable): _____

075 CSAS

*New York residents remit applicable sales taxes.
*Canadian residents remit applicable GST and provincial taxes.

MIRA | HARLEQUIN®
www.Harlequin.com

MMS1011BL